MW01134780

Into Magnolia

Sandy Cove Series Book Three

Rosemary Hines

To the many students who called
me Teacher

"Let us not become weary in doing good, for at the proper time we will reap a harvest if we do not give up."

Galatians 6:9

CHAPTER ONE

Amber Gamble sat on the floor beside her bed. *I hate them. All of them,* she thought to herself. This was her third foster home in one year. She was sick and tired of having to move and live with people she didn't even know. *I don't need any of them. I'd be better off on my own!*

She opened her backpack and pulled out the photo of her mom, her dad, her little brother, and herself. It looked like a normal enough family, but Amber knew better. "Jerks," she said aloud as she glared into her parents' faces. Where were they when she needed them most? How dare her dad take off and leave them? And then her mom's breakdown. She could still see her huddled on the floor in the corner of her bedroom crying and saying she wished she were dead. Ever since then, she'd been worthless as a mom, in and out of psychiatric hospitals and drug rehabs.

Fine. If that was the way she was going to be, she wished her mom were dead, too. Might as well be. Some mother she turned out to be.

At first she'd believed that her mom would get better. She and Jack would just be living in separate foster homes for a month or so while Mom got over the whole affair with Dad. That's what the social worker had told them. "I'm sure your mom will be fine in a few weeks. Then she'll be able to take you both back home."

What a lie. That social worker was a jerk just like the rest of them. It had been almost a year. Her mom was in the looney bin again, her dad was off with his girlfriend somewhere in Arizona, and she and Jack were still living in these stupid foster homes. It didn't help that she had to keep moving from one home to another. Who wanted a fourteen-year-old loser like her? They all pretended to care for a few weeks or even a couple of months, and then they'd find some excuse to get rid of her.

"This sucks," she told Bonnie Blackwell the last time the social worker had come to tell her she'd be living with another family.

"I know it's hard, Amber. But you are in short-term foster care. That means you're being placed with people who only care for kids for a few weeks or months at a time. The good news is that the court thinks you and your mom will be reunited soon. Then you can go back to living as a family — you, your mom, and Jack."

"Right," she replied with a sarcastic tone.

Amber looked back down at the picture, this time focusing on Jack.

"I'm calling him right now. We're out of here," she said to the wall.

She took out her cell phone — the one and only decent thing the social worker had given her — and punched in Jack's number.

"Hello?" a woman's voice answered.

"I need to talk to Jack," Amber demanded.

"Is this Amber?"

"None of your business. Just get Jack."

"I'm sorry. Jack's asleep. It's almost eleven."

Amber looked at the phone, scowled, and hung up. "Jerk. What? She thinks I can't tell time?"

She rifled through her backpack and found the pack of cigarettes at the bottom. Pulling one out, she lit up and went to sit on the window seat, blowing her smoke out the window as she tried to swallow back her tears.

When she felt trapped, the cigarettes were her only friends. Thank God she'd met Adam. At least he understood her. And he got her cigarettes whenever she needed them.

"I swear I'm getting out of this prison," she said with determination. "And I'm taking Jack with me."

Michelle Baron felt a rush of adrenalin. The day had finally arrived, and she eagerly climbed the brick stairs leading up to the entrance of Magnolia Middle School. It was hard for her to believe that she was finally a full-fledged teacher! A childhood dream was about to become her new reality. Now she stood before the school, her spirit soaring and her heart racing as she took it all in.

It was still early and only a few students were in sight. Off to one side of the parking lot a couple of boys showed off their skateboarding skills. A group of three girls clustered at the top of the stairs comparing class schedules. The girls looked her way as she passed them. "Good morning, ladies," Michelle offered with a smile.

Pushing open the heavy glass door, she inhaled the smell of floor polish that told the tale of a busy weekend of cleaning and preparation on the part of the janitorial staff. Magnolia School gleamed, and the bulletin boards lining the halls displayed crisp pictures and announcements for the incoming students. A new year! Michelle's emotions soared as she considered the possibilities.

Then her mind shot back to her departure from home thirty minutes earlier. Her daughter Madison was dressed in her first-day-of-school skirt and ruffled tee shirt. She looked so confident with her new pink backpack and 'Best Friends' binder. Was it really true that their baby was in kindergarten already? Where had the years gone?

Michelle dreaded telling her little girl she would have to leave for her first day of teaching before Maddie's bus came to pick her up. Instead, Steve would be there for their daughter's first walk to the bus stop. The school had an introductory program where parents were allowed to ride the bus with their kindergarteners the first day. Steve had carefully arranged his schedule at the law firm to accommodate this big event.

"Don't worry, Mommy. We'll be fine," Madison said as she gazed up at Steve. "Daddy knows where the bus comes."

"That's right, pumpkin," Steve confirmed with a nod and a smile.

Still, Michelle wished she could have been there to see Maddie climb those steps into the school bus. There was a price to pay for her new teaching job, and she knew this was just the first of many instances when she would realize it.

Drawing her mind back to the present, she thought about all that she needed to do before class began. First stop, the office to pick up her roll sheets. As she stepped into this hub of the school, the receptionist greeted her with a smile. "Hey there, Michelle! Are you ready?"

"I think so," Michelle replied, returning her smile and walking over to the myriad of mailboxes. Near the top of the left row of boxes, she saw her name and teaching assignment: Michelle Baron — Language Arts. A stack of papers rested inside. Included in the pile were her roll sheets, announcements for the week, and packets to give her first period students.

As she flipped through the papers, the principal, Daniel Durand, walked up. His tall, stocky build and curly gray hair gave him the appearance of a retired athlete. "Good morning, Michelle."

"Good morning, Mr. Durand," Michelle said, hugging the papers to her chest.

"No 'Mr. Durand' stuff, please. You'll make me feel old." He gave her a warm smile and a friendly but innocent wink. "Just call me Dan."

Michelle blushed. "Okay, Dan."

"So, is there anything you need for your first day?" he asked.

"I'm a bundle of nerves, but other than that, I think I'm ready," she replied.

He smiled again and reassured her that she would be fine once the day got under way. As they parted, Michelle headed out the office door and down the hall to her new classroom.

Room 107. There it was. Michelle's hand shook as she inserted the key into the lock and opened the door. The room looked great. All her hard work on bulletin boards and furniture arrangement had transformed the space from a dull shell into a bright, cheerful, and inviting haven. The freshly scrubbed carpet smelled of shampoo, and the desks waited eagerly for their occupants.

She began sorting her papers on the table at the front of the room. In addition to the office handouts from her mailbox, she had her course syllabus and an outline of her behavior standards ready to give her new charges. The spelling books were stacked on the back counter beside the aging literature and grammar texts.

So much to accomplish this first day! She went over the notes she had written on a large index card, and placed it securely on her podium. Today would set an important tone for the year ahead, and she was determined to make her students feel comfortable and at ease while maintaining an air of professionalism and respect.

Cassandra Gibralter, her master teacher during the prior term of student teaching, had given her a wonderful example as well as some timely and treasured advice. "Always remember, Michelle, that you are not teaching curriculum, you are teaching students. They will look to you to be their guide and example, whether they're willing to admit it or not." Glancing over her syllabus for the last time, Michelle smiled to herself as she remembered those words.

When her eyes came to rest on her behavior guidelines and standards, she could almost hear Mrs. G (the name the students fondly called their teacher) as she instructed Michelle. "You are not here to be their friend. Trust me, they have plenty of friends. What they need is your leadership and example, your encouragement to become the best men and women they can be. Sometimes this will mean you are not the most popular teacher, but you will become one of the most loved."

By the end of her semester as a student teacher, Cassandra's words had unfolded as prophecy. The kids really did love her — even the ones who murmured about her strict rules or high expectations. Some of the most glowing remarks in her yearbook that June had come from the unexpected sources of the "troublemaking" kids. Michelle knew she was called to this ministry of teaching. She could almost feel God's mantle of trust placed upon her shoulders this first day of work.

A rap on the door revealed Mrs. G peeking in through the small window. Apparently Michelle had forgotten to turn the key to the unlock position when she'd entered the room. She hurried over and pulled the door open.

"Michelle, everything looks great in here!" Cassandra said, smiling as her eyes surveyed the class.

"Thanks, Mrs. G," Michelle replied with a smile.

"Cassie," she corrected her, opening her arms and giving Michelle a hug. "You'll be great this year," she said warmly. "Well, I'd better scoot and make sure I'm ready when that bell rings."

"Okay. And thanks for coming by. I'm glad you're right down the hall."

"Feel free to call me anytime, Michelle. I mean it. There are so many questions that arise in the first few days and weeks. I'm more than happy to help in any way I can." With that, she gave Michelle's arm a little squeeze and left the room.

As Cassie exited, a young girl — who looked a little frightened and intimidated— peered in. "Are you Ms. Baron?" she asked softly.

"I am. Are you in my class?" Michelle walked over to the girl, who was still holding the door open as if waiting to be invited inside.

"Yes. First period." The girl handed Michelle her schedule. *Katy McGolderick.* She looked too young for eighth grade, her short stature and slight frame topped by baby fine brown hair and enormous chestnut eyes.

"Hi Katy. It's nice to meet you," Michelle said, extending her hand and giving the girl back her schedule.

"Is it okay if I stay in here until the bell rings?" the timid girl asked as she looked around the room.

"It's fine. In fact, I could use your help."

Katy's eyes lit up, and she smiled. "Sure. What can I do?"

"See those spelling books on the back counter?"

She looked back and nodded.

"You can put one of them on each desk."

"Okay," she replied, heading to the back of room.

Michelle got her blank seating charts out of a folder and placed them on her podium. "Do you have a favorite place to sit, Katy?" she asked the girl, who was now busy dispersing spelling workbooks to the empty desks.

"Not really. The front somewhere, I guess."

"The front it is then. I'll put you up on the left side by the window, right across from my desk."

Katy smiled and set her backpack on the chair of that desk then returned to her task with the books. As she placed the last one on her own desk, the passing bell rang.

Michelle walked to the door, opened it wide, and wedged the doorstop to hold it in place. Standing there, she greeted students who began streaming into the room.

As the final few entered, the tardy bell rang. Michelle looked over the class. Thirty-six students filled the desks, many of their faces lit with anticipation. In that initial glance, she noticed a group at the back of the room, already slouching in their seats, eyes fixed on her as if to dare her to try to teach them anything that year. She made a mental note to disperse those students throughout the room when she made her official seating chart later in the week.

Mrs. G taught her that it was best to let the kids sit wherever they wanted the first few days. It gave her a chance to see whom they already knew, and how they naturally clustered into their cliques. This would be helpful information later.

Michelle stepped to the podium and took a blank seating chart from the stack. "Welcome to room 107," she began. "My name is Mrs. Baron." She gestured to the board, which read:

Mrs. Baron Room 107 Language Arts

Then she asked them to check their schedules to make sure they were in the correct room.

"While I'm taking roll, I'm going to pass around a blank seating chart, and I'd like you to write your first and last name on the square that represents the desk where you are currently sitting. This will be your seat assignment for the remainder of the week."

She handed the blank chart to Katy, who promptly wrote her name and passed it to the student behind her.

Michelle called roll, making phonetic spelling notes beside the names she mispronounced as well as writing down any nicknames the students requested for themselves. She noticed that several of the students in the back row were chewing gum. Wondering to herself whether or not she should correct them on this violation of school rules, she heard Mrs. G's voice in her mind. *The first week sets the tone in the room. If you let them get away with things the first week, they will expect that leniency in the future as well."*

Without looking directly at the offenders, she said, "I'd like to start the year off with a brief overview of what we will be learning in language arts this year as well as the behavioral expectations I have for my students."

Standing at the front of each row, she counted out the syllabi and handed them to the students sitting in the front. As the kids began passing the handouts back through the rows, Michelle noticed that even the students who had been slouching in the back, leaned forward to receive the papers.

"Let's begin with an overview of the curriculum," Michelle said as she held up one of the handouts and pointed to the front top section. Referring to her roll sheet, she randomly called on students to read the paragraphs that described the academic goals of the course, as well as the materials required and the reading list.

"Great," she said with a smile. "Now let's look at the behavioral standards at the top of page two."

The sound of papers flipping filled the air as the students moved to that section of the handout. While the class read through the rules, she noticed the gum chewers return to their slouched postures, attempting to hide behind the rest of the students.

"Summer's over, but I'm sure it's hard to leave some of the pleasures of that season behind. If you are chewing gum right now, please deposit it in the nearest trash can."

Several students stood and followed her directive. She noticed that one of the girls in the far corner of the back continued to chew defiantly. She glanced at the name on the seating chart. *Amber Gamble.*

Looking directly at her, Michelle said in a clear but kind voice, "Amber, would you mind getting rid of your gum, too, please?"

All eyes turned to look at the culprit. Amber rose slowly to her feet and meandered over to the wastebasket. She clutched the gum between her front teeth then pulled it with her fingers, making a long strand of the sticky substance extend from her mouth. Then she chomped the string of gum, chewed a few more times, and finally spit it out.

"Thank you," Michelle said evenly. "While you're up, would you mind grabbing a stack of those literature books for your row, please? And if each student at the back of the rows would do the same, we can get these books passed out to you today."

By the end of the period, all the students had their three books – spelling, literature, and grammar – and they had their first assignment – to go over the syllabus and behavior guidelines with their parents that night, getting them to sign the bottom of the second page and provide their daytime phone numbers and email addresses.

As quickly as the period had passed, the subsequent classes also seemed to rush by in a blur. At

3:00, Michelle looked out over the empty room, smiled a weary smile and sighed. Day one. She had survived.

Michelle's husband, Steve, arrived home that evening to find little Maddie at the kitchen table earnestly at work on a crayon drawing. "How's my favorite girl?" he asked as he bent over and planted a kiss on the top of her head.

"Oh, Daddy," Maddie replied without taking her eyes off of her artwork.

Michelle shut off the water in the kitchen sink and turned to face her little family. "Hi, hon." Her eyes sparkled but her lopsided grin revealed a weary woman.

"How was your day?" Steve asked, pulling her into a hug. He felt her cling to him tightly for a moment before pulling away.

"It was great. Seems like most of my classes will be good. First period has a few kids who will be a challenge. But overall, I'd say everything went smoothly."

"I'm proud of you, babe. Those kids are lucky to have you."

Michelle looked up and gave him a kiss.

"Look, Mommy!" Maddie's voice demanded. "I'm finished!" She held up her drawing of a brown triangle sitting on grass with some lollipop trees in the background.

"Wow! That is great, honey," Michelle replied.

"What's the picture for?" Steve asked.

"Well, Daddy, it's my homework assignment. We had to draw a picture of something we did this summer. See? Here's our tent in Yosemite."

"Oh, yeah. I see it. Good job." He patted her on the back, his heart swelling with love for their little girl.

Michelle smiled at them both and announced, "Time to wash up, guys. Dinner's in five minutes."

"Let's go, pumpkin." Steve took her little hand in his, and they headed to the restroom to wash up.

By 10:00 that night, Michelle was exhausted. Thankfully Steve had taken over the kitchen clean up while she bathed Madison and got her settled in bed. Three bedtime stories and two Eskimo kisses later, Maddie had succumbed to a deep and needed sleep.

"I'm beat," Michelle said as she picked up a few stray toys and books in the living room.

"Me, too. Let's call it a day."

They walked upstairs together, their cat Max bolting ahead as if racing them to the bedroom.

"So, do you have everything ready for tomorrow?" Steve asked, as they got ready for bed.

"I think so," Michelle replied, slipping between the sheets. "Oh, this feels so good!" she added with a smile, sinking down into her pillow. As she closed her eyes, she found herself thinking about the group in the back of first period. Somehow she had to figure out a way to reach those kids.

"What was that sigh about?" Steve asked, cuddling up against her.

"Oh, just thinking about that first period class."

"You'll figure them out." He kissed her gently then turned out the light.

But Michelle couldn't shake an unsettling feeling. Amber Gamble was going to be a real challenge.

CHAPTER TWO

As Michelle stopped by the office the following morning, she noticed Amber sitting on a chair near the door to the assistant principal's office. Michelle looked from Amber to Daisy, the receptionist at the front desk. Daisy's raised eyebrows acknowledged Amber's predicament as she nodded at Michelle and sighed. Apparently Amber's reputation was off to a poor start at Magnolia Middle School.

Retrieving her mail from her cubby, she headed to class.

When first period began, Michelle noticed that Amber was not in the room. "Does anyone know where Amber is?" she asked.

"Probably got suspended," one boy remarked. Several students laughed in response.

"It's a bit early in the year to be getting suspended," she replied skeptically.

"Not for Amber," someone in the back popped off.

"Okay. Let's get started," Michelle said, pointing to the board. "Here's your warm up activity. Please take out a piece of notebook paper and begin writing."

The prompt on the board asked the students to write about their bedrooms. It encouraged them to use as many descriptive words as possible and to be specific. "Paint a picture with your words so I can see your room in my mind," the final sentence read.

Michelle watched as most of the students opened backpacks, pulled out binders, removed paper and began to write. Several nudged others around them to borrow paper or a pencil. Then the room got quiet as they began to write.

A few moments later, Amber showed up. She dropped her backpack with a loud thump and slumped down into her desk.

"I'm glad you're here, Amber. We're doing a quick write for our warm up this morning," Michelle added as she pointed to the board.

Amber rolled her eyes, tapped the girl next to her and asked for paper and a pencil, then started to write. A minute later, she raised her hand.

"Amber?"

"I'm finished."

Michelle could feel her irritation rising as Amber stood and strolled to the front of the room. She tossed her assignment on Michelle's desk, turned, and slowly sauntered back to her seat. Smiles and uneasy laughter replaced the quiet and focused atmosphere of the room.

Michelle glanced down at Amber's paper — *I don't have a bedroom. THE END.*

"Amber, I'd like to see you for a minute after class," she said.

Amber shrugged and rolled her eyes.

After collecting the warm up quick writes, Michelle asked the students to clear their desks. She began distributing a pretest for grammar. "This test will not go into the grade book," she reassured them. "It is a measure of how much you already know, so I can create a plan that will best fill in any gaps. If you finish before the end of the period, you may begin working on your homework for tonight – pages 3-4 in the grammar workbooks."

Later, when the bell rang and the class poured out of the room, Amber managed to escape with the masses. Michelle thought about calling the office or sending a call slip to Amber's next class, but the busyness of the daily schedule swept her away. It wasn't until the end of the day that she realized she had not addressed Amber's defiant disappearance.

Gathering up the stack of 180 quick writes and the students' pretests for grammar, she stuffed them into her canvas bag and erased the board. Her cell phone buzzed, and she noticed a text message from Steve.

Still in court. Can't pick up Madison.

On most days, their close friend, Kelly, would be getting Maddie at the end of the school day and taking her to their house until Michelle could pick her up. Kelly's little boy, Luke, was a year and a half older than Madison and the two little ones, Lucy and Logan, were four and two. But today Kelly had an appointment, so Steve was planning to pick up Maddie.

Michelle sighed, added her lesson plan book to the paperwork in her bag, and headed for the office, punching Maddie's school number into her cell phone to let them know she would need to go to daycare for about half an hour.

As she turned in her roll sheets, she ran into Ron Black, the assistant principal.

"Hi Michelle," he greeted her with a smile, unable to disguise the fatigue in his eyes.

"Hi, Ron. Long day, huh?"

"Yep. It's starting early this year," he replied. "We usually get at least a week or two's reprieve at the beginning of September, but we started out with a bang this morning. One of our girls was caught smoking in the bathroom."

"Amber Gamble?"

"Yeah. How did you know?"

"She's in my first period class. I saw her sitting by your office before school."

"That girl is a handful, Michelle. Keep an eye on her. She's got lots of baggage."

Michelle nodded.

"You should check her file when you get a chance," he suggested as he turned to go to his office.

She glanced down at her watch. 3:30. Better get over to pick up Madison at the after-school daycare. Amber's file would have to wait.

The evening disappeared before she knew it. At 11:30 that night, she finally pushed aside the stack of quick writes and tests, glanced over the details of her lesson for the next day, and headed for bed.

Steve was sound asleep when she slipped in beside him. She almost forgot to set the alarm clock before drifting off to sleep.

CHAPTER THREE

Michelle was startled awake by the shrill buzz of the alarm. Forcing herself out of bed, she shuffled to the bathroom and splashed cold water on her face. "Steve, can you get Maddie up?" she called out to her husband who was now getting out of bed himself.

"Okay, babe. I'm on it," he replied.

After quickly getting dressed, Michelle began applying her makeup.

"Mommy, I don't feel well." Maddie stood at the door of the bathroom hugging her teddy bear.

Michelle turned and looked at her daughter. She appeared to be fine with good color in her cheeks, although her hair was in complete disarray.

"What's up, honey? Does your tummy hurt?" she asked.

Maddie nodded her head, squeezing her bear tighter to her chest.

This was Madison's typical response to stress. Her stomachaches were the red flag that something was bothering her.

Michelle took a deep breath. She wanted to get to school early to pull Amber's file. Looking up at Steve, who was now standing behind Maddie, she gave a silent plea for help. Their cat, Max, was pacing back and forth at the entrance to the bathroom, crying for attention himself.

"Hey, pumpkin. Let's go downstairs and feed Max. Then we can sit together in the big chair for a few minutes."

"Okay," Madison replied softly, her eyes downcast.

Michelle nodded her gratitude at Steve and hurried to finish getting ready.

Steve cradled his oversized baby in his arms as they snuggled in the soft rocker recliner in the family room. "How's your tummy, Princess?"

"Better, Daddy," Madison replied, resting her head against his chest.

"Everything okay at school?"

"I guess." She snuggled deeper into his arms.

Steve hesitated. Madison had never complained about anything at school in the past, but he could tell from the resignation in her voice that something was not right.

"Tell me about Mrs. Tucker."

"She's okay. She put my Yosemite picture up on the bulletin board."

"That's great, honey. She must really like it," Steve added, giving her a squeeze.

Madison nodded and was silent for a few moments. "Daddy?" she asked.

"Can Mommy take me to school today?"

"I don't think so, Maddie. She has to be at school early, remember? We talked about that this summer — how Mommy will have to leave for school before the bus comes."

She sighed and nodded, then pushed herself upright and looked into Steve's eyes. "Mommy's really busy." Her voice cracked.

He could tell she was trying not to cry. "Yes she is, honey. Let's give her a little time to get settled into her new job. Maybe it will be better after that."

"Do you think so?" Madison asked, a glimmer of life returning to her eyes.

"I hope so, sweetie," he replied. "Let's go upstairs and get ready. We'll let Mr. Bear come with us to the bus stop today," he added, patting her bear on the head.

Madison giggled. "You're funny, Daddy! His name is Teddy."

Warmth rushed through Steve's heart as he looked at the smile on his daughter's face. To think he almost missed this moment. He shot up a quick prayer of thanks for the gift of their daughter. Two years of infertility had almost robbed them of this precious little girl. But that was seven years ago, and now they were off to kindergarten.

Michelle only had a few minutes to rifle through Amber's file. A red folder marked CONFIDENTIAL was inserted into the back. She quickly pulled it out. There was a court order regarding the temporary placement of Amber and her brother Jack into the care of the state foster system.

"Foster care," she said quietly under her breath.

"What?" Daisy asked from her desk. "Did you ask me something?"

"No, I'm just talking to myself," Michelle replied. She glanced at her watch. There was no time to read the enclosed report by the social worker. She'd have to come back to the office and pour over it later. Seemed she was always in a hurry. This was going to be a hectic year.

After entering her classroom, she quickly wrote the date and the day's agenda on the board, then sat down at her desk to record the quick writes and pretests into her grade book. She flipped on her computer, scanned the school emails, and noticed one from Ron Black. The subject matter: Smoking Incident.

Michelle clicked on the email and began to read.

Yesterday morning, a female student was caught smoking in the girls' bathroom. Please report any tobacco smell you notice to the office. I would appreciate it if the female teachers would periodically stop by the girls' bathrooms, and the male teachers the boys' bathrooms, to check for smokers.

Unfortunately this is becoming a problem at Magnolia, and we want to nip it in the bud. Any students caught smoking must be brought directly to the office. This is an automatic referral. Please help us send the message that our district has a zero tolerance policy for smoking on campus.

The email ended with a reminder about the staff meeting that day after school. Michelle groaned. After Steve told her about his conversation with Madison, she'd wanted to try to slip out right after school and surprise her daughter with a trip to the ice cream shop. Instead, she'd have to text Steve and let him know that she would be home late. Hopefully he could break away and pick up Madison.

The bell rang as Michelle closed the email. Soon students filtered in, and Michelle remembered that she'd have to address Amber's failure to stay after class yesterday. As the period began, she directed the students to the front board.

"Please take out a piece of paper and copy the sentences on the board, making all the necessary corrections in punctuation, capitalization, and spelling."

The students unzipped backpacks and clicked open their binders. Then the room fell silent as they began to work. Michelle walked between the rows looking at the various students and their work. She ended her tour at Amber's desk. Tapping her gently on the shoulder, she signaled Amber to follow her out the back door.

Once they were out in the hall, Michelle spoke softly to Amber. "You did not stay after class yesterday."

"Oh, yeah. Guess I forgot." Amber stared into her eyes unblinkingly.

Michelle could feel her heart racing. "Listen, Amber. I want to get us off to a good start this year, but I need your help." Michelle prayed silently as she returned Amber's stare.

No response.

"Do you understand, Amber? I want us to get along, but it takes two to do that. You do your part as a student, I'll do mine as a teacher."

Amber looked off to the side as if fixing her gaze on something behind Michelle. "Whatever," she muttered.

Michelle gently rested her hand on Amber's shoulder, and the girl looked back into her eyes. "I really care about you, Amber. I mean it. Let's give this another try."

Amber paused and replied, "Whatever you say."

Michelle withdrew her hand and gestured toward the door, following Amber back inside the classroom.

That afternoon during her conference period, Michelle slipped the red confidential folder out of Amber's file. Sitting down at the worktable, she began flipping through the pages. The heading, SOCIAL

SERVICES REPORT, at the top of the third page flagged Michelle's attention.

The report began with some basic information about Amber's parents' divorce and the court-ordered custody arrangement granting Mrs. Gamble physical custody of both of the minor children, Amber and her brother Jack. It detailed the rights of Mr. Gamble to have visitations with the children during their school breaks and for one month during summer vacation.

Another entry further down the log indicated some special health circumstances with Mrs. Gamble requiring intermittent hospitalizations and court-ordered drug rehabs. After Mr. Gamble refused the option of caring for his children, they were placed in temporary foster care. Apparently, there were no other relatives except an elderly grandmother on the east coast and an uncle, who traveled continuously as a military reporter.

Specifics of each foster home in which the children had been placed followed this section. Although Jack had been able to remain in his initial foster home, it appeared that Amber was on her third placement. The former two homes had complained of Amber's sullen attitude, her disrespectful and often defiant behavior, and her smoking as reasons for terminating their care.

Amber currently lived with a middle-aged woman, who housed two other foster children as well — a five-year-old girl and her three-year-old brother. Cecilia Harte was a former bank teller. She and her husband, Paul, had no children of their own. Apparently, they had opted to become foster parents. When Paul died suddenly of a massive heart attack, Cecilia continued the process of providing short-term care for needy youngsters.

The social worker's log chronicled the decision to leave Amber's brother Jack in his original foster home and place Amber under Cecilia's temporary custody, with the hope that their mother, Stacy Gamble, would respond to the latest treatment for her severe depression and be able to resume her role as a parent.

Oh, Lord. How can I help her? With all these students, how can I make a difference for this poor girl? Michelle made a mental note to call Ben and Kelly and ask them to put Amber on the prayer chain at church. Without disclosing Amber's identity, she could certainly ask for prayer for an unnamed but hurting young lady at her school.

Amber sat on the grass and waited outside the front of school for her foster mom to pick her up. Her body was crying for a cigarette, but she knew she didn't dare light up here. She picked at the grass beside her and watched her peers walking out to climb into cars awaiting them at the curb.

Why did Cecilia always have to be late? Probably too busy with her soap operas, Amber thought. Or those two snotty nosed brats that lived there. Amber didn't even like to acknowledge Tessie and Todd by name. To her, they were just another reminder that her brother was stuck at another house somewhere and that both of them had loser parents.

As Amber watched for Cecilia's beat up Ford Bronco, she noticed Mrs. Baron coming down the front walk.

"Hi, Amber," her teacher's voice greeted her.

"Hi," Amber replied without making eye contact.

"Waiting for someone?"

What business is it of hers, Amber thought, but she replied, "Yeah."

"See you in the morning," her teacher said, continuing toward the faculty parking lot.

"Right," Amber replied.

As she disappeared around the corner of the building, Amber spotted Adam sauntering across the lawn toward her. He was a junior at the high school a few blocks away, and they had met last spring when he walked past Magnolia on his way home and struck up a conversation with her.

"Hey, Amber."

"Hey," she answered.

He plunked down on the grass beside her and propped his elbows on his knees. "Got a cigarette?" he asked with a laugh.

"Funny, Adam," she snapped.

"Whoa. Aren't we *touchy* today?" he said with a grin.

"Sorry. I'm just sick of all the stupid rules at this school and how that jerk, Harte, keeps me waiting every time she comes to pick me up."

"Let's ditch this place," Adam suggested.

"And go where?"

"I don't know. The beach maybe."

She leaned over and looked him in the eye. "Seriously?"

"Yeah. Seriously. We could hitch a ride down there, have a smoke, and then hitch another ride back to your place later."

Amber smiled. "Sounds good."

They stood up and walked off, Adam carrying her backpack for her. That's what she liked about him. He took care of her.

An hour later, Amber and Adam were stretched out on the sand. They'd gotten a ride with a high school senior Adam spotted coming their way about two blocks from the middle school. It was some guy Adam's brother hung out with on the weekends, so Amber felt totally safe taking the ride.

Once they got to the beach, Adam pulled a cigarette out of his jeans pocket. It was a little bent, but he straightened it out and lit up. He and Amber took turns taking long drags on the cigarette. She could feel herself unwinding. The sound of the surf, the relief from her nicotine cravings, and the presence of Adam all worked to relax her.

They both stretched out on the sand, lying on their backs as they talked about school and their messed up lives. Adam's alcoholic dad had gone into one of his tirades the night before, and he and his brother were trying to stay clear of him. Ever since Adam's mom died two years ago, it seemed like neither of them could please him.

He rolled onto his side and propped his head up facing her, as he quietly studied her face.

"What?" she asked defensively.

"You know something, Amber?"

"What?"

"You have great eyes."

"Right, Adam. Knock it off."

"I'm serious. You do."

Amber could feel her adrenalin beginning to surge. She had a thing for Adam, but so far they'd just been friends. She turned her face toward his, and before she could say another word, she felt his mouth gently cover hers. Closing her eyes, she relaxed into his kiss.

Adam pulled away for a moment and then came back for more. She responded by moving toward him and parting her lips for the deep, passionate kisses that followed. Her body was responding in ways Amber could not control. She knew she should stop, but every fiber of her being wanted more.

31

As Adam inched his body up against hers, she felt his hand start to travel down her body and slip under her shirt. At that moment, Amber's cell phone started vibrating in her pocket. It startled her, and she sat up.

"What's wrong?" Adam asked, looking bewildered.

"My phone. Wait a sec."

Amber looked at the name on the screen of the cell phone. *Jack.* "I've got to get this. It's my brother."

Sitting up, Adam took out another cigarette and lit up.

"Jack? Are you okay?" Amber asked.

"I'm fine. Where are you?"

"I'm at the beach with a friend. Why?"

"At the beach? Are you nuts, Amber? Mrs. Harte just called. She said she's been looking for you for almost an hour."

"She'll get over it, Jack."

"I don't think so, Amber. She said she's calling the social worker, and if you don't show up soon, she's calling the cops."

"Great," Amber replied sarcastically. "I can't even spend some time with a friend without the warden checking on me."

"You'd better call her, Amber. I mean it. Call right now."

"Fine, Jack. I'll call her. Anything else?" She glanced over at Adam and rolled her eyes.

"Yeah. Did you call me last night?"

"Oh, yeah, I did. The witch you live with told me you were asleep."

"Mrs. Goodwin isn't a witch, Amber."

"Whatever," Amber replied, flipping her hair back over her shoulder.

"So what did you want? Why did you call?"

Amber could tell that Adam was getting restless. "Just checking on how you are. That's all."

"Right. Why don't you come over one of these days and see for yourself?" Jack asked, implying that he resented Amber for not keeping her word about visiting him.

"Yeah, little brother. I'll do that soon." Adam handed the cigarette to her, and she took a long drag before finishing. "Gotta go, Jack."

"Call Mrs. Harte."

"Okay already! I said I'd call, didn't I?" Amber snapped.

"You know Mom wouldn't like the way you are acting these days, Amber."

"You're kidding, right? Mom doesn't care about us, Jack, or she'd have come for us by now."

"That's not true and you know it."

"Whatever."

Jack was quiet on the other end. Amber felt like a jerk talking to her brother that way, but sometimes he could be so stupid.

"Listen, Jack. I've got to get off the phone," she said, pushing Adam's hand away from her shirt buttons as he teased her and laughed.

"Just promise me you'll call Mrs. Harte before she calls the cops or something."

"I promise. And I'll come by in a few days."

"Yeah. Bye, Amber."

"See ya." Amber flipped her phone shut and turned to Adam.

"Trouble?" he asked.

"My foster mom is freaking out. I have to call her." She opened her phone again and dialed the number, bracing herself for the barrage of questions to follow.

After she had reassured the woman she was okay, she promised to be home in an hour.

"Guess we'd better get going," Adam said as he got up and grabbed Amber's backpack. He reached out a hand and pulled her up beside him. They walked toward the street hand-in-hand, and for the first time in a year, Amber felt some hope for her future. With Adam around, she'd at least have someone to love who could love her back in return.

CHAPTER FOUR

The social worker was waiting on the porch when Amber got home. "I hear you've had a little adventure this afternoon, Amber," Bonnie Blackwell said, her voice revealing her chagrin.

"What? Spending time with a friend is a felony now?" Amber asked sarcastically.

Bonnie shook her head and sighed. "You know that's not it, Amber. You took off without telling Mrs. Harte. She was worried sick."

"I doubt that," Amber replied.

"Here's the deal, Amber. You have a good home here for a while, but not if you keep up this kind of attitude. Mrs. Harte cares about you, whether you like it or not. And she's doing her best to take care of you and Tessie and Todd."

Amber didn't say anything. She just stared at the street lamp.

"You should be helping her, not making life harder for her."

Silence revealed the wall around Amber's heart.

"Look, I know this is hard on you, too, but I heard from your mom's doctor today. It sounds like you may be here longer than we thought."

"Great. Thanks for the good news." Amber looked up at the sky. She did not want this lady to see the tears that were swimming in her eyes.

"Do you want me to look for another placement for you?" Bonnie asked softly as she placed her hand on Amber's shoulder. "Or do you think you can buck up and follow Mrs. Harte's rules?"

Amber shrugged and looked away. "I don't care where I live," she lied. "I just want to stay at Magnolia."

"Okay, then let's give it another try here."

"Fine." Amber slung the backpack over her shoulder and walked inside without saying goodbye.

"Sorry I'm late," she muttered as she walked by Cecilia Harte in the front room. The kids were watching cartoons, and Amber could smell dinner cooking.

"Wash up," Cecilia replied. "Dinner's ready." She walked over to the TV and turned it off, triggering protests from Tessie and Todd. "You two need to wash up, now. You can watch the rest of the cartoons after dinner."

Amber tossed her backpack down at the foot of the stairs and followed the little ones into the bathroom. She'd try to help out a little, like Bonnie suggested. Maybe then Cecilia would be more open to the idea of Amber spending time with Adam after school.

Stacy Gamble sat on the edge of her bed, holding her head in her hands. A suffocating fog of hopelessness engulfed her. An image of Amber and Jack playing on a playground somewhere in the photo album in her mind brought a rush of tears and a deep ache in her chest. "My babies," she murmured softly.

An attendant came into the room holding a small paper cup in her hand. "Time for your medicine, Stacy," she said matter-of-factly. She handed Stacy the paper cup and retrieved the water bottle from her bedside table.

Stacy looked at the pills in the cup. She knew they would dull the pain and give her a temporary escape that only sleep could provide. Without another thought, she upended the cup and swallowed them.

Maybe tomorrow would be better. Maybe tomorrow she would somehow find a way to see her kids again. With those thoughts swirling in her mind, she eased herself down into the bed and drifted off to sleep.

Michelle could smell the smoke on Amber's clothes as she entered class later that week. The pungent odor clung to Amber and followed her like a gray storm cloud. Michelle hesitated to write a referral and send her to the office because it would disrupt her teaching and shift the focus away from the lesson. Besides, she hadn't actually seen her smoking.

While most of the students worked on the warm up activity on the board, Amber slipped a black journal out of her backpack and flipped it open. As Michelle began her routine walk through the room, Amber kept glancing her way. She reluctantly closed the journal as Michelle neared her desk.

In a soft but firm voice, Michelle reminded her to begin working on the warm up.

"I don't have any paper," Amber muttered.

"How about a sheet from that?" Michelle pointed to the journal.

"That's not for class stuff."

Michelle could feel herself growing tense and could hear the edge in her voice as she replied, "Then what is it doing out on your desk?"

"Sorry." It was clear from her tone that Amber was not sorry at all. She rolled her eyes, slid the journal off her desk, and crammed it back into the backpack. "There. Satisfied?" she asked with a smirk.

Michelle simply shook her head to herself and walked away. She knew she was not handling this right, but something about that girl got under her skin. Besides, the timer was signaling the end of the warm up exercise, and she had a class to teach.

As she went over the correct answers to the exercise with the rest of the students, she could see Amber pull out her journal again and begin reading whatever was inside.

During lunch break, Michelle looked for Mrs. G but couldn't find her in the lounge area. She sighed and sank into one of the chairs at the teachers' lunch table.

"Rough morning?" Ron asked as he passed through the lounge on his way out to supervise the kids in the quad.

"It's Amber Gamble. She's making me crazy."

"Hang in there, Michelle. Don't let one kid upset you. This school's got a handful that are walking along the edge of the cliff. But most of them are just hurting kids."

"I know. I don't know why I let her get to me this way," Michelle confessed as she shrugged her shoulders.

"It's because you want to be a winner with each and every one of your students. That's what makes you a great teacher. But it can also be the sure road to frustration and burn out."

"Yeah. You're right."

"Here's a suggestion. Tomorrow, or even this afternoon, look around and mentally count all the students who are on task. You'll find that the majority of them are right there with you."

"Thanks. I'll do that." Michelle smiled and waved as Ron backed out of the lounge with a nod.

Michelle tried to follow Ron's advice. For the next several days, she did her best to shift her focus from the fringe kids to the ones who were really working. Although it helped reassure her that she was actually getting through to most of them, she couldn't shake her aggravation with Amber.

Time after time, Amber pushed her buttons. If she wasn't tardy, she was insolent and unproductive. The scowl on her face spoke volumes about her feelings for the class and for Michelle as a teacher. At least once a day, Amber would find a way to defy her or disrupt the lesson.

Michelle didn't want to take her frustrations home with her, but she could see this dilemma starting to intrude on her conversations with Steve and Maddie.

"Honey, are you listening?" became a frequent query over the dinner table, as Steve observed her pensive expression.

Finally, Michelle decided she would take action. She'd go visit Amber's foster home and see what kind of world this girl inhabited.

It was 4:00 p.m. Wednesday afternoon when Michelle found herself standing on the sagging front porch of Cecilia Harte's weathered home. She could hear the boisterous sounds of cartoons coming from the television and had to knock three times before a tired looking woman pulled back the curtain and peered outside.

The door moaned slightly on its hinges, as it swung open. "Can I help you?" the woman asked.

"My name is Michelle Baron. I'm Amber's language arts teacher."

"What has that girl done now?" Cecilia asked, introducing herself and inviting Michelle inside. "You two turn down that television!" she called out to the youngsters in the adjoining room.

As the volume receded somewhat, she gestured to the couch and asked Michelle if she'd like something to drink.

"I'm fine, thanks," Michelle replied with a smile she hoped looked genuine.

"So what's with Amber now?"

Michelle could see that Cecilia Harte was just as frustrated and concerned as she was. Where should she start? And would it be fair to unload her burdens about Amber on someone who was already shouldering what seemed to be an enormous load? She was just opening her mouth to say something about wanting to just get to know her students better, when Amber flung open the front door.

"What's going on?" she asked. "Am I in some kind of trouble?"

"Your teacher just got here, Amber."

"Actually, I was in the neighborhood and wanted to drop by," Michelle said.

"Right." Amber replied, with a tinge of sarcasm. She cocked her head to the side and looked at the ceiling.

"Amber!" Cecilia chided. "Watch your manners."

Amber rolled her eyes and started to walk out of the room, tossing back over her shoulder, "I'll be in my room."

After Amber had darted upstairs, Cecilia looked at Michelle and shook her head. "She's got a lot of baggage. I was hoping she'd be reunited with her mom in a week or two, but it's looking like that won't be happening for a while." A sudden cry from the other room diverted her attention, and she excused herself to referee a fight between the two little ones.

Michelle's stomach ached. This had not helped at all. Sure, she understood more about the environment where Amber lived, but it did not seem to justify the hostility and rebellion Amber exuded at school.

This sure isn't working like the teacher movies in the theater, she thought to herself. Wasn't this the way the heroine in those stories always began to make an impact on troubled students?

Cecilia came back into the front room with a little girl straddling her hip. Tear-streaked cheeks and a pouty mouth told Michelle that this little one had lost the fight. Her thoughts shifted momentarily to Madison. It hadn't been that long since Maddie was the age of this girl. She wondered how such young kids had ended up in foster care, and it made her heart ache to be home with her daughter.

She rose to her feet. "I'd better be going."

"Thanks for dropping by," Cecilia said with a weary smile. "Amber needs more people in her life who care. Call me if she gives you any trouble."

Michelle nodded and thanked Cecilia for her time, smiling sympathetically at the little girl in the woman's arms before walking out the front door.

CHAPTER FIVE

Amber slouched down against the headboard of her bed, her cell phone pressed to her ear. The room was strewn with clothes and her backpack sat unopened on the floor just inside the door. With her foot resting on her bent knee, she wiggled nervously as she listened to the fifth ring. "Come, on. Pick up," she mumbled under her breath.

"Hey, Amber."

"Adam! Are you busy?"

"No. What's up?"

Amber lowered her voice, glancing over at the closed door. "I need to get out of this place."

"Cool. Want me to come get you?"

"Yeah. I was thinking maybe your brother could take us down to the beach."

"He's off with some friends somewhere, but he left his car. No one's here, so maybe I'll just take it."

"Are you crazy, Adam? You don't have a driver's license."

"No, but Troy let's me drive sometimes. It'll be fine. We just have to get back before he does."

She knew it probably wasn't the best idea, but Amber was desperate to get out of the house. The beach would be the perfect escape. "Okay. I'll meet you out front."

Slipping on her flip-flops, she cracked open the bedroom door and listened. Cecilia was in the bathroom giving the kids a bath. She'd never hear Amber leave with all the ruckus those two were making in the tub. Amber hung a "Do Not Disturb" sign on her doorknob and left music playing in her room. She and Cecilia had an agreement that Amber could have privacy in the evening as long as she came and told her goodnight before she went to sleep.

Heading down the stairs and out front, Amber checked her pocket to make sure her cell phone was there. As she approached the curb, Adam drove up in a beat up Ford sedan.

She hopped in the front door, and started to fasten her seatbelt. "Hi!" she said with a smile.

Adam patted the center seat. "Over here," he said, reaching for her hand.

She slid next to him and dug into the cushion to find the seat belt.

He tapped his hand on the steering wheel to the beat of the music on the radio. "Ready?"

"Yeah."

"Okay. Off to the beach!" Pulling the car from the curb, they took off.

A full moon illuminated the streets, and Adam maneuvered the car carefully, constantly checking his rearview mirror for any signs of a patrol car.

Soon they were parking on a quiet street parallel to the sand. Amber slid out through Adam's door, and he took her hand, leading her toward the water. The beach was empty — a sure sign that summer was over.

They walked quietly along the water's edge, heading for a cluster of driftwood logs where they could sit.

"So what's up?" he asked as they sat down.

"Nothing. I just had to get out of that prison for a while. All I hear around there are those two brats fighting or the warden telling me what to do."

Adam nodded, his gaze on the horizon. Silence hung between them, as the waves lapped the shore. He gently pulled his hand out of hers and placed it on her shoulder.

Amber turned to face him. As he leaned forward to kiss her, she eagerly responded. *Finally, someone who loves me. Someone who's here for me when I need him.*

Soon they were stretched out on the sand, caressing and exploring each other's bodies. Just as Adam was beginning to unbutton her jeans, her cell phone rang.

She pulled it out and glanced at the number on the screen. It was the social worker. She wanted to hit the mute button, but what if it was about Jack? Her brother might be in trouble or something.

"Yeah?" she asked.

"Amber? It's Bonnie Blackwell. I've got some news about your mother."

Amber pushed herself up in the sand, watching Adam flip onto his back and stare into space.

"What? What is it?"

"The psychiatrist has decided to give your mom an opportunity to try an outpatient program for a week. She'll be going home this weekend, but will be coming in for daily group and individual counseling sessions. If it goes well, you and Jack may be able to return home in a few weeks. I thought you'd want to know."

"Yeah. Okay, thanks."

"It's just a first step, Amber. We'll see how she does. But I'd like to take you and your brother to see her once she gets settled at home."

"Okay. Does Jack know?"

"I'm calling him as soon as I get off the phone with you. Can I talk to Cecilia for a minute?"

Amber's heart started to race. "Uh, well, she's kind of busy right now. She's giving the kids a bath."

Looking over at Adam, their eyes made contact, and he sat up. "Can I have her call you back?"

"Sure. That's fine. In the meantime, I'll call your brother."

"Sounds good," she replied. "And thanks for letting me know."

Flipping the cell phone shut, she pushed herself up to a standing position. As she buttoned her shirt, she said, "We've gotta go."

Adam swore under his breath. "So when she says 'jump' you jump?"

"It's not like that. But I've gotta have Cecilia call her back, or we'll be busted again. Maybe we can come back tomorrow night."

"Right." Adam moved slowly, clearly communicating his disappointment and frustration.

When they got into the car, she sat in the middle again and rested her hand on his lap, but this time Adam did not hold it. Pulling up to the curb, he kept the motor running and stared out the windshield as she slid over and exited the passenger door. "See you tomorrow after school?" she asked.

"Yeah. Sure."

As soon as the door was closed, he pulled away without so much as a glance in her direction.

Michelle tried to listen to Maddie as she chattered away about her day at school from her little rocking chair in the family room. Meanwhile her mind was pulled to the stack of papers that awaited her as soon as her daughter was off to bed. She also needed to go over her lesson plan for the next day, adding in the various state standards she would be covering, since her principal was requiring the teachers to post this information daily on the front board of class.

Making a final sweep through the room to pick up discarded shoes and toys, she heard Maddie add with exasperation, "…and then she took my paper and wrote her name on it!"

Michelle paused and looked at her daughter. "Who took your paper, baby?"

"I'm not a baby, Mommy!" Maddie rolled her eyes.

"You're right, honey. Sorry. So tell me again who took your paper." Michelle set the shoes and toys on the bottom stair and turned back to Madison.

"That sassy brat, Alonna! She always takes my papers."

"Did you talk to your teacher about it?"

"I can't or she'll call me a tattletale." Maddie's eyes started to tear up.

Michelle went over and knelt in front of the rocking chair. "Did you try asking Alonna to give you back your paper?"

"Yes. She finally did when Liam told her she'd better." Maddie smiled through her tears. "I like Liam, Mommy. He's my friend."

"That's good. Do you want me to talk to Mrs. Spencer about Alonna?"

Big sigh. "No. It's okay."

"Okay, pumpkin. You let me know if you decide you want me to."

Maddie nodded.

"Time for bed," Michelle announced, pushing herself up from the floor and holding out her hand. Maddie sighed dramatically again, and the two of them headed upstairs, Michelle pausing to pick up a handful of items awaiting their journey to the closet and toy basket. With Steve working long hours on a new case, it was up to her to help Maddie with her bedtime routine. It would be an hour before she could tackle the papers and plans that awaited her in her school bag.

By midnight, the words on the papers became a blur to Michelle. She'd only graded three of the five classes and hadn't touched her lesson plans. She was splashing cold water on her face, when Steve snuck up behind her.

"Hi, beautiful," he said, nuzzling into the back of her neck.

"Steve! You scared me."

"Sorry, babe. What are you doing up so late? I thought you'd be asleep a long time ago, especially after such a busy day."

She wrapped her arms around his waist and rested her head on his chest. "I wish. I've still got at least two hours of grading and plans to work on."

"No way. You've got to get some rest. Come on," he reached for her hand and led her to their bedroom amidst her feeble protests.

Before dawn, Michelle slipped out of bed and softly padded downstairs. Starting the coffeemaker, she retrieved her lesson plan book and her charts of the state standards. She flipped open the standards and began hunting for the labels she needed for her board.

By the time her second cup of coffee was done, she'd finished the lesson plan and had graded another class's papers. The sun peeked in through the kitchen window. *Thank you, God. No rain today.*

She made the lunches for Steve, Maddie, and herself, and then headed for the shower. Steve was just rolling out of bed as she stepped under the warm water. "Need any help in there?" he called.

Michelle shook her head, smiling wearily to herself. Not too long ago, that would have meant a playful start to the day. Now it was a reminder that she had so little time or energy for her man.

"Sorry, honey. Almost done." She rinsed herself off and stepped out. "Would you go start waking up Maddie?"

"I'm on it," he replied, exiting the room with the razor buzzing against his morning stubble.

Amber swore at the alarm clock as she slammed her hand down on the knob. *Another day in paradise. Right.*

She flashed back to the night before. Adam sure left in a huff. All she needed was her boyfriend acting like a jerk, too. She sure hoped her mom would get her act together soon, so they could be together as a family again. What was left of the family, at least. As far as her dad was concerned, he could fry in hell. His girlfriend, too.

"Amber? Are you up?" Cecilia called from the hall.

She groaned. "Yeah, I'm up." Pushing herself out of bed, she stared at the clothes in her closet. She grabbed a pair of tight, holey jeans and a low cut tee shirt. Looking at herself in the mirror after dressing, she smiled. *This will get Adam's attention.*

As she headed through the kitchen on her way out, she grabbed a candy bar out of the snack basket on the counter.

"Amber, what are you wearing?" Cecilia asked. "Isn't there a dress code at Magnolia?"

Amber looked at her and shook her head. "It's fine." She quickly left before the next lecture about breakfast. Shoving the candy bar into her backpack for later, she made her way to the bus stop.

As Michelle sat at her desk trying to get a few more papers graded before school began, Katy poked her head in the door. "Do you need any help, Ms. Baron?"

Remembering the standards she needed to post on the board, she replied, "Sure. You can write some things on the board for me."

Katy beamed. "Great!"

After she'd listed the state standards for the lesson, Michelle also had her write the names of the students who were missing assignments. About a third of the kids in each class had failed to turn in the essays she was currently grading. That meant there would be many more to grade if she could collect the rest of them.

Several minutes later, the bell rang and students began to wander in. Michelle had posted a warm up assignment on the board, and several of them got out their binders and went to work. A few moments after the tardy bell, Amber and her friends strolled in the back door and took their seats, making no effort to start writing.

As Michelle walked to her podium, one of the kids called out, "Why's my name on the board?"

Pointing to the list Katy had neatly written, Michelle explained, "These are the names of those who still owe me the first essay – your autobiographical incident."

Several groans erupted followed by questions about how late the assignment could be turned in.

"I'm giving those of you who haven't finished yet a chance to work on it in class today. Whatever you have done by the end of the period is what I'll collect. It's half credit for essays turned in today."

"What were we supposed to write about again?" Amber asked without waiting to be called on. Her friends laughed.

"A time when you learned an important life lesson. Just write it like you are telling me the story of what happened."

"Right," Amber replied.

"The rest of you will have a chance to do your homework in class. We are reading the first story in the literature book and answering the questions on page 7. Use complete sentences please." Michelle wrote the assignment on the board, and returned to her podium to make a new seating chart. It was time to split up the group in the back.

As Michelle sat down at her desk to eat lunch, she glanced over the late essays she'd collected from her students. Amber's caught her eye, and she began reading it.

One day my dad decided he didn't want to be my dad anymore. He found a girl at the gym. So now he's all about his new girlfriend. He told us he'd come visit sometimes, but I guess he forgot about that. *So he walked away and is having fun, my mom is screwed up, my brother is living somewhere else, and I'm stuck here.*

Life lesson: Don't ever get married or have kids.

Michelle's heart sank. What a mess. She thought about her own parents and how they had taken care of her and Tim. She'd never had to deal with any of the stuff Amber was facing. Then she tried to picture Steve walking away from her and Madison. She couldn't fathom how Amber's dad could do such a thing.

Poor girl. She needs to see the other side – a couple who are committed to each other and their kids. How could Michelle reach Amber? Maybe if she talked to her foster mom again, she could arrange for Amber to do something with them on a weekend.

She'd love to get Amber to the youth group at church, and then maybe they could have a picnic at the park. It would be great if she could include Amber's brother, too. Michelle's mind wandered as she considered the possibilities. Before she'd even finished her sandwich, the bell rang and the next group of kids started streaming in the door.

During her conference period, Michelle decided to stop by the counselor's office and share her thoughts about Amber. By this time, she was getting pretty excited about her ideas.

"Be careful, Michelle," Karen Stafford warned. "Kids like Amber are tough to reach. And the church thing is iffy. She's got to really want to do it, or you could look like you are trying to breach the separation of church and state."

"So how do I approach it?" Michelle asked.

"Talk to your husband first. Make sure he's onboard with this. If he is, I'd suggest you mention something about the youth group to Amber's foster mom and see how she reacts. If she's open, you can try talking to Amber. If not, you'll need to back off."

Michelle nodded.

"You know, we used to have a Christian club on campus. The teacher who sponsored it left a couple of years ago. Would you be interested in being the sponsor for something like that?"

"Sure. What would I have to do?"

"Your role would be to supervise the kids while they met during their lunch break. The club itself has to be student initiated and run to meet the state requirements. They used to have a local youth pastor who came and did a Bible study with them. He was invited by a few of the students who went to his church."

Michelle thought about how busy her life was already. But how could she say no to a Christian club? And this might be a chance for Ben to reach out to the community on behalf of their church. "Just let me know what to do, and I'll do it."

"I'll talk to some of the eighth graders who were in the club as sixth graders. Maybe they'll want to get it going again."

Michelle stood up.

"Hey, thanks for caring so much about Amber. I hope you can work something out with her foster mom."

"Thanks," Michelle replied, heading out the door. Before returning to her classroom, she pulled Amber's file and scribbled Cecilia Harte's phone number on a piece of scratch paper. She'd talk to Steve and see what he thought, and then try to reach Cecilia that night.

"I don't think this is a good idea, honey," Steve said. He thought of all the legal implications of what Michelle was suggesting. Just having that girl in their car was a liability. And the church thing – that was a potential lawsuit waiting to happen.

"I know you care about her," he added as Michelle studied his face. "But you can't solve the world's problems. You've already got enough on your plate."

"What's the use of teaching, then? If I can't impact my students' lives, why am I there?"

Steve could sense the tension rising along with her voice. They'd just gotten Maddie to bed, and he didn't want her overhearing an argument. He reached over and put his hand on her shoulder. "I think it's wonderful that you want to help Amber. I'm just not sure this is the way to do it. We have to consider Maddie, too. Do you really want her around kids like Amber?"

Michelle looked away, shaking her head in frustration. "I hear you, Steve. I'm just trying to figure out how to connect with this girl. She's so needy, and the people who she should be able to rely on have let her down. I want her to see what a healthy family looks like, and to have a chance to connect with the kids at church."

"Maybe you could persuade her to come to the Christian club," he suggested.

"Right, Steve. Like she's going to be interested in that."

"Okay, well how about if you try having lunch with her at school. Are you allowed to do that?"

"Yeah, I'm sure that would be fine. If I can get her to show up."

"Try it. See what she says. And I'll talk to Ben. Maybe he can think of another way to reach out to her."

Michelle nodded in agreement, but he could tell she was disappointed. She began twisting a strand of hair at the nape of her neck as she gazed off into space. Steve reached over and gently guided her hand away from the frayed clump of hair, then caressed her long, dark tresses. "I love you, babe," he said tenderly.

She looked into his eyes. Leaning forward, she kissed him, and he pulled her into his arms. Desire drew them out of the kitchen and up the stairs to their bedroom, leaving the scrap paper with Cecilia's Harte's number sitting on the table.

CHAPTER SIX

Amber called Adam around 8:30. His brother agreed to take them down to the beach for a while, promising to pick them up before midnight. Amber had figured out a routine of sneaking out during the kids' bath time and then returning after Cecilia was asleep. *Good thing she at least respects my privacy at night*, Amber thought, as she once again left the radio playing and the "Do Not Disturb" sign on her doorknob.

This time Adam brought a blanket and a joint with him. They smoked the joint together, and then stretched out on the blanket.

Amber rolled over on her side and propped herself up on her elbow. "Adam?"

"Yeah?"

"Do you ever think about getting out of here?" she asked.

Now he rolled over and faced her. "What do you mean?"

"I mean leaving. Getting out of Sandy Cove."

Adam scooted closer and rested his other hand on her stomach. "Not really. Why?"

"I don't know. Just wondering. Don't you get sick of listening to your dad yelling at you and your brother?"

He looked away for a moment then shrugged. "Sometimes. But that's life. Besides, where would we go?"

Amber stared up into the sky. "Anywhere but here. I just want to get Jack and get out of here."

"You're crazy, Amber," he said, bending over and kissing her.

Soon their bodies were pressed together, and she could feel him unhook her bra and unbutton her jeans. Before she realized what was happening, she'd crossed a line she could never regain. *So this is love.* It hurt some, but now she and Adam were definitely together. He told her not to worry about getting pregnant. He said it couldn't happen the first time. Next time he'd bring protection.

As Amber lay in bed hours later, she realized how attached she was getting to Adam. Although part of her felt a little sick that they'd actually done it, another part felt not so alone anymore.

Amber's social worker called the following day. It was Saturday, and she wanted to get Amber and Jack together at a neutral location in order to discuss the visitation with their mother.

"I've arranged for Mrs. Harte to drop you off at the park by the lighthouse," Bonnie Blackwell told Amber. "I'll pick up Jack and meet you there."

"Okay," Amber agreed. This would work out well, especially since she'd been promising to come see Jack but had ended up spending most of her free time with Adam.

"See you there around eleven," the social worker added before hanging up.

Amber got up and stretched. She really wanted a cigarette, but it was too risky during the day, with the kids running around the house, and Cecilia expecting her to come downstairs for breakfast. Pulling on an old sweatshirt and the jeans that were on the floor beside the bed, she ran a brush through her hair. Then she reached into her pocket and found the extra joint Adam had given her the night before. Better hide this somewhere, she thought.

Opening the closet, she spotted a cosmetic bag that she kept her extra makeup in. She unzipped it, pulled out a small box that held some toe rings and put the joint under the cotton square at the bottom. Then she closed the box and dug down into the makeup to bury it beneath a myriad of eyeliners, blushes, and applicators. *There. That oughta do it.* She smiled as she zipped the bag and returned it to the corner of the closet.

She managed to make it through breakfast and the annoying cartoons blaring from the living room, and then asked if she could take a walk 'to get some fresh air' before Cecilia drove her to the park.

"I guess that would be okay," she heard her foster mom say as Amber headed out the door. A few houses away, she pulled a cigarette and matches and lit up, careful to watch for any neighbors who might spot her and report back to Cecilia. Taking deep drags, she felt herself beginning to relax and her hands to stop shaking. She flipped open her cell phone and called Adam.

No answer.

Probably sleeping in, she thought to herself with a smile as she replayed their passionate encounter from the night before. If only there were some way she and Adam could just get away from Sandy Cove and move in together. She knew she was pretty young to be thinking of stuff like that, but there was no way she wanted to wait until she was 18 to get a place of her own. Plus, she could just imagine being able to be with Adam whenever she wanted. No school, no foster parent breathing down her neck, no social worker trying to get her to live by someone else's rules.

She allowed herself to fantasize about having a cute apartment where she and Adam could live. Maybe Jack could live with them, too. She and Adam could drop out of school and get jobs to pay for the place. Adam would be able to get his driver's license in a month, so he'd be able to drive them wherever they needed to go. He could even take Jack to school and sports or whatever. She'd show her mom she didn't need her or anyone else. Adam was the only one she needed. He understood her and knew how to make her forget all her problems.

Just as she was beginning to decorate their imaginary apartment in her mind, the buzzing of a vibrating cell phone in her pocket broke her train of thought.

Jack.

Even though he couldn't see her, she immediately dropped the cigarette on the ground and smashed it with her shoe.

"What's up, little brother?"

"I just wanted to make sure you're still coming to the park to meet us," he said.

"Yup. I'll be there."

"Okay, good. I think Ms. Blackwell has some news about Mom."

Amber shook her head and rolled her eyes. Poor Jack. He still believed that their mom would get better, and they could all live as a family again.

"Amber? Did you hear me?" he pressed.

"I heard you, Jack. Just don't get your hopes up. You know how Mom is. She starts to get better and then does something stupid again that lands her back in the looney bin or in rehab."

There was silence on the other end, and Amber felt bad for bursting Jack's bubble. But someone had to help him see the reality of the situation. Unless she and

Adam could figure some way to get out of Sandy Cove and get a place of their own, both of them would probably be in foster care for a long time.

She heard him sigh into the phone. "See you at the park," was all he said before hanging up.

As Amber slipped into the house a few minutes later, she avoided Cecilia and the kids and quickly bolted up the stairs to change clothes and spray some cologne on her hair. She didn't want to deal with any accusations about smoking today.

It was a beautiful day to go to the park, and Michelle was looking forward to her time alone with Maddie. The first week of school had sapped her of the energy she was used to giving their daughter.

But after a good night's sleep, she was thrilled to see the sun streaming through the window. Although she'd long ago reconciled herself to the cloudy, drippy weather that blanketed Sandy Cove much of the year, her southern California roots still craved the warmth of the sun and rejoiced when the weather cleared.

Steve had left early that morning for a jog and a breakfast meeting with their pastor and friend, Ben. They were planning a men's Bible study that they hoped to start two Saturday mornings a month at the local Coffee Stop.

Since Maddie was still sleeping, Michelle helped herself to a cup of coffee and went out into the backyard with her Bible. The bright blue sky and the golden warmth of the sun awakened her senses.

She listened to the birds chirping and soaked in the solitude she rarely experienced these days. Setting her Bible down beside her, she sipped her coffee and reflected on her new life as a middle school teacher and mom.

Michelle had such high hopes for the kids in her classes, and her mind was preoccupied with them even when she was at home or church. Their high energy kept her on her toes, and she knew she'd have a busy year just trying to keep them focused and learning.

Maddie seemed to be adjusting well to her school routine, in spite of the little ups and downs with some of her peers. Her teacher was a perfect fit for their daughter, and Maddie loved learning new things. It was quite a contrast to the eighth graders in Michelle's classes, whose primary focus was impressing their peers.

Still, Michelle loved the age group. It wasn't hard for her to remember her own teen years and how much energy she'd poured into her friendships. Always battling her shy nature, she had to make even more of an effort to connect. Thankfully she'd always had Kristin, her best friend, to share her life issues, hopes, and dreams.

I should call her, she thought. *Maybe this afternoon after the park.*

But there were lots of papers to score, lesson plans to complete for the following week, and of course the usual weekend routine of laundry and cleaning. Opening her Bible, she flipped to the book of James. Ben had begun a series of sermons in this book, and she tried to read through each chapter in advance. Skimming over the first chapter, she paused at verse seventeen.

Every good and perfect gift is from above, coming down from the Father of heavenly lights, who does not change like shifting shadows.

She let the truth of that passage soak into her heart and mind. So many good and perfect gifts – Steve, Maddie, their little home in Sandy Cove, and now an opportunity to fulfill her dream to teach. God had truly blessed her. Tears of joy mingled with the wordless praises that overflowed from within. For several peaceful minutes, she allowed herself to bask in His love.

Then a sound interrupted her reverie.

"Mommy?"

Michelle turned to see her little girl standing at the door in her princess nightgown, her teddy bear hugged to her chest.

"Good morning, sweetheart. Mommy's just enjoying the sunshine out here." She held open her arms, and Maddie shuffled her slippered feet over and climbed into her lap, leaning her head against her heart.

"Are we still going to the park?"

Michelle smiled as she caressed her daughter's curls. "You bet! Mommy will fix breakfast, then we'll get you dressed and ready to go." She paused and added, "How about pancakes today?"

"Yipee!" Maddie exclaimed as she turned and hugged her mom. "I love you, Mommy!"

"Love you, too, sweetie."

It doesn't get any better than this, Michelle thought as she snuggled her daughter close.

Amber spotted the social worker and her brother sitting at a picnic table up on the grassy hillside of the park. Pushing the car door open and grabbing her backpack from the floorboard, she threw a "See ya," over her shoulder to Cecilia as she climbed out of the old Ford and headed their way.

Jack was straddling one of the benches and tossing a football up in the air while Bonnie looked through some paperwork on the table.

"Hey!" Amber called as she crossed the grass, her backpack slung over one shoulder.

"Amber!" Jack exclaimed, grabbing his football and heading her way. He nearly collided with her in his enthusiasm.

"Whoa! Slow down!" Amber grabbed him into a rough hug then pulled the football out of his arm. "Fall back for the pass."

Jack ran backwards, his hands outstretched for the ball. Amber lobbed it his way, and he easily caught it. Letting her backpack fall to the ground, she ran after him, chasing him around a few trees before tackling him to the ground. They both sat up and laughed.

"Wanna go on the monster slide?" Jack asked.

"Maybe later," she replied, retrieving her backpack and walking toward the picnic tables.

"Hi, Amber," Bonnie Blackwell said with a smile. "You two look like you were having a lot of fun out there."

"Yeah," Jack replied with a grin. Amber just nodded her head in acknowledgment.

"Are you ready to talk?"

"Sure," Amber said, plunking down on the bench.

"I've just been going over some visitation paperwork," Ms. Blackwell began. "Your mother will be staying at Glen Haven, which is a supervised half-way house, for the next month. She can have visitors anytime in the evening until nine thirty, but she'll be in group and individual therapy during the day."

Amber nodded and Jack sat silently running his fingers over the stitching on the football, studying it as if seeing it for the first time.

"I'd like to set up some mid-week visits for you guys starting next Wednesday." She looked over at Jack. "I can pick you up at six thirty, then we can go over to get Amber. How does that sound?"

Jack looked at Amber, and they both nodded.

"We'll just stay an hour or so the first time and see how it goes. Your mom is eager to see you guys, but she's really tired after all her therapy sessions."

Poor Mom. Right. "Whatever," Amber replied.

"It's just the first step, Amber. Let's hope she is able to return home soon with the two of you."

"That'll be the day," Amber replied, feeling a little guilty when she saw Jack's hurt expression. "I just don't want you to get your hopes up, kid," she told him.

"Let's all try to think positively about this. Your mom needs to know that you two believe in her and want to be back with her again. Okay?"

"Sure," Amber said, softening her tone for Jack's sake.

"Then it's settled. I'll let your foster parents know about our plans. Just be sure you are home when I get there."

Amber draped her arm around Jack's shoulder. "No problem."

"Well if you two want to visit for a while, I can check my phone messages and do a little paperwork here," Bonnie offered.

"Yeah," Jack replied. "Let's go over to the equipment."

"You're on!" Amber stood and grabbed her backpack from the table.

"You can leave that here, if you want," Bonnie suggested, gesturing to the pack.

Amber's thoughts immediately went to the joint in the zippered pocket inside. "No, that's okay."

She and Jack walked across the park toward the equipment, Jack tossing his football in the air as they did. There were two areas of swings, slides, and various climbing apparatus on the far side of the park. One was designed for toddlers and younger kids, the other for older elementary ages like Jack.

As they approached Jack's monster slide, Amber thought she heard a familiar voice from the other playground. Looking around the pirate's tower, she saw her English teacher, Ms. Baron, with a little girl who looked to be five or six years old. They were on the swings, laughing and talking as they pumped together higher and higher.

"Look at me, Mommy!" the little girl said excitedly.

"I see you! You are almost flying!"

So that was her daughter.

Amber couldn't help but stare. Ms. Baron and her daughter looked so happy just swinging on the swings together. Wow. Amber never thought of her teachers as having kids. Ms. Baron was a pretty strict teacher, but she looked like a fun mom.

"Come on, Amber," Jack whined. "Let's go on the monster slide."

"Okay, okay. I'm coming," she replied, forcing herself to refocus on Jack. *Some people have all the luck*, she thought to herself as she compared her relationship with her mother to the one she'd just observed on the other playground.

CHAPTER SEVEN

After dinner that night, Michelle helped Madison with her bath. Then they setout her clothes to wear to church the next day. Maddie liked to try to get ready all by herself in the morning, so it helped if they chose her outfit the night before.

Tucking her daughter into bed, she sat down and rested against the headboard to read her a story. Twenty minutes and three books later, she told Maddie it was time for lights out.

"I had fun today, Mommy," her little girl said, as she snuggled into her bed.

"Me, too, honey." Michelle smiled. She kissed Madison and headed downstairs to start the schoolwork she'd put off all day.

Steve was just placing a file into his briefcase when she walked into the family room. "She asleep?" he asked.

"Almost."

He reached for her and pulled her into his arms. Michelle rested her head on his chest, the sound of his heartbeat causing her to relax momentarily. Then she pulled back and said, "Gotta get my lesson plans started for next week."

Steve moaned. "Can't it wait until tomorrow? I haven't seen you all day." He pulled her back into an embrace and kissed her head.

She felt so torn. Though she would love to cuddle with her husband, if she didn't get some of her work done tonight, she'd be busy all afternoon after church tomorrow. Then she'd miss a chance to spend time with Maddie again.

"Let me work for about an hour. I promise I'll stop after that."

"Okay, babe," he replied. "Mind if I turn on the TV?"

"No, that's fine. It won't bother me. I'll sit in here with you while I do my lessons." Michelle gave him a squeeze, then retrieved her school bag from the coat tree and pulled out her lesson plan book and the grammar text. While Steve watched a police drama, she mapped out her goals and plans for the upcoming week. An hour melted into two, and it was almost midnight before she put her books away. Steve had fallen asleep on the couch, the remote control resting on his lap.

She gently slipped it out of his limp hand and punched the power button, silencing the late night news. "Come on, honey," she whispered. "Let's go to bed."

Steve stirred from his sleep, rubbed his face with both hands, and got up. "Okay." He grabbed the box of cookies from the coffee table and deposited them in the kitchen, then took her hand as they walked upstairs together.

"Guess I was more tired than I thought," he said.

"Yeah. I'm pretty beat myself," she agreed.

As they entered the bedroom, Michelle noticed that she hadn't even made the bed. There was so much to do every day. She hoped she could keep things together at home while she tried to make a go of being a teacher. Pulling the covers into place from the foot of the bed, she recalled her time at the park with Maddie and smiled.

Tomorrow was another day. Maybe after church they could all do something together. But she did have a stack of grammar packets to score, too.

CHAPTER EIGHT

Amber had mixed feelings as the three of them approached Glen Haven. Jack was unusually quiet, and Ms. Blackwell was acting very business like and matter-of-fact. The place looked like a normal house, except for the wooden sign out front with its name displayed in green letters.

The evening clouds were rolling in, and their dark shadows contributed to Amber's uneasiness. What would her mother look like, and how would she act? Amber was as much concerned for her brother as she was for herself. Mom had always seemed a little too emotional, and Amber could remember often reassuring her, when it really should have been her mother's job to do the reassuring.

Would she be really quiet and weepy like the last time they saw her? Amber didn't think she could handle another hour of watching her mother cry and try to explain to them how hard life was for her. It was pretty hard for them, too, and it was basically her fault that they were stuck in foster homes.

"When we first walk in, I'll be talking to the housemother," Bonnie explained. "Then we will go to see your mother in another room."

"Are you sure she wants to see us?" Amber asked.

"You don't need to worry about that. They wouldn't have suggested this visit if your mom wasn't ready for it."

Amber noticed Jack biting his fingernail. She nudged him to stop, but he shook her off then shoved his hands into his pockets.

They walked up the steps to the large porch. Several rocking chairs faced the street, and a variety of potted plants gave it a welcoming, homey look. Bonnie rapped on the door and a gray haired woman in a flowery apron opened it up.

"Mrs. Greene? I'm Bonnie Blackwell from social services and these are Stacy's kids, Amber and Jack."

"So nice to meet you," the woman replied as she gestured them to enter.

The house had a pleasant fragrance of homemade cookies. "Smells good in here," Bonnie observed.

"I just finished baking a batch of my famous oatmeal chocolate chunk cookies," she replied. "I thought they might be a nice addition to your visit. Stacy said you both love cookies."

Amber felt Bonnie nudge her to respond. "Thanks," she said as she watched Jack nervously looking around the room.

"Your mom is in our rec room, right through those doors. Why don't you all just go on in, and I'll bring the cookies as soon as they are cool enough to transfer to a plate."

Bonnie escorted them through the swinging door and into a cheerful room with several sofas and easy chairs as well as an entertainment center housing a large television. Their mother was sitting in a rocking chair by the window, and she immediately stood up and came over to them.

"Oh, my babies!" She wrapped her arms around them both and drew them close. "I have missed you so much!" Then she pulled back. "Let me take a look at you." She studied them both. "Jack, you look like you've grown six inches! And Amber, you are beautiful as always."

"You look good, too, Mom," Jack piped up, suddenly losing his nervous expression.

"Yeah, you do," Amber agreed.

Amber noticed that her mom seemed flustered by their compliments, starting to smooth her hair and clothes nervously. It was clear that she'd spent time getting ready for their visit. Her hair was clean and curled, and she was wearing what looked to be a new outfit. She even had make up on. Amber couldn't remember the last time she'd seen her mom wearing eyeliner or blush. Maybe she really was getting better.

"Let's sit over here," Stacy suggested, taking them both by the hand and leading them over to a denim sofa that faced the entertainment center. She sat between them, squeezing their hands and repeating, "I have really missed you two."

"That's a pretty cool TV," Jack said, pointing across the room. "Do you get cable here?"

"Of course they do, dummy," Amber said, immediately regretting her remark.

It was silent for a minute. Just as Bonnie was about to say something, Mrs. Greene pushed open the door and brought in the cookies. "Here they are," she said, placing the plate on the coffee table in front of them.

"Cool! Thanks!" Jack replied, helping himself.

Bonnie and Mrs. Greene chuckled, and Amber saw her mom smile.

"Would you like one, Amber?" Stacy asked.

Amber's stomach churned. It was just too weird visiting her mom at this place and everyone acting like it was a normal thing to do. "No thanks."

She felt her mother stiffen and loosen her grip on her hand. *Here goes. Now she'll probably clam up or start crying.*

Instead, her mother took a cookie and turned to Jack. "How's school going, sport?"

Amber winced. That was the term their dad used for Jack.

But Jack didn't seem to notice or care. "Fine. I just got an 'A' on my last spelling test."

"That's great. Congratulations!" Her mom turned to her and asked, "How about you, Amber? How are your grades?"

"So-so."

Stacy tried again, "How are your teachers?"

Amber shrugged. Why were they talking about this dumb stuff? "When do you think you'll get out of here?" she asked.

Stacy was quiet for a moment. "I don't know, honey. Pretty soon. They're helping me get my medication levels stable."

"Oh." That could mean anything. "So, do you like it here?"

"Yes."

"That's good. It sucks where I live."

"Amber!" Bonnie said.

"Sorry. Just thought she might want to know."

Her mom looked deflated. The smile she wore when they entered had vanished, and Amber could see the tears beginning to well up in her eyes.

Oh brother. Now I've done it again. She'll start crying, and we won't see her for another month. Whatever. I'm sick of pretending everything is fine.

Jack started biting his fingernail again.

"I know you're eager to move back home, Amber," Bonnie said. "Your mom's doing the best she can to follow all the doctor's orders and get the therapy that will help make that possible."

Amber nodded, turning her thoughts to Adam. She pictured their spot on the beach and could imagine his embrace, his kisses, and the way his hand moved over her body. "Maybe we should go now," she suggested.

Stacy blotted at her eyes, looking lost.

"I think that might be a good idea," Bonnie agreed. She turned to Stacy. "We'll try this again in a week or so. I'll be in touch with your therapist."

Stacy nodded and tried to smile. She squeezed both of their hands again. "I love you guys. Thanks for coming to see me."

"We love you, too, Mom," Jack said, throwing his arms around her neck.

"Yeah," Amber replied as she stood up. "Get well." She gave her mom a perfunctory kiss on the cheek and then turned and walked toward the door.

It seemed like forever before Amber could hear Cecilia take the kids into the bathroom for their bath. She'd been waiting for over an hour to sneak out and go to the beach with Adam. Finally she heard the water running in the tub. Grabbing her cell phone, she made the call.

"Okay, I'm ready," she told Adam.

"On my way."

She peeked out the bedroom door to be sure it was safe, then headed out to meet him at the curb.

When they got to the beach, Amber suggested they take a walk. It was a clear night with a full moon reflecting off the water's surface. Adam took her hand and led her down the stretch of sand toward the lifeguard station near the lighthouse.

"How'd it go with your mom today?"

"Great," she replied sarcastically.

"Sounds like it. Want to talk about it?"

"Not really. She's her usual pathetic self. I doubt if she'll ever be half a mom again. Not that I need a mom, but I feel bad for Jack. He really thinks she'll get better, and we'll all be back together – just one big happy family!" She sighed and looked up at him.

"What? What are you thinking?"

"I just wish we were a little older and could get a place somewhere. Then maybe we could take care of Jack or something."

"Whoa. Sounds pretty serious to me." He pulled her into his arms, and they stood silently holding each other as the waves lapped the shore.

"Yeah. Never mind. I'm just glad we can come here. It's the only part of my day that doesn't suck."

Adam bent down and kissed her. She immediately responded, yielding to her craving for his love.

"It's kind of light out here tonight," he said, pulling away for a moment. "Maybe we should go up in the lifeguard stand where we'd have more privacy."

Amber smiled. She pulled him in that direction.

Soon they were entwined in each other's arms. "Did you bring it?" she asked.

Adam dug into his jeans pocket and swore under his breath. "Don't worry. I'll stop in time," he promised.

But Amber went home feeling more than worried. A load of guilt along with the fear of becoming pregnant made it difficult for her to sleep that night.

The next day at school, she couldn't concentrate on anything any of the teachers were saying. Even her friends had to repeatedly ask her if she was listening when they said something to her in the halls or at lunch in the quad.

She knew that she could be getting herself in a bigger mess than her life was already in. But that evening, as soon as it was safe, she found herself calling him again.

The part of her that longed to be held in his arms was stronger than the part that told her to stop.

CHAPTER NINE

As Michelle sat praying for her students before the first bell rang Monday morning, Amber Gamble came to mind. She thought back to her conversation with Steve and his suggestion to have lunch with Amber sometime.

An hour later, the first period class was almost over, and the kids were packing up their books. Michelle patrolled the classroom looking for any messes left on the floor.

Walking past Amber's desk, she paused for a moment. "Amber?"

"Yeah?"

"I was wondering if we could have lunch together today."

"Why? Did I do something wrong?"

"No. I'm just trying to get to know my students better, and I thought maybe I'd try lunch with some of you."

"Oh." She hesitated, glancing around to see if any of her friends were paying attention, but they all seemed focused on getting their stuff put away so they could bolt out the door when the bell rang.

"So what do you think?" Michelle asked, breathing a silent prayer for a yes.

"Uh, yeah, sure. I guess that would be okay."

"Great. Why don't you come by here after fourth period and we'll find someplace outside where we can eat and talk."

The bell rang and the kids started to leave. "See you at lunch," Michelle said.

"See ya," she replied.

Five minutes after the passing bell for lunch, Michelle sat at her desk praying that Amber would show. With only a 30-minute break, they'd have precious little time as it was, but Michelle hoped it would lay the groundwork for building a relationship of some kind.

The clock ticked away, and she nibbled at her sandwich and chips. *Please, Lord. Please prompt her to come.*

As she turned her attention to her computer and began checking her school email account, the door opened, revealing a suddenly shy-looking Amber Gamble.

Michelle's spirit soared. "Hi, Amber. Come on in."

Amber approached her desk and stood there looking lost.

"Do you have lunch with you, or can I get you something at the cafeteria?" Michelle asked.

"I don't usually eat much," Amber replied.

"Well, I'd be happy to get you a burger or something if you'd like."

"That's okay. I have a candy bar." She pulled it out of her backpack to show Michelle.

Michelle didn't want to lecture her about her choice of lunches, so she just smiled and nodded. "My favorite kind."

Amber smiled. "Mine, too."

"Would you like to go outside somewhere or just stay in here?" Michelle noticed the clock. Only twenty minutes left until the end of lunch break.

"Here's fine," Amber replied.

"Okay." Michelle gestured to her sandwich. "My lunch. Mind if I eat while we visit?"

"No, go ahead."

Michelle nodded. "So tell me a little about who Amber Gamble is."

"What do you mean?"

"If you had to introduce yourself by telling three things about you, what would you say?"

Amber hesitated. "I don't know." She turned away and started playing with her hair.

"How about if I go first?" Michelle asked.

Amber looked back at her. "Okay."

"Well, I'm a wife — I've been married for eight years. I'm a mom – we have a little girl named Madison. And this is my first year as a teacher. Now your turn."

"Uh…okay, I'm a student, I have a brother named Jack, and… oh, yeah, I have a boyfriend named Adam, who goes to SC High."

"Really? What grade is Adam in?" Michelle asked, trying to appear casually interested.

Amber looked down at her hands. "He's in 10th."

"Wow. Older."

Amber nodded. "Yeah. Most guys at Magnolia are jerks."

"I see." Michelle made a mental note to see if she could find out more about this Adam kid. "What's Adam's last name?" she asked.

Amber looked up. "Wilson, why?"

"Just wondering. Did he go to Magnolia?" Perhaps Cassie knew him from a prior year.

"Yeah. So did his brother, Troy."

"How old's Troy?" Michelle asked, hoping this wasn't beginning to sound like an interrogation.

Amber shifted nervously in her seat. "He's 18. He's a senior."

"So what do you and Adam do together?" Michelle asked, wondering how seriously they were dating.

Amber looked away and flipped her hair over her shoulder. "Mostly just go to the beach to hang out." It was pretty clear she didn't want to talk about it any further. "Is that your daughter?" she asked, pointing to a picture on Michelle's desk.

"Yeah, that's my Maddie. She just started school this year at Cove View Elementary."

Amber picked up the picture and looked more closely. "She's cute."

Michelle smiled. "Thanks."

"You guys go to the park by the lighthouse, don't you?" Amber asked as she put the picture back onto the desk.

"Sometimes. Why?"

"I saw you there over the weekend. Your daughter looked like she was having lots of fun."

Michelle nodded. "Do you like to hang out at the park, Amber?"

"Not usually. I was there with my social worker and my brother."

"Oh. What were you guys doing there?" she asked.

"We were having a meeting about going to see my mom. She's living at Glen Haven – it's a halfway house sort of for people who are...you know, messed up in their heads." She squirmed a little.

"I know about Glen Haven. Our church has considered doing a little Bible study there once a week. Do you think your mom would go to something like that?"

"I doubt it. She's not into the God thing much."

Michelle just nodded. "So how's it going at your foster home?" she asked, wanting Amber to tell her own story rather than relying on the office file.

"Okay, I guess." It was clear from Amber's tone of voice and the subtle shaking of her head that she was not happy with the arrangement.

"It must be hard." Michelle leaned in, hoping Amber would look up.

"Yeah. It sucks."

"Jack doesn't live there, does he?" she asked.

Amber shook her head.

"That's too bad. So do you get to see him very often?"

"No. Only when Blackwell arranges it."

"Blackwell?"

"Our social worker. She decides when we get to meet up."

"I see." Michelle could see the pain in Amber's face when she talked about her brother. "Do you think it would help if I offered to hang out with you and Jack at the park sometimes when I take Maddie?"

The look of surprise on Amber's face showed how much this caught her off guard. "Seriously? You'd do that?"

"Sure. Why not? I'm already there. If she wanted to, she could drop you two off for an hour or so while Maddie plays on the equipment. I really wouldn't mind, as long as it was just the two of you."

"Who else would it be?" Amber asked.

"I mean if you don't bring your boyfriend along. Just a chance for you and your brother to visit."

"Oh. Yeah. I doubt if Adam would want to come anyway. He's more of a beach person."

"Well, if you're up for it, I can see if I could talk to your social worker about it."

79

"Yeah. That would be great. Thanks," Amber smiled the first genuine smile Michelle had seen from her.

"Okay. I'll look into it," she promised. Noticing the clock, she added, "The passing bell is about to ring. I'd better head over to the office to check my mailbox for messages. Let's do this again soon." She gave Amber a warm smile and rose from her seat.

"Yeah. That would be cool." Amber rose to her feet, slung her backpack over her shoulder, and walked out, opening the candy bar wrapper as she left.

Michelle spotted Cassandra in the office after school that day and immediately thought about her lunch with Amber. "Hey there," she said.

"Michelle! How are things going?"

Michelle set her stack of papers on the counter. "Great! I think I'm getting organized."

"That's the biggest thing. If you can keep on top of that, you'll be fine," Cassie replied with a smile.

"Hey, I wanted to talk to you about one of my students. Do you have a minute?"

"Sure. What's up?" Cassie turned and leaned against the counter.

"I've got this girl in my first period named Amber."

"Amber Gamble?"

"Yeah."

"I've heard a lot about her. She sounds like a handful."

Michelle nodded. "She really pushes the limits. But I think I'm actually starting to make some headway with her."

Cassie looked intrigued. "Yeah? Tell me."

"Well, I dropped by her foster home and met her guardian. She seemed really surprised that I made the effort. Then I asked Amber to have lunch with me today, and she agreed."

"That's huge," Cassie replied. "How did it go?"

"I think it went pretty well. But here's something I wanted to ask you about. She's got this boyfriend from the high school. His name is Adam Wilson. I was wondering if you had him in your class a few years ago."

"Wilson. Hmmm." Cassie stared off into space for a moment. "Sounds familiar. What year is he now?"

"Sophomore."

Cassie thought for a moment and pulled an old yearbook off the shelf. She flipped through to the Ws. "Wilson, Adam. Oh yeah, here he is. He came into my class mid-year. Transferred from the honors class."

"What do you remember about him?" Michelle asked.

"Not too much. Seemed like a shy kid. I think he had an older brother, too."

"Yeah. Troy's his name."

"Troy Wilson. Now that's a kid I definitely remember. He was quite the ladies' man, even in eighth grade. The girls were always trying to get his attention."

"Hmmm. Wonder if his brother is trying to follow in his footsteps by choosing a younger girl he can impress."

"Wouldn't surprise me. Does Amber seem like the vulnerable type to you?"

"Yes and no. She's got a pretty tough exterior, but she seems like she's hungry for someone to love her."

"Uh, oh. Bad combination. I'd keep an eye on that one."

"Yeah. I think I will," Michelle replied. "She really misses her little brother, Jack, so I volunteered to supervise them at the park sometime."

81

"That's really sweet of you, Michelle. Just be careful that you don't get in over your head. Kids like Amber can really sap you if you let them. And you've got your own family to think about, too," Cassie added.

She nodded. "Yeah. Thanks." Retrieving her papers from the counter and her mail from her mailbox, she said goodbye and headed out to the parking lot.

CHAPTER TEN

"Going somewhere?" Cecilia asked Amber as she opened the bathroom door. The two little ones were disrobing for their bath, and she realized she'd left their pajamas in their bedroom.

"Uh…well…yeah. I was going to go to the library to study with a friend."

"The library? How were you going to get there?"

"My friend is picking me up in a few minutes," Amber replied.

"And you were going to leave without telling me?" Cecilia asked, adding, "I think I hear your radio playing in there."

Amber glanced back at her bedroom. "Oh, yeah. I'll go turn it off. Sorry about that."

"Wait. Before you do that, I want to know whenever you are leaving to go anywhere, okay?"

"Yeah. Got it."

"What time do you think you'll be back?"

"In a couple of hours. By ten."

"Okay. Take your cell phone with you. Is your friend bringing you home?"

"Yeah. He — I mean she will bring me back. Her mom, I mean."

Cecilia studied Amber's face. She knew the girl was probably lying, but she wanted to build some trust in the relationship. Plus she had two other kids to tend to, and the bathwater was probably getting pretty high in the tub by now. "Home by ten. No later."

"Right."

"And turn off the radio before you go."

Amber opened her bedroom, flipped off the music, and shut the door firmly behind her, bolting down the stairs to meet Adam at the curb.

"Splish, splash," Madison sang as she played with a baby doll in the bathtub. Michelle smiled and pushed a stray hair out of her face as she leaned over to wash her daughter's back.

"Does the baby get a shampoo tonight?" she asked Maddie.

"Yup!"

"Okay. Here's a squirt of shampoo for her." Michelle squeezed the bottle and allowed a small amount of the no-more-tears formula to fill Madison's outstretched palm.

"Okay baby," Maddie said in her singsong voice. "Rub a dub dub! Time to wash your hair."

"You're next, sweetheart," Michelle added.

"Oh, Mom," came the whine.

"No 'Oh, Mom' pumpkin. Remember, when baby gets a shampoo, so do you."

Maddie sighed. "Okay," she said forlornly.

As Michelle began massaging the shampoo into her golden curls, she asked, "How about going to the park again soon?"

Madison's frown was replaced by a smile. "Really, Mom? Can we go tomorrow?" The excitement in her voice made Michelle grin.

"Not tomorrow, baby. But later this week, okay? Tomorrow Mommy has a meeting after school, so you're going to Auntie Kelly's house to play, remember?"

"Oh yeah. Goody! Auntie Kelly is so much fun! And I can play with Luke, Lucy, and Logan."

"That's right. And we'll go to the park another day." Michelle gently rinsed the suds from her hair. "Maybe we'll bring one of my students along," she added.

Maddie looked up at her. "I thought your students were all big?"

"They are, honey."

"But aren't they too big for the park?"

"Mommy's not too big for the park, am I?"

Madison thought for a moment. "No, but you're a mommy. Mommies come to the park for their kids. But big kids don't like the park."

"Is that so?"

She nodded her head with a serious expression. Michelle tried to keep a straight face.

"Why would we take a big kid with us, Mommy? Don't we want to just play the two of us, like we always do?"

"I just thought it might be fun to bring a girl I know named Amber. She likes to play at the park with her little brother."

"Can't her mommy take them to the park?" Madison asked earnestly.

"No. Their mommy is sick. She can't go to the park." Michelle knew that was a half-truth, but the reality of Amber's life was far beyond Madison's comprehension.

Just then, Steve poked his head in the door. "How's it going in here? I'm ready to read a story to my favorite princess."

Madison clapped her hands, sending bubbles into the air.

"Time to get out, honey," Michelle said with a chuckle.

Steve knelt down beside his daughter's bed as they prayed together. "Bless Mommy and Daddy, and Max, and my teacher, and Grandma and Grandpa, and Auntie Kelly and Uncle Ben, and all my friends, and Amber and her brother and their mommy."

"Who's Amber?" Steve asked.

"She's one of Mommy's big girl students. Her mommy's sick, so we might take her and her brother to the park sometime."

"Really?"

"Yeah. Mommy said so."

"Oh. Okay. Well it's time for you to go to bed now, little one. Climb under those covers, and I'll get you all tucked in." Steve held the sheet and comforter open as she slid in to bed.

Brushing the curls away from her face and kissing her forehead, his heart swelled with love for her. He prayed silently, thanking God for her as he thought once again about all the infertility tests and procedures they'd faced to usher her into their family.

"I love you, princess," he whispered.

"I love you, too, Daddy."

"Night night," he added before clicking off the bedside lamp and quietly leaving the room.

He found Michelle down in the kitchen finishing up the dinner dishes. "Need some help?" he offered.

"No, I've got it," she replied, smiling at him over her shoulder. "Thanks."

Steve sat down at the table and glanced through the mail. "Madison added a few people to her prayer list tonight."

"Really? Who?"

"One of your students named Amber and her brother and mother."

Michelle put the last dish into the dishwasher and turned to face him. "Really."

"Yup. She said you might be taking them to the park this week," he added.

"I'm just thinking about it."

"Isn't Amber the girl that gives you so much trouble in class — the one who's in that foster home?" Steve tried to sound matter-of-fact, but he could feel his hand starting to clench.

Michelle leaned back against the counter and crossed her arms. "Yeah. That's her."

"Do you really think it's a good idea to take her to the park with Maddie?"

"I'm trying to build a relationship with her," Michelle began. "The two of us had lunch together, and she confided in me that she hardly ever gets to see her little brother. I thought maybe I could work it out with their social worker to supervise the two of them at the park once a week or something, so they could have time together."

"That's really noble, Michelle. But what about Madison?"

"What about her?"

"Do you really feel comfortable having her around this troubled teen?" He took a deep breath, trying to keep his voice calm and even. He couldn't believe Michelle thought this was a good idea.

"I'll be there, Steve. She's not going to do anything stupid. It's just a chance for her to be with her brother."

"But isn't the point of your park time with Maddie that it's a chance for just the two of you to be together? You're so busy these days with school, grading papers, lesson plans and stuff. I thought you wanted your play time at the park to be quality time together."

"I do, Steve," she replied, an edge to her voice. "I'm sure Amber and her brother will hang out on the older kids' equipment. I'll still be able to keep an eye on them and play with Maddie at the same time."

Steve studied her face. "I'm not really comfortable with this, `Shell. Give it some more thought before you go any further."

Michelle nodded. "Okay. It may not work out anyway. I haven't had a chance to talk to the social worker or anything yet." She looked a little hurt.

He got up and walked over to her, wrapping his arms around her and breathing in the fragrance of her cologne. "You're a good Mom and a good teacher, honey. Just don't try to mix the two, okay?"

She nodded and leaned into his embrace. "I'm beat," she said with a sigh.

"Me, too."

Their cat Max scurried out of the room ahead of them as they walked out of the kitchen, Steve's arm draped over her shoulder.

Amber could feel her stomach churning. The sound of the waves and the reflection of the moon on the surf usually brought her a sense of peace. Coming to the beach at night with Adam was what she looked forward to all day. But tonight was different. Three weeks had passed since she'd given herself completely to him, and something wasn't right.

"I'm late," she said.

"What do you mean, late?"

"I mean my period is late." She looked away, feeling her cheeks burn as she tried to swallow the lump in her throat and the shame that caused it.

Adam cursed under his breath.

"Hey, don't get mad at me," Amber shot back defensively. "You were the one who was so sure nothing would happen."

"So now what?" he asked.

"I don't know. I guess I'll get a pregnancy test at the drugstore." Amber wished she hadn't even told him. She should have done the test first, just to make sure.

Adam was quiet. He just glanced over at her then looked back out to sea. She couldn't tell what he was thinking or feeling. "I'm really sorry, Adam. Maybe it's nothing."

He turned to her again and attempted a smile. But all Amber could see was sadness or disappointment. She brushed aside a tear, hoping he didn't see it.

"Maybe I'd better take you home."

Amber stared at him. She just wanted him to take her in his arms and tell her everything would be okay. Instead, he looked like he'd rather be anywhere but with her. Their blanket was still folded beside them on the sand, and her hopes of being rescued slipped away into the night.

She stood up, brushed the sand off her jeans, and walked toward his car without a word.

As they drove off, he asked if she wanted him to stop by the pharmacy. "I don't have any money with me," she replied.

"I can pay for it." He opened the glove box and pulled out a wallet. "Just take whatever you need."

When she opened the wallet, she saw five twenties. "Where did you get all this money?"

"I sold some stuff."

"What stuff?"

"Just stuff. Don't worry about it. Just take what you need." He seemed really edgy, and she didn't want to upset him any more than he already was.

"Okay. Thanks." She took the money and shoved it into her sweatshirt pocket.

Adam pulled the car into the lot and found a parking place near the entrance.

"Be right back," she said, opening the door and stepping out.

He nodded. "I'll be here."

Amber worked her way through the aisles until she found the pregnancy tests. Examining a couple, she chose one that looked easy to read and headed for the check out. She was relieved to see an older woman at the register. The lady rang up her purchase and bagged the test.

Before she could even say a word, Amber handed her the cash. Once the change was in her hand, she walked quickly back to the car.

"Got it?" Adam asked.

"Yeah."

"So how long does it take?"

"I think it's just a few minutes," she replied, slipping it out of the bag to look over the directions.

"Are you going to do it tonight?"

Amber studied the directions. "It says to do it in the morning."

"Oh. Okay. Well, should I take you home?"

Amber wished she had a real home to go to with a real mom who wasn't in some rehab. A mom who would hold her close and tell her what to do. She knew she wouldn't be able to sleep tonight, and she wished she and Adam could just go back to the beach, spread out the blanket, and stay together until morning.

"Amber? What do you want to do?" Adam pressed.

"Whatever."

Adam tapped the steering wheel with his palm. "Listen, if you want to wait awhile, we can go back to the beach." He said the words she wanted to hear, but his heart wasn't present in the offer.

"No. It's okay. Just take me home." She turned and looked out the passenger window, watching the flashing neon light of the local liquor store advertise a brew.

Adam started the car and pulled out of the parking lot. They rode in silence back to the house.

"Amber?" Cecilia's voice called through the bathroom door the next morning. "Are you almost finished in there? The kids need to brush their teeth before I take them to meet the social worker."

"Just a sec!" Amber replied. She stared at the test stick in her hand. The blue plus sign was clear. She was pregnant. Shoving it into her pocket, she washed her hands and retrieved the box and directions from the counter. She folded the box into a tight wad and crammed it, along with the slip of instructions, into her makeup bag.

She almost knocked into the two kids waiting outside the door. "Sorry," she muttered under her breath, heading into her room and shutting the door. Once she heard them in the bathroom, she took the test stick out of her pocket again. Still positive.

What am I going to do? she thought, her heart racing.

Retrieving her cell phone from the nightstand, she punched in Adam's number. He didn't answer. Voicemail instructed her to leave a message after the tone.

"Adam, it's me. I need to talk to you. Call me." She flipped the phone shut and threw it into her backpack, then went downstairs, grabbed a couple of cookies, and headed to school, never even telling Cecilia she was leaving. Usually she gave Amber a ride to school, but this morning she had an early appointment with the other kids' social worker, and Amber had agreed to walk.

As she walked the two miles to school, she tried to imagine all the possible scenarios that lay ahead. Maybe she'd have a miscarriage. Her mom had said she'd had one between Amber and Jack. Or maybe she'd have an abortion.

The thought made her shudder. She really didn't want any doctor messing around with her down there. Plus she felt bad for the baby. It wasn't his or her fault.

Maybe she could convince Adam that they could drop out of school and have the baby. He could get a job, and they could get welfare or something until she could start working, too. Her social worker would know about how to do that.

Amber tried to picture being a mom and living with Adam. They could have cute little apartment somewhere. She really didn't care where they lived.

Maybe Jack could come live with them until Mom was well enough to have him back with her. They might even be able to become his foster parents and get some money from the state. That would help.

Amber started to feel better. She hated school anyway, and she was pretty sure Adam did, too. Why should they waste their time sitting in classrooms? They had something much more important to do now that she was going to have a baby.

She knew she'd hear tons of arguments from adults trying to tell her she was too young to be a mother. But didn't girls used to get married and have babies when they were her age? She would be fifteen before it was born. And Adam would be almost eighteen. They could make it work.

Then she'd have someone to love her always – a baby of her own – plus she wouldn't have to live in foster care anymore, and she could stay with Adam all night every night.

As Amber approached the school, she noticed there weren't any other kids hanging around outside. She flipped open her phone and looked at the time. School had started five minutes earlier. She skipped going to her locker and headed straight to English.

CHAPTER ELEVEN

Michelle was in the middle of her second example of a complex sentence when Amber slipped into the room. The class turned their attention to the back of the room, watching her take her seat.

"Amber, come and get a tardy slip," Michelle said.

Amber sullenly moseyed up to her desk, taking the tardy slip from the box on the corner and then proceeding back to her seat.

Michelle could feel her frustration rising. She redirected the class back to the example and continued with her lesson. After completing the explanation and answering their questions, she directed them to the independent assignment on the sideboard. "If you finish early, you may begin your homework," she added.

A few minutes later, Amber approached her desk. "May I borrow a pencil?" she asked.

"Sure," Michelle replied, handing her a new pencil, freshly sharpened that morning. "Did you miss the bus? You were pretty late today."

"I don't take the bus. I usually get a ride, but I had to walk today." Amber leaned over and gazed at the picture of Madison on Michelle's desk. "Your daughter is so cute," she added.

"Thanks. We think so," Michelle replied with a smile.

Amber nodded and started to walk back to her desk. Then she paused, turned around, and asked, "Did you find out about the park thing yet?"

Michelle thought back to her conversation with Steve and winced inwardly. She should never have mentioned her idea to Amber without first thinking it through and checking it out with the social worker and her husband. She shook her head. "Not yet. I'll let you know."

"Okay. Thanks." Amber gave her a slight smile and walked back to her seat.

"I'm telling you, Steve, I'm getting through to her." Michelle followed him into the family room, carrying a stack of papers in her arms.

"I'm sure you are, honey. And I'm glad you can see that. But why do we have to involve Maddie in this? Don't you think it's a good idea to keep your work separate from your home life?" He glanced at the papers in her arms and raised his eyebrows as he awaited her response.

As much as he loved seeing Michelle so passionate about her teaching, the hours she spent grading papers and working on lesson plans in the evenings and on weekends were really eating into their time together. Now she wanted to add one of her students into her one-on-one time with their daughter on their after school park excursions.

"Can I just try it once, honey? If it interferes with Maddie, I won't do it again. But if Amber and her brother just hang out where I can see them and don't cause any trouble, what's the harm?" She clearly wasn't going to drop the issue easily.

Steve looked at her and hesitated. Her earnest expression and beautiful big eyes pleading for understanding softened his stand. "Okay. One time. But you promise you will be honest with me and yourself about how it pans out?"

"Promise. If there are any problems at all, I won't do it again."

"Do you think I should join you guys? I could look over my calendar for the next couple of weeks and pick a day when I won't be in court."

"That's really sweet. But I don't think it's necessary. Unless you want to, of course."

He pulled her into his arms, crushing the papers she was holding. "I always want to spend time with you and Maddie."

She looked up at him and smiled. "If it works out, I'm sure Maddie would love it, too." She kissed him softly and then set her papers on the coffee table. "I'll call the social worker tomorrow and see what she says."

"Okay. I'll check my schedule at work, and if she says it's a go, we'll see if we can find a day that works."

"Thanks, honey."

Her smile melted his resolve to work on his opening comments for tomorrow's court case. "Do you really have to grade all those papers tonight?" he asked, running his finger down her arm.

"Mr. Baron! Are you suggesting I put you above my career?" she asked with a playful tone.

He took both her hands in his. "And if I were, what would be your response?"

She feigned dismay with a dramatic sigh. "Then I suppose I would have to comply." She moved closer and kissed him again.

Steve inhaled her cologne and drew her into an embrace. "I love you, Mrs. Baron."

She pulled him toward the stairs and they headed for bed, all the paperwork left behind.

It took Michelle a few days of playing phone tag before she was able to connect with Bonnie Blackwell, Amber's social worker. She was pleasantly surprised by Bonnie's friendly manner and her eagerness to accommodate Michelle's request.

"It's not very often that we have teachers willing to help our kids outside of school hours," the woman explained. "Amber is very blessed to have you in her life right now. She needs positive female role models, and I think it will be great for her to see you in your interactions with your daughter as well."

"My husband was thinking of tagging along with us, too," Michelle added.

Bonnie did not respond immediately. "I know he's probably trying to be helpful offering to join you. But my concern is that we have to be so careful about who we allow access to our kids. All our employees and volunteers, as well as the foster parents, must be fingerprinted and subjected to background checks.

"I know you have already had both of those to be a teacher, so I'm confident in allowing you to supervise Amber and Jack at the park. But to add your husband into the mix, I'd need to do that kind of paperwork on him."

"I hadn't thought of that," Michelle replied. "But it makes sense. I'll just explain that to Steve. I'm sure he'll be fine with me doing this on my own, He just wanted to help out."

"Okay. Great. Well let me know which day is good for you, and I'll make the arrangements with the kids' foster parents. I'm free to drop them off at the park most afternoons next week. My only late meeting is with one of my kid's teachers on Wednesday around four. Other than that, you name the day and I'll get it set up."

"Thank you!" Michelle was suddenly very excited about the prospect. What had started as a charitable idea was now becoming a new way to show Amber that she really cared.

After going over the conversation with Steve and looking at her calendar, she decided on Thursday as the best day. She called Bonnie, who promised to have Amber and Jack at the park at four. That would give Michelle time to wrap things up at school and get over to pick up Maddie at Kelly's house before meeting them there.

Amber approached her after class the following day. "My social worker told me that we are going to the park on Thursday."

"That's right. I'm going to stay there with you and your brother for an hour or so."

"Cool. Thanks." She pointed to Maddie's picture. "Your daughter will be going, too, right?"

"Yep. I'll play with her on the little playground, and you and your brother can hang out on the other side where the big equipment is."

Amber nodded. "Does Jack know?"

"I assume so. I think Bonnie called him last night."

"Okay. Well, better get to my next class."

"Yeah. See you in the morning. Don't forget to study for the vocabulary test."

"Right." Amber gave a mock salute and walked out the door.

Amber was late to class the morning of the park date. She looked pale. "Are you feeling alright?" Michelle asked, wondering if they would need to postpone their plans.

"My stomach's just a little upset. I'll be fine." She took her seat and pulled out a piece of notebook paper to begin working on the warm up.

By the end of the period, she seemed to have perked up. Michelle had noticed her sneaking a few crackers out of her backpack to nibble on during class, but she didn't want to cause any rifts by calling her out on it.

"See you at four," she said as Amber passed her desk on the way out the door.

"Yeah. See you then."

The day was a mixture of pleasant surprises and the usual irritations. Her morning classes scored remarkably well on the vocabulary test she gave them, but the behavior in her afternoon groups was so off task and borderline disrespectful that she nearly gave them all zeroes on the quiz and had them spend the rest of the period writing an essay about proper classroom etiquette.

Four of her worst offenders received office referrals before the period was over, something Michelle hated to do. She wanted the administration to know that she could control her own classes, but these boys were making it nearly impossible for the rest of the kids to focus and finish their quizzes.

She thought back to her student teaching experience the year before. It sure helped to be able to tag team with the troublemakers. She and Cassie had a great system. Whoever was teaching the lesson would give a warning to any disruptive students, then the other teacher would remove troublemakers from the room if they persisted in their antics.

Although Michelle really enjoyed this age group, it was frustrating and disheartening to carefully prepare lessons to teach the state standards, and then have a few students sabotage the process by refusing to listen or behave. Calling parents sometimes helped, but often even the parents were at a loss as to how to correct their child's actions in class.

Students like Amber helped Michelle see the bigger picture. Many of her kids were hurting, and the last thing they cared about was English. Sometimes she wondered if she should have become a counselor instead of a teacher, but she had a passion for helping them learn and hoped that somehow she could funnel their energy into their studies rather than their obsessive desire to impress their peers.

She was pretty tired by the time the final bell rang. After the last student left the room, she walked the aisles, straightening the haphazard rows and re-shelving random books that had been left in the baskets under the seats.

Walking through the teachers' lounge on her way to the parking lot, she noticed the coffeemaker still had a little brew left in the bottom. It looked burned, but she needed the lift. Pouring it into a Styrofoam cup, she added some creamer, gave a quick stir, and took a sip. Maybe this would revive her before she got to the park.

Pulling up in front of Ben and Kelly's house, she saw Maddie watching for her through the front window. The door flew open, and she raced out exclaiming, "Mommy! Mommy! Are we going to the park?"

"Hi, sweetheart. Of course we are. I promised, remember?" She smiled at Kelly who was following Madison to the car.

"She had a peanut butter sandwich and some cookies and did her homework paper," she told Michelle. Handing her Maddie's pink backpack, she added, "Have fun at the park. Let me know how it goes with Amber and her brother. I'll be praying."

"Thanks! And thanks for feeding my little munchkin."

"Anytime." She smiled. "Better get back in there. I left some cookies cooling on the counter, and you know how those boys are."

"Okay. See you tomorrow." Michelle helped Maddie into the car, and they headed for the park.

Amber and Jack were sitting on a bench with Bonnie Blackwell when they pulled up to the curb to park. Michelle waved at them and turned to her daughter in the back seat. "That's my student, Amber, and her brother," she said, pointing to the park bench.

"She looks nice," Maddie replied.

Michelle smiled at her daughter's sweet innocence. *May she always look for the good in people*, she prayed silently.

They got out of the car and walked over to the bench as Bonnie rose to greet them. "So this is Madison," she said warmly, extending her hand to the little girl. "It's nice to meet you."

Maddie looked up at Michelle, who nodded and smiled. "It's okay, sweetie. You can shake Ms. Blackwell's hand." Maddie held out her little hand and grasped Bonnie's, who gently shook it. Then she said, "Maddie, this is Amber and her brother Jack."

"Hi," Madison said with a wave.

Amber waved back and both kids returned her greeting.

Then Bonnie turned to Michelle. "I've told both foster moms that I'll have the kids back by five thirty, so I'll pick them up a little after five. It's not a lot of time, but it'll be a good first run." She turned to Amber and Jack and added, "You two need to stay within sight of

Ms. Baron at all times and start watching for me a little after five."

They nodded, Amber looking over at Jack. "Let's go over by the log bridge."

Michelle nodded her approval, and they walked in the direction of the equipment.

"Can we go on the swings, Mommy?" Maddie asked.

"We sure can," Michelle replied, smiling at Bonnie. "See you in an hour." Then she led her daughter by the hand to the swing set.

Michelle periodically glanced over to where Amber and Jack were hanging out. They seemed to be talking most of the time, but they did climb some of the log equipment, and Jack showed his sister a few tricks on the bars. She noticed that Amber watched her and Maddie quite a bit. She almost seemed torn between being with her brother and coming over to hang out with them.

Shortly before five, the two kids ambled over. "Hi Maddie," Amber said in an endearing voice. "Are you having fun on the swings?"

Maddie grinned and nodded vigorously.

"I'll bet it's really fun to come to the park with your Mommy," Amber added.

"Want me to push you?" Jack asked.

"Yes!" Maddie replied.

Jack drew the swing back as high as he could before letting go, smiling as Madison squealed in delight. "More!" she cried, and he pushed her higher, glancing over at Michelle for her approval.

"It's fine, Jack. Just not too high," she said. Watching Amber and Jack interact with Madison really tugged at her heart. How she wished she could make everything right for these two kids. Maybe if she talked to

Steve again, he'd agree to let her continue seeing them outside of class and possibly even invite them to church.

Her thoughts were interrupted by the sound of Bonnie's voice calling out to them. She was walking their way and waving.

Michelle thought she heard Amber curse under her breath. "What did you say?" she asked.

Amber blushed. "Oh…nothing. Just wish we didn't have to leave so soon."

"We'll try to do it again soon, okay?"

"Yeah," she replied.

Bonnie walked up to them and asked, "So did you two have fun?"

Jack nodded. "Yeah, I showed Amber my flips off the bars."

"Great! Amber, how about you?"

"Yeah. It was good," she replied.

Bonnie turned to Michelle and thanked her. "We'll talk again soon," she promised.

"Bye!" Maddie called out as they walked away.

Amber turned back and smiled at the little girl then waved. She made eye contact with Michelle and mouthed the words *thank you*.

Michelle thought her heart would burst as she whispered to the breeze, "You're welcome."

CHAPTER TWELVE

Amber did not get a chance to see Adam that night. Cecilia asked her to watch the kids while she ran out to the store. Although Adam offered to come over to her place, Amber didn't think it would be a good idea. She wanted to remain in Cecilia's favor since she was hoping to get another park day with Jack soon.

As she sat watching television with the other two foster kids, she thought about her teacher, Ms. Baron and what a good mom she was.

Her pregnancy was starting to give her morning sickness, and whenever she thought about it, Amber got really scared. She knew Adam would try to talk her into having an abortion, but that scared her almost as much as the idea of having a baby. She really needed to talk to someone, but who?

I can't think about this right now.

She forced herself to concentrate on the show that blared from the television screen. She had plenty of time to decide what she was going to do. Plus, there was always the chance she'd have a miscarriage and wouldn't have to do anything.

Adam promised to meet her after school the following day. They were planning to tell Cecilia she needed to go to the library for a study group and wouldn't be home until nine. That would give them lots of time to hang out at the beach.

When school let out the next day, Amber stopped by her locker and got some cookies she'd brought from home. It seemed like eating helped settle her stomach, and she didn't want to feel nauseous while she was with Adam. She knew he'd use every excuse, including that one, to try to convince her that an abortion was her best answer.

As she exited the building to the front lawn of Magnolia Middle School, she noticed Adam standing on the sidewalk talking to a couple of boys. It looked like he gave them a bag and got an envelope back from them.

"Adam!" she called, smiling as she waved to him. He nodded in her direction, said something to the boys, and then left them behind as he sauntered her way.

"Hey," he said, taking her backpack and slinging it over his shoulder.

"Hey," she replied with a grin. She reached over and took his hand as they walked over and got into his car.

"What was that about?" she asked, gesturing toward the two boys, who were still standing together on the sidewalk.

"Nothing."

"What was in the bag?"

"Nothing," he replied, an edge to his voice.

"Okay. Whatever you say." Amber tried not to sound upset, but it really bugged her when he shut her out of stuff.

"So did you tell Cecilia about the library?" he asked, obviously trying to change the subject.

"Yeah. She bought it. I think it helped that I watched the kids last night for her. I'm good until about nine."

"Cool. Wanna get a burger before we go to the beach?"

Amber's stomach was starting to bother her again. "Yeah, that sounds good."

Adam drove to the local fast food restaurant and shut off the car. "You stay here. I'll go in and get them."

"Okay, no cheese on mine."

"No cheese. Got it." He swung open his door and squeezed her hand before sliding out. "Be right back."

As he walked into the restaurant, Amber noticed the envelope on the floorboard. She picked it up and looked inside. It was full of money. Lots of money.

"What's all this?" she asked when he returned with the burgers.

Adam cursed as he grabbed the envelope from her. "What are you doing snooping in my stuff?"

Amber felt like she was going to cry. The last thing she wanted was Adam mad at her now. "Sorry," she said, her voice quivering a little.

Adam sighed, staring straight ahead out the windshield. "Just don't mess with my stuff, okay?" he said in a much softer tone.

"Okay."

They were both silent as he drove to the beach. Amber got the bag of burgers and her cookies from the seat, and Adam retrieved the blanket from the trunk. Then they walked down to the sand.

After they sat down, Amber started nibbling on her burger, suddenly feeling sicker.

"Are you okay?" he asked, watching her pick at the food.

"I guess. My stomach is just a little upset."

"You sick?"

"No, I think it's just ... you know."

"I thought that was just supposed to be in the morning."

"Me, too. Guess it can happen anytime. I'll feel better after I finish eating."

Adam nodded and looked away. A few moments later, he said, "So I've been thinking about everything."

"Yeah?"

"And I think we're just too young for this, Amber. It's not a good time for us to be thinking about having a baby. I mean, you aren't even in high school yet, and I've still got two years to finish before I graduate."

Amber could feel her stomach ball up into a tight knot. She knew she'd cry if she said anything, and that would just upset him more.

"So what do you think?"

She looked out over the ocean and just nodded.

"You agree, right?"

Amber took a deep breath and tried to steady her stomach and her emotions. "Do we have to talk about this today?"

"When did you want to talk about it?"

"I don't know. Just not today." She turned away and brushed a tear from her eye, hoping he didn't see it.

"Are you still upset about the envelope?"

"Should I be?" she asked.

"No. I just needed to make a little quick cash, in case you need it. For...you know... for the procedure."

"So what were you doing, selling weed?"

"I was just helping a friend make a delivery. He gives me half."

"Great." She couldn't keep the disdain from her voice. The last thing she needed was Adam getting busted for dealing.

"Hey, I did it for you, Amber. I don't have that kind of cash lying around. Do you?"

She shook her head. "If you get busted, what happens then? What about me and the baby?"

"It's not a baby, yet, Amber. That's the whole point. We can end this thing before it's too late. I've got enough money now to pay the clinic. My brother's been through this before with his girlfriend. He said it's really easy. You just give them the cash, and they take care of everything. No one ever has to know. It only takes an hour or two."

Amber couldn't speak. Clearly Adam had made up his mind. But she was far from deciding that abortion was the answer. "Maybe you should just take me home."

Adam stared at her. "You seem really upset about this. I thought it would be a relief to you to know that I took care of getting the money and everything."

"I'm just not ready to make that decision, Adam. Okay?"

He sighed. "Okay. Whatever you say." He reached over and turned her face toward his. "We'll just forget about it for today."

Leaning down, he kissed her. She reached for him and they fell back into the sand, wrapped in each other's arms, as they tried to forget the baby growing in her womb.

"I'm just saying it went really well today," Michelle said as she stirred the simmering sauce on the stove.

"That's great, honey," Steve replied.

"So what do you think?"

"About what?"

"About me doing it again, maybe on a regular basis for a while."

He put the mail aside and turned to look her in the eyes. "I've already told you what I think, Michelle. You need to be careful about getting too involved with this girl and her troubles. Besides, I don't want your time with Maddie compromised."

"It really wasn't like that, Steve. Amber and her brother just hung out on the other playground where I could see them. I spent my time with Maddie, not them."

"Let's just think about it and discuss it more later." He walked over and leaned forward to smell the sauce. "Yum. Smells great."

Michelle nodded. "Thanks."

He wrapped his arms around her from behind and nuzzled into her neck. "If you want to set up one more time at the park with them, I'm fine with that. Just don't make promises for the future."

Michelle brightened and turned to face him. "I promise I won't make any long term commitments. We can take it one week at a time."

"Okay. That sounds good. But you've got to level with me if you see Maddie being affected by this."

"Of course. You know she's my first priority."

"Speaking of which, I'll go check on her and have her wash up for dinner." Steve gave her a peck on the cheek and walked out to the family room where Maddie was watching cartoons and coloring.

Thank you, Lord, Michelle whispered in her heart. Then she turned to serve up the dinner.

"Honey, did Madison fall at the park today?" Steve called out from the bathroom, where he was helping their daughter get ready for her bath.

Michelle walked to the doorway. "No, why?"

"Look at this bruise on her back," he said as he turned Maddie to show her.

Michelle saw the large purple mark on the right side of her back. "Maddie, what happened, honey?" she asked as she knelt down beside her daughter to get a better look.

Madison looked confused. "Nothing, Mommy."

Michelle and Steve looked at each other puzzled. Steve's raised eyebrows communicated the same concern she was feeling.

"Did you fall at school today?" he asked.

"No."

"Did one of the kids hit you?"

Madison shook her head. "Can I get into the bath now, Daddy?"

Steve looked at Michelle, concern written across his face.

Michelle turned to Maddie, "Sure, honey. Mommy will help you get in." She made eye contact with Steve and mouthed, "Later." There was no point alarming Madison, who clearly denied any known cause for the bruise.

After she was settled into bed, they broached the subject. "So what do you think happened?" Steve asked.

"I have no idea. It's a strange place to get a bruise."

"Maybe you should ask Kelly about it tomorrow. She might have seen the kids roughhousing or something before you picked Maddie up for the park."

"Yeah. Good idea." Michelle nodded. "I'll ask her tomorrow."

Michelle pulled into the driveway of Ben and Kelly's house the following afternoon, exhausted from a lengthy staff meeting. Continuous subtle pressure to teach to the annual state tests was now coming in the form of guest speakers who were invited to share "helpful tips."

Seasoned teachers challenged the administration on effective instructional practices as well as interrupting the speakers with pointed, but valid questions. To a shy, non-confrontational person like Michelle, the tension in the room was stressful enough without the added demands to employ strategies she also questioned privately.

"Remember the kids," Cassie had said after the meeting was over. "That's why we are here. Not for the tests. Don't let this stuff get to you. Just keep doing what you know is best. What these kids need is so much more than grammar and literature. They need your compassion and the connection you are building to their lives. Those are the things they will remember ten years from now, not how well you taught them the parts of speech."

Michelle nodded, a weary smile replacing her furrowed brow. "Thanks, I needed that. I always leave these meetings in knots, never feeling like I'm doing enough or doing it in the right way."

"That's because you are a good teacher, Michelle. You care about the kids and about bringing learning to life for them. Don't lose that."

Now as she approached the house, she tried to refocus her thoughts and energy on her role as a mom. The conversation with Steve from the night before had haunted her on and off all day. What was the big bruise on Maddie's back? She hoped Kelly might have some simple explanation.

"Hi, Michelle," Ben greeted her as he opened the door. "Kelly's in the kitchen with the kids."

"Okay, thanks." She walked into the kitchen to find Maddie and Lucy coloring at the table as Kelly hunted for something in the refrigerator.

"Hey," she said.

"Mommy!" Maddie exclaimed with a grin. "Come see my picture!"

111

Kelly stood from a crouching position and closed the refrigerator door. "Hi, friend," she said. "How was your day?"

Michelle looked at her and rolled her eyes.

"One of those, huh. Another staff meeting?"

"Yep."

"Look at my picture, Mommy," Madison chimed again. "I'm drawing it for Daddy. It's a picture of us at the park. So he can see us playing."

Michelle leaned over and examined the drawing. "That's great, honey. Who's that?" she asked as she pointed to someone in the picture.

"That's Amber. See, she's smiling. I think she likes me." Maddie beamed.

"I'm sure she does. She asks about you at school sometimes."

"Really?"

"Really."

Kelly handed Michelle a cup of fresh brewed coffee. "You look like you could use a little pick-me-up."

Michelle smiled. "Thanks. Can I snag one of those cookies, too?" she asked, pointing to the fresh baked peanut butter treats on the counter.

"Help yourself. Take some home, too. We don't need all these," Kelly said, digging into a drawer and pulling out a plastic zip bag.

"Steve will love that. Peanut butter's his favorite."

"Ben's, too. That's why I need to get rid of some of these. He'd eat the whole batch if I let him."

They both laughed. "Come on, honey. Time to go. Go get your backpack," Michelle said. As Maddie and Lucy left the room, she turned back to Kelly. "I almost forgot. I need to ask you about something."

"What's up?"

"Last night, Steve showed me a bruise on Maddie's back. I just wondered if anything happened here

112

yesterday – like the kids roughhousing or something – that might have caused it."

"Not that I can recall. Did you ask Maddie about it?"

"Yeah. She didn't remember anything from school or from here."

"That's weird. Kind of a strange place for a bruise."

"That's what we thought." Just then Madison returned with her backpack. "I'm ready, Mommy."

"Okay." Michelle turned back to Kelly. "I'm sure it's nothing to worry about, but I just wanted to check with you to see if you remembered anything."

"No. Sorry. If I think of something, I'll call you." Kelly followed them to the front door holding the bag of cookies in her hand. "Don't forget these," she said as they walked out the door.

"Thanks. And thanks again for watching Madison."

"You know we love having her," Kelly replied. "Tell Steve I said hi."

"Will do."

As they climbed into the car, Michelle wracked her brain about what she could fix for dinner. Seemed like some days never ended.

"Did you talk to Kelly about Maddie's bruise?" Steve asked after their daughter was in bed.

"Yeah. She said she couldn't think of anything that happened at her house."

Steve shook his head. "Do you think she's okay?"

"I don't know. I'm kind of worried. She has two new bruises on the tops of her legs. I asked her about them, but she said the same thing. She can't remember getting hurt at school."

"You don't think she's being bullied or anything, do you?" Steve asked.

"No. I'm sure it's nothing like that. She loves school."

"Yeah. You're right." Steve sunk down into the couch and rubbed his face with his hands. "Do you think you should call the doctor?"

"I hate to make too big a deal out of this, but maybe that's a good idea. I'll see about getting her an appointment after school one day this week."

"Okay. Let me know if you need me to take her," he offered.

"Thanks. I'll try to work it around my meetings at school." Michelle sighed and pushed away the stack of papers in front of her.

"Why don't you just relax tonight and forget about school." Steve reached over and rubbed the back of her neck. "You seem so stressed lately."

Michelle leaned her head back into his massaging touch. She moaned softly as he worked on a knot that had been bothering her all day.

"Hurt?"

"A little. But don't stop," she replied, closing her eyes and willing the tight muscle to release its spasm.

A little while later, the house was quiet as Steve looked over his notes for court and the dishwasher hummed in the background. Michelle flipped open her laptop and typed a search into the web browser: *bruising in children*. Multiple links appeared on the screen, some from medical sites and others from a variety of sources such as parenting magazines and blogs.

Most article descriptions began with the assurance that childhood bruising was common and unavoidable.

She was relieved to see that they seemed to be in agreement that most children bruise easily.

Then a site caught her eye: *Diseases that Cause Bruising in Children*. She clicked on the link and began reading. Her brows furrowed as she scrolled through the article.

"What are you reading, babe?" Steve asked, closing his briefcase.

"An article about bruising in children."

He leaned over and looked at the computer screen. "Leukemia? Whoa." He closed the laptop and turned her face toward his. "Let's not go borrowing trouble here, honey. Just make the appointment with Dr. Gold, and see what he says before you go searching for answers on your own."

Michelle sat back and sighed. "Yeah. You're right." She put the laptop on the coffee table and leaned against him. "Do you think she's okay, Steve?"

"I think she's fine."

But she could detect a worried tone in his voice.

CHAPTER THIRTEEN

Michelle was in the middle of passing out some vocabulary tests when the phone on her desk buzzed. "Katy, would you please get that for me?"

Her eager assistant popped up from her desk in the front row and hurried to answer. "Mrs. Baron's room, student speaking."

After a short pause, Katy held out the phone. "It's the office. They need to talk to you."

Giving the test papers to the last row, Michelle instructed her students, "As soon as you have your test, you may begin. Don't forget your name and student number at the top." Then she took the phone from Katy. "This is Michelle."

"Sorry to bother you, Michelle, but the nurse at your daughter's school is on hold. She said she needs to talk to you," the secretary said.

"Thanks. Go ahead and put her through."

"Mrs. Baron?"

"Yes? Is Maddie alright?"

"She's got a pretty bad nosebleed, and we're having trouble getting it to stop."

"What happened? Did she trip or fall?" Michelle's eyes surveyed the room, looking for students who were off task.

"No. She was on her way to recess when it started."

"Can you hold on for a second?" Michelle asked, noticing a couple of kids whispering in the back row. She covered the mouthpiece of the phone and spoke to them. "Did you have a question, Brandon?"

"No. Just needed a pencil," he replied.

"Okay. Back to work. Eyes on your own paper." She turned her attention back to the phone. "Sorry about that."

"No problem. I know it's hard when your class is interrupted," she replied. "I can keep Madison here resting on the cot until someone can pick her up. Do you want me to call your husband?"

"He's in court all day. Let me see if I can get someone to cover my classes for the rest of the day. I'll call you back."

After hanging up and making sure all the students were working on their tests, Michelle sent Katy to the office with a note for the office manager, asking her to try to get a sub to cover her classes for the day.

About ten minutes later, the school counselor appeared in her doorway. Karen was able to take her class for the rest of the period, and Cassie was going to take the next class. They were still working on a sub for the remainder of the day, but Karen reassured her that they'd work something out.

Before leaving, Michelle reminded her students about their homework assignment and encouraged them to work on it when they finished their tests. She gave Karen the tests for the rest of the periods, grabbed her purse, and headed out the door. As she walked out to the parking lot, she called the nurse to let her know she was on her way.

A short time later, she was walking into the nurse's office at Madison's school. Spotting Maddie stretched out on the cot, she went right to her and sat on the edge of the little bed. "Are you okay, baby?"

Madison started to cry, and Michelle gathered her into her arms. A gauze pad fell from the little girl's nose, revealing bright red blood.

"I'm glad you were able to come right over. She's been a little trooper, but I could tell she was scared," the nurse said, handing Michelle a fresh gauze.

"Hold this up to your nose, honey," Michelle said. "Mommy's going to take you home."

Maddie swallowed hard, clearly trying to calm herself as she held the white pad up to her little nose.

"I noticed she's got quite a few bruises, too," the nurse added.

"We've also been noticing those," Michelle replied. "In fact, her dad and I were just talking about making an appointment with the pediatrician."

"That's probably a good idea. Her nose seems to be slowing down, but it should have stopped bleeding by now."

Michelle nodded.

"Has she had nosebleeds before?"

"No, but I've been noticing her gums are bleeding when she brushes her teeth at night."

"Well, it's probably good to just check in with her doctor. Who does she see?"

"Dr. Gold. Donald Gold."

"He's great. Let me know what he says," the nurse replied. Then she turned to Madison. "Just keep that gauze pad up against your nose until the bleeding stops, okay?"

"Okay," Maddie replied with a nod. She scooted off the cot and took her mom's hand.

"Thanks for taking care of her," Michelle said. "Off we go, pumpkin. Maybe we can have a special treat for lunch today."

Madison smiled behind her gauze. "Okay, Mommy."

Later that afternoon, as Maddie was taking a nap, Michelle called Dr. Gold's office and made an appointment for the following day, October 21st at four.

I've got to talk to someone, Amber thought as waves of nausea threatened to send her racing to the bathroom once again. She sat on the floor leaning up against the bed. Reaching for her cell phone, she hit speed dial for Adam. It went straight to voicemail.

Great. He's probably hanging out with his brother somewhere.

She hesitated, and then scrolled through her phone to find the number for her mother's rehab facility. After being transferred from the front desk, she heard her mom voice at the other end.

"Amber?"

"Yeah. It's me, Mom. Can you talk?"

"Sure, baby. But they just gave me a sedative for the night, so I'm a little groggy."

"Oh. Maybe I should call back tomorrow."

"It's okay. Go ahead. Tell me what you called about."

Amber paused, not sure how to begin. "Well, you know I've got a boyfriend named Adam, right?"

"Mmm hmm. I remember you saying that."

"So anyway, we've been spending lots of time together."

No response.

"Mom? Are you listening?"

"What baby? What did you say?"

Amber rolled her eyes. It took all her focus to keep from throwing up as her stomach continued to churn. "I said we've been spending lots of time together."

"That's nice, honey." Her mother's voice was slurred, and Amber could tell she was almost asleep.

"You sound tired. We can talk later."

"Okay. You... take care, Amber."

"Right. Bye, Mom." She pushed the end button and tossed the phone on the bed before running into the bathroom and losing her dinner.

A few moments later, she heard a knock on the door. "Are you okay in there, Amber?" her foster mother asked.

Taking a deep breath, she tried to steady her voice. "Yeah. I'm fine."

"Alright, well I need to get in there to give the kids a bath. Are you almost finished?"

Amber quickly flushed away the evidence. "Yeah. Just a sec." She washed her face with some cold water and swished some mouthwash to clear the acid taste that had become her constant companion. Checking her face and straightening her shirt, she opened the door, brushed past Cecilia, and took refuge in her bedroom.

Pushing her backpack aside, she stretched out on the bed and hugged a towel to her chest. She'd learned to keep it close in case she couldn't make it to the bathroom. Closing her eyes, she tried to figure out what she was going to do.

As she lay there in the dark, a deep loneliness engulfed her. She could feel tears seep from her eyes and roll down her cheeks, but she didn't make any effort to brush them away. If tears were her only companion, so be it.

Without even getting undressed, she slipped into a deep, numbing slumber.

Amber managed to escape the next morning without having to converse with Cecilia, who was always trying to get her to eat breakfast. There was no way she could force anything down in the mornings these days. She just hoped she'd be able to avoid the dry heaves until she could force down a cracker or two in the middle of the morning.

As she entered her English class, she noticed Mrs. Baron preparing a PowerPoint. Her teacher sure worked hard to help them understand stuff. Too bad Amber would probably have to drop out of school in a few months.

When she thought about Mrs. Baron and her family, it seemed like she had the perfect life. Amber wished she could get a good career, and that Adam would marry her so they could raise their baby together.

"Hi, Amber," her teacher said with a smile. But something about Mrs. Baron was different today. Her usual upbeat countenance was replaced by a seriousness that Amber usually only saw when some of the kids were really pushing her buttons.

This was the first class of the day, and it hadn't even started yet, so something else must be bothering her. Amber returned her greeting and took her seat in the back.

The bell rang a minute later, and they were soon viewing the PowerPoint about symbolism in literature. Amber tried to concentrate. Mrs. Baron was one of the few adults who seemed to really care about her, and she didn't want to make any waves, when she could tell her teacher was upset about something.

While they worked on the follow-up assignment, Amber noticed Mrs. Baron was staring at the picture of her daughter on her desk.

She sure loves that little girl.

Soon the bell rang signaling the end of class, and Amber was one of the last students to leave. "Mrs. Baron?"

"Yes, Amber?"

"Could we talk sometime?"

"Sure. Why don't you stop by at lunch?"

Amber nodded. "Okay. Thanks." As she turned to leave, she heard the teacher's cell phone ring. Whoever it was, her teacher seemed pretty serious about the call.

Michelle was quickly organizing her paperwork. The school day seemed to drag by, and she was eager to get going. The pediatrician's office called that morning to verify their appointment after school.

Although Steve had urged her not to borrow trouble, she couldn't help but worry about Maddie. Something had to be really wrong to be causing all these unexplained bruises, the bloody nose, and the bleeding gums she'd noticed the night before.

Preoccupied with her concerns for her daughter, Michelle had forgotten about her appointment with Amber. As she was slinging her purse over her shoulder, her troubled student walked through the door.

"Hi, Amber," She said, glancing at the clock and pulling her keys out. "What's up?"

"You look like you're in a hurry," Amber observed, her eyes on Michelle's purse.

"Yeah. I've got an appointment in half an hour." Michelle could see Amber's expression fall. "What happened at lunch? I thought you were going to come by."

"Sorry. Just some stuff with my boyfriend."

"I thought he was at the high school."

"Yeah. We were texting about something."

"Oh." Michelle felt torn. Something was clearly bothering Amber, and she wanted to help. She'd been trying to forge a relationship between them, and apparently Amber was beginning to trust her. But the appointment for Maddie was her top priority. Steve had agreed to pick up their daughter at school, and he was probably already leaving there to head for the doctor's office.

"It's okay if you're busy," Amber said.

"I'm really sorry. Can we talk in the morning? I can get here early if you'd like."

"Mornings are kind of hard for me. Maybe tomorrow at lunch," Amber replied. "I promise I'll show up."

"Okay. Sounds good." Michelle escorted Amber out to the hallway, locking the door behind them. "See you tomorrow."

"Yeah. See ya." Amber walked off as Michelle hurried out to the parking lot.

Dr. Gold's friendly smile and casual questions about school helped Madison relax. While she chatted about her teacher and new friends, Michelle and Steve watched him examine her bruises, look in her ears and eyes, check her reflexes and gently feel for swollen lymph nodes.

"Okay, princess. We're done. You can put your dress back on," the doctor said.

Madison slipped off the examining table and pulled her dress back over her head. "Now do I get a lollipop?"

"You sure do," the nurse replied with a smile, holding out a basket of brightly colored candies.

As Maddie carefully chose her treat, Dr. Gold turned to Steve and Michelle. "I'd like to run some blood tests. There's a lab downstairs, and I think you can make it there before they close."

"What do you think it is?" Michelle asked anxiously.

"I won't be able to make a diagnosis without the blood work," he replied.

"How long will it take to get the results?" Steve countered.

"We should have them back within a week. I'll have the front office call you to set up an appointment as soon as they're in."

Michelle needed more information. Pressing the doctor, she asked, "What kinds of things are you testing for?"

"When we see bruising and bleeding issues like this, we need to check for conditions like leukemia and other diseases that include bleeding disorders."

Michelle noticed Madison watching her closely. She didn't want to alarm her little girl, but the mention of leukemia brought a level of fear that threatened to overtake her completely.

Steve was quick to step in. "But there are other things that could be causing this, right?"

"Yes. There are conditions like Von Willebrand disease that can mimic the symptoms of leukemia. That's why it's important to do the blood tests. After I see the results, I can refer you to a specialist who will determine whether or not to run further tests."

Dr. Gold turned to Madison and squatted down to her level. "How's the lollipop?" he asked.

She nodded her head as she sucked on her treat. He ruffled her hair gently. "Mommy and Daddy are going to take you downstairs to the lab. They're going to take a little of your blood from your arm, so we can find out why you are getting all these bruises. They have a treasure chest in the lab that is just for little princesses. After your blood test, you can pick a special toy to take home with you."

"Will it hurt?" Maddie asked.

"Just a little pinch," he replied reassuringly. Straightening up, he extended his hand to Steve and then Michelle. "Try not to worry. Let's just focus on getting the proper diagnosis for now."

"Thanks, Doctor," Steve replied. He held one hand out to Madison and the other to Michelle as they left the office and headed downstairs to the lab.

CHAPTER FOURTEEN

Michelle was awake most of the night, tossing and turning in a battle of fear versus faith. She'd maintained a strong, upbeat exterior for Madison throughout the lab experience and the following evening. But when she'd finally stepped into the shower before bed, the gravity of the doctor's words engulfed her.

Leukemia. After all they'd been through to have a child, the infertility tests, the insemination procedure, the wait for DNA results – now to face the possibility that their precious daughter might have a life-threatening illness – it was more than she could bear.

Please God. Please help us. Don't let it be cancer.

She stayed there for a long time, letting the warm water pound on her back as her tears coursed down her face. Had she ever imagined in her pre-mommy days the depth of love she now felt for her little girl? She knew she'd trade places with Maddie in a heartbeat if she could spare her little girl any of the possible pain that lay ahead.

"Honey, are you okay in there?" Steve's voice called from the bedroom.

Michelle shut off the water, wrapped a towel around herself, and stepped out. "Yeah."

She threw on a robe and walked into the bedroom, towel drying her hair on the way.

"You look like you've been crying," Steve said, placing his hand on her shoulder.

She turned away and nodded, feeling the tears starting to well up again.

"Hey," he said softly, drawing her into his arms.

Michelle buried her face against his chest. "It's not fair, Steve."

He stroked her damp hair with one hand as he held her tightly with the other. "I know. Here, let's sit down and talk." He led her over to the edge of the bed and eased her down beside him. Lifting her chin with his finger, he looked into her eyes. "We can't assume the worst."

"I know. It's just hearing the word *leukemia* coming out of the doctor's mouth. I guess I really didn't expect it."

Steve sighed and gazed across the room. "Me neither."

"I should have never taken the teaching job this year. I've been so busy, I feel like I haven't been the kind of mom I want to be. If I wouldn't have been so preoccupied with my lesson plans and grading papers, maybe I would have noticed something sooner."

"Come on, Michelle. Don't start second guessing everything. We've got to hold onto our faith right now and pray that this turns out to be nothing serious."

She nodded, but her thoughts kept circling back to her greatest fears.

"You need your rest, babe. Why don't you go dry your hair, and then let's go to bed. Things will look better in the morning."

Michelle looked at him and tried to smile. Pushing her weary body up, she walked into the bathroom.

As they stretched out in bed a little while later, she thought she heard Madison crying. She tiptoed into their daughter's room and found her sleeping, her teddy bear hugged to her chest. Carefully pushing Maddie's hair off her face, Michelle leaned down and kissed her cheek. "I love you," she whispered softly.

Madison moved in her sleep and clung tighter to her bear. Adjusting the covers over her sleeping form, Michelle walked out of the room without a sound.

Steve held her in his arms while he fell asleep, and Michelle dozed off for a short time, only to be awakened by Max, who jumped up on the bed and plopped down beside her.

In the darkness, with no one to talk to, her imagination began to explore all the devastating outcomes that might await their little family. As her spirit fought to illuminate her faith and the hope that only God can give, the forces of darkness whispered fear and despair into her heart and mind.

Michelle walked into her classroom early the next morning, trying to shake off her sleepless night and be prepared for her meeting with Amber. Thankfully, the day's lesson was primarily student task oriented, so she wouldn't have to be on her feet quite as much.

When first period began, Michelle noticed that Amber was absent.

After giving her students their assignment, she sat down to look over her plans for the rest of the week.

Pray, Michelle. Pray hard.

It was as if God had tapped her on the shoulder. What was it? Was He urging her to pray for Maddie? Her heart began to race.

Pray for Amber. Pray now.

Amber? What was it now?

Michelle walked to the back of the classroom where she could see all the kids working. As she leaned against the counter, she stared at Amber's vacant desk and silently prayed.

Something was very wrong. She could feel it in her spirit.

Returning to her desk, she called the attendance office. In a quiet voice, she asked, "Have you gotten a call this morning about Amber Gamble?"

"Gamble. Let me check." There was a pause and then, "Nope. Probably truant again."

"Okay. Thanks." Michelle shook her head.

Pray Michelle. Keep praying.

While she walked the aisles checking on her students and helping them with the assignment, she continued to pray silently for her troubled student.

"Just go in and talk to them," Adam said.

Amber stared out the car window at the clinic. Her stomach churned. "I don't want to do this," she said.

"What? Go talk to them. What's that going to hurt?"

"You know what I mean, Adam." Amber tried to hide her frustration. "Can't we just talk about it some more?"

"What do you want me to say — that I'm all for quitting school, going to work, and supporting you and a baby? I'm only seventeen, not twenty-five. I don't want to give up my friends and my life and start playing house."

Amber felt like a knife had been jammed into her heart. She avoided looking at him as she shook her head and tried not to cry.

Adam's voice softened. "I know you're upset. I get it. No one's saying you have to make a decision today. Just go in and talk to them."

She nodded.

"I'll go with you if you want."

"No. I'll go by myself." She pushed open the car door and got out. Without looking back, she walked into the clinic.

The entire day, Michelle's mind kept flitting back and forth between Madison and Amber. She tried to pray whenever she felt her fears rising for her daughter. How was she supposed to concentrate on teaching when Maddie's very life might be hanging in the balance? And why did she feel such an urgency to pray for Amber?

To top it off, a student's parent left a hostile voice mail on her school line. The boy had been disrupting class for several weeks and was non-responsive to all the measures Michelle had tried. She'd called his mom and left a message informing her of his behavior and asking for back up from home. Instead, the mother's message indicated that she blamed Michelle for her son's actions.

"He's an angel in all his other classes," she claimed. "He's never had problems at school until your class. I think you've just decided to use him as an example rather than to examine your own shortcomings."

Michelle was stunned. She'd never gotten this type of feedback from a parent in the past. She decided to turn to Cassie for advice. Surely she'd know what Michelle should do now.

"Are you okay, Michelle?" Cassandra asked, as Michelle walked into her room during break.

"No, actually I'm not." Michelle's eyes blurred with tears.

"Sit down. Let's talk," Cassie replied, gesturing toward a chair next to her desk. "Tell me what's up."

Michelle began by pouring out her heart about Madison and the test results they were awaiting.

"I had no idea. You didn't mention any of this to me, did you?"

"No. It's all happened so fast. I couldn't believe it when the doctor said the word leukemia."

"How long did you say the test results take? A week?"

"At least a week for the blood test. Then we might have to do more tests."

"I'm so sorry. How can I help?" Cassie asked.

"Nothing for now. In the meantime, I came to talk to you about something else. I've got a parent who left me a very accusatory voicemail claiming I'm the cause of her son's disruptive behavior."

"Oh, brother."

Michelle reached over, picked up the phone on Cassie's desk and dialed her voicemail box. She handed the receiver to Cassie. "Listen."

Cassie rolled her eyes and shook her head as the message played in her ear. "Michelle, this lady's wacko. You can tell by her voice and her accusations that, in her mind, her little darling can do no wrong."

"So what am I supposed to do?"

"First, don't take it personally. Like I said, she's a wacko. Next, contact all of this boy's other teachers. Find out the real scoop about how he's doing in their classes."

Michelle nodded. "Good idea."

"And talk to Ron. This mom sounds like one who will probably be storming into the office to complain if her son gets anything other than a stellar grade in your class, especially for citizenship."

Michelle sighed. "Okay. Will do."

"We all get calls like this from time to time, Michelle. It's not you. Some parents just don't accept the fact that their junior high kids are not the perfect little students they may have been in elementary school. Kids change. And if they're ever going to push the envelope, it will be in junior high. If you let this mom intimidate you, and you back down with this boy, you'll be sending him a message that will create ripples for a long time."

"Yeah. You're right. I just wish I didn't have to deal with this on top of everything else."

Cassie nodded sympathetically. "Speaking of students, how's Amber Gamble doing these days?" she asked.

Michelle told her about the bridges she had begun to build with Amber, including their successful park day.

"That's great. You are really making headway with her," Cassie replied, smiling.

"I hope. But I'm kind of concerned about her today. She asked to meet with me yesterday, but then didn't show up for our lunch appointment. When she came by after school, I was in a hurry to get to the pediatrician's office. We rescheduled for today, but she's absent." Michelle paused. "Something's really wrong. I can feel it."

"Wouldn't surprise me. Hopefully she'll be back tomorrow, and you can get to the bottom of it."

The bell rang, signaling the end of their break.

"Don't worry about that phone call, Michelle. I mean it. There are lots of crazies out there. Just do what you know is right. And don't forget to talk to the other teachers and Ron. I'm sure they'll reinforce what I said."

"Thanks, Cassie. I will." She stood and headed back to her classroom.

CHAPTER FIFTEEN

Amber sat on the edge of the examining table hugging her body as the doctor spoke of her options. Halloween decorations of skeletons and spider webs with giant tarantulas added to the macabre mood.

"A simple D & C procedure might still be possible. There's no need for your parents to give consent," she explained.

Amber nodded.

The doctor seemed to take this as an affirmative decision on her part. "The girl at the front desk can set up an appointment for you. You'll need someone to drive you home afterward, but you should be fine to go to school in a day or two."

"Wait," Amber heard herself say.

"Yes?"

"What if I decide to have the baby?" she asked.

"Well, that's a pretty big decision. Having a baby is a life-changing event, Amber. At your age, I'd recommend against it. You still have school to finish." She flipped through the paperwork on the clipboard in her hand. "You're only fourteen years old. Very few girls would want to be saddled with a baby to care for at your age."

Amber looked away and gazed out the window. "I'll think about it."

"Okay, you do that. But don't wait too long. The later in your pregnancy that you terminate, the more complicated it becomes." The woman put her hand on Amber's shoulder. "This is just one of those difficult situations that we can easily resolve."

"Like I said, I'll think about it."

The doctor nodded and excused herself to see her next patient.

Amber scooted off the examining table and quickly dressed again. She was eager to get out of the clinic. Something about it made her nausea even worse.

As she walked out the front door, a girl who looked to be about nineteen or twenty walked up to Amber and held out a brochure. "You might be interested in this," she said.

Amber took the brochure and glanced at the cover. *Living Water Ministries, Hope for Women in Crisis Pregnancies.* She felt her face flush with embarrassment. Quickly stuffing the brochure into her bag, she thanked the girl and hurried over to Adam's car.

When she opened the door, he pulled the ear buds from his iPod out of his ears and sat up from a slouched position. "So, how'd it go?" he asked.

"I'm definitely pregnant. The doctor said I'm still early enough to ..." Amber's voice broke, and she started crying.

Adam just stared at her. He looked completely lost.

"Sorry," she said, trying to pull herself together. "Can we talk about this later?"

"Sure. Whatever you say." Adam started the car and backed out of the parking space. "Want to go home?"

"Can we go to the beach?"

"Yeah," he replied.

They sat watching the waves for a while, neither speaking a word. Finally, Adam asked, "What did that girl give you?"

"What girl?"

"The one in front of the clinic."

Amber reached into her bag and pulled out the brochure. She handed it to him.

"Looks like a church thing," he said. "Probably some propaganda."

"Let me see it," she replied, holding out her hand. As she read through the inside content, the icy cold grip on her heart started to melt away, and for the first time she began to feel hope.

"So what does it say?" he asked.

"It's about alternatives to abortion."

"That's what I thought. Propaganda."

Amber tried to hold onto the relief she'd felt a moment before, in spite of Adam's cynical response. "Why do you say that? Isn't it possible that there are other things we could do?"

"Like what? I already told you I'm not ready to be a dad. We're not getting married, Amber, or anything crazy like that."

"Yeah. You made that pretty clear," she replied bitterly. "But maybe I could put the baby up for adoption."

"Man, Amber, what is it with you? You're too young to have a baby. Do you really want everyone in school to know that you got pregnant in eighth grade??"

"No, but I did, Adam. I just feel bad for the baby."

"What baby? It's not a baby yet, Amber. That's the whole point," Adam said, exasperation raising the volume of his voice.

"Maybe not to you. Maybe not to that doctor in the clinic. But that doesn't mean it's not a baby to me." Amber started crying again. "Maybe you should just take me home." She got up and started walking back to the car.

"Wait a minute. Don't just walk away from me like that. This is my kid we're talking about here. I should have a say in this, too," Adam said, strutting through the sand toward her. "Amber, stop."

She stopped and turned to look at him.

"Think about this," he urged. "You've heard the stories about how adopted kids go looking for their real parents. They show up on their doorsteps twenty years later, and then everything gets messed up. Do you want to take a chance of having that happen to you someday?"

Amber couldn't speak. She didn't have the answers for his questions. All she knew was that the brochure from Living Waters had given her a feeling that somehow things could work out all right. She definitely didn't have that feeling at the clinic.

"I can't talk about this right now, Adam. I just want to go home."

He shook his head and followed her to the car.

"Living Waters, Lisa speaking," the voice on the other end of the phone said.

"Uh, hi," Amber began. "I, uh, wanted to get some information about your place."

"Sure. How can I help you?" The voice sounded young, and she seemed friendly and safe.

"Well... I was wondering if you help teenagers, too."

"Everyday. We don't have any age requirements for our services."

Amber breathed a sigh of relief. "Okay, well, I'm only fourteen. But if you don't have any age requirements, I guess that's okay, right?"

"Absolutely. Would you like to give me your name?" Lisa asked.

Amber hesitated for a moment.

As if reading her mind, she added, "First name is fine."

"Okay. Yeah. It's Amber."

"Can you tell me a little about your circumstances, Amber?"

"I'm about seven weeks pregnant. I wanted to find out about adoption." Although she felt nervous, Amber sensed she could trust this place.

"Okay. We can help you with that. Would you like to come in and talk with one of our counselors? They can guide you through all your options," she added.

"Yeah. That sounds good. Afternoons would be best. After school, like around four."

"We can do that. How does tomorrow sound? We have a counselor available at four thirty. You're welcome to bring a parent or friend with you, if you'd like."

"Can I talk to my boyfriend and call you back? I need to find out if he can give me a ride over," Amber explained.

"Sure. We'll be open until seven tonight and again in the morning at ten."

"Okay. I'll call back after I talk to him." As Amber flipped her cell phone shut, she started to cry. But these tears were tears of relief.

Hopefully Adam would agree to take her to Living Waters tomorrow and she could find out what she needed to know to make her decision.

"I'm not going to any church place that's going to try to talk you into having this kid, Amber," Adam said the next day. "You're crazy to even think about this."

"It's not a church. It's just a crisis pregnancy center."

"You know what I mean. All those places are run by churches. And they have one goal – to lay a guilt trip on you so you don't have an abortion."

Amber turned away, but he grabbed her arm. Spinning back to face him, she said, "Don't you feel bad for the baby? Don't you care about it at all?"

"Don't start with me, Amber. You know it's not a baby yet."

"How do you know? You've seen those pictures in the science books. They look like babies to me," she retorted.

"They talked to you about this at the clinic already, remember? They said it was just tissue."

"Whatever," Amber replied sarcastically.

"Yeah. Whatever," he parroted back to her. "You do whatever you want, Amber. It's your body. But don't expect me to be part of your fantasy about becoming a mom. 'Cause I'm not going to throw away my life for some kid when I'm only in high school."

"Thanks for the help. Guess I'll have to find another way to get there," she said, turning and walking away.

Adam did not follow.

Michelle noticed the red light flashing on her cell phone as she forced herself to eat her lunch. The pending blood test results for Madison had her stomach in knots these days, but her lack of sleep, coupled with no food, would leave her completely depleted for her afternoon classes.

Pulling up the home screen of her phone, she saw the text indicating that she had voicemail. A moment later, she was listening to a message from the nurse at Dr. Gold's office.

"Madison's blood work is in, and Dr. Gold has consulted with a hematologist, who would like to order further testing. Please call Dr. Morris to schedule a bone marrow test. His office is expecting your call, and they will be able to see you this week."

Michelle's heart stopped. *Bone marrow test? Pediatric hematologist?* She'd spent the past week trying to convince herself that all of Maddie's blood work would come back normal, and that she was worrying for nothing.

Now her hands trembled as she dialed the doctor's office. The switchboard answered her call, saying that Dr. Gold's office was closed for lunch. She'd have to wait until after school.

She tried to call Steve on his cell phone, but he didn't pick up. I've got to talk to someone, she thought, panic threatening to overtake her.

As if in immediate response to her cries, God's presence enveloped her. She closed her eyes, now brimming with tears, and began to pray in ways she'd never prayed before — prayers of desperation from the heart of a mom.

She remembered how God had taken her through the crisis with her father's suicide attempt. He'd also faithfully answered her prayers for a child in the face of her husband's infertility. And He'd opened a door for her ministry at Magnolia Middle School at a time when it was almost impossible to find a teaching position anywhere.

I know the plans I have for you, Michelle. They are plans for good and not for evil. Plans to give you hope and a future.

Her favorite verse from Jeremiah replayed in her mind over and over as she grasped for a promise from God, something she could cling to through the possible trauma awaiting her.

"Please, God – don't let it be cancer," she begged.

Another verse from Proverbs spoke to her heart. *Trust in me with all your heart. Lean not on your own understanding. I will direct your path.*

Peace washed over her. A confident assurance that God would be with them replaced the panic she'd felt just moments earlier. Surely He would get them through this. Somehow.

The sound of the school passing bell pulled her back to her classroom, which was now beginning to fill with raucous eighth graders returning from their lunch break. She dropped her cell phone into her purse and walked to her podium, grabbing the attendance sheets from the corner of her desk on her way.

A couple of students with questions about the homework from the previous night awaited her attention. Shifting her focus to them, she shot up a silent prayer of thanksgiving to the God of the universe who had taken time to join her for lunch.

It was already getting dark when Steve and Michelle sat across the desk from Dr. Morris late in the afternoon on November 2nd. A heavy-set older man with a round face and jowls, he exuded a kind and gentle temperament.

"Your daughter's platelet count is lower than we like to see, and she has a slightly elevated white blood cell count. Her numbers are not too far out of range with the white count, so they could even reflect a minor infection her body is working to fight off. The bone marrow biopsy will help us make a more conclusive diagnosis of what is causing her bruising and bleeding issues."

"What do you think it is?" Michelle asked, the word *cancer* looming over her like a dark cloud.

Dr. Morris scanned Madison's lab results again. "I'd rather not speculate too much at this point. Leukemia remains a possibility, but her blood work is inconclusive. Did Dr. Gold discuss bleeding disorders with you?"

"Yes. He mentioned leukemia and Von something disease."

"Von Willebrand," he offered.

"Yeah."

"We'll need to wait a couple of weeks for the lab results on the Von Willebrand factor tests, but since we're seeing some issues with the platelets and white count, I'd like to go ahead with the bone marrow biopsy in the meantime. If we *are* looking at leukemia, we'll want to begin treatment as soon as possible."

"And if it's not leukemia?" Michelle asked hopefully.

"Then we'll wait until we get the results back on Von Willebrand and other possible clotting disorders."

"What exactly does the bone marrow biopsy entail?" Steve asked, taking Michelle's hand in his.

"Madison will be admitted to the hospital early in the morning. She'll need to fast from midnight the night before because we'll be using anesthesia during the procedure. Other than the placement of the IV, the actual aspiration process will be easy for her since she'll be asleep," he explained.

"The bone marrow will be taken from the iliac crest – on her back, just above her hip. I'll be using a special needle with a syringe to remove some of the marrow from the bone. The entire procedure only takes about twenty minutes."

"Will we be allowed to be in the room with her?" Michelle asked anxiously.

"You can stay with her while they prep her and set up the IV. You'll meet the anesthesiologist and can be with Madison until she is asleep. Then you'll wait in an adjoining room while we do the aspiration and biopsy. As soon as she's in recovery, you can be with her again, so she'll see you when she wakes up."

Michelle nervously twisted the hair at the nape of her neck. "Will she be in a lot of pain afterward?"

"She'll be groggy the rest of the day and will have some discomfort for a couple of days, but it will be easily manageable with some mild pain killers. In a few days, she'll be back to her old self."

Dr. Morris paused and gave them both a warm smile. "I know this seems pretty scary, but Madison will do just fine. If she has a favorite doll or stuffed animal, she can bring it with her. Sometimes that helps kids relax. The hospital has a family educator who will meet with you in advance to walk you through everything."

"How soon can we get this done?" Steve asked.

"Would next Monday, the seventh, work for you? I have an opening that morning."

Steve looked at Michelle. "What do you think? Can you get off school?"

"Yeah. I'll get a sub for the day. How about you?" she asked.

"I've got a deposition after lunch, but I can have Roger cover it for me."

Michelle nodded.

Turning back to the doctor, Steve said, "Let's book it."

Sheila listened to the phone ringing at Michelle's house. She was about to hang up when she heard her son-on-law's voice at the other end. "Hello?"

"Hi, Steve. It's Sheila. I'm surprised to catch you home this early."

"We had a doctor's appointment for Maddie," he explained.

"Oh. Did Michelle have a faculty meeting after school?" Sheila asked, assuming that was why Steve had taken Madison to the doctor.

"No, she's right here. Let me put her on."

"Hi, Mom," Michelle said.

"Hi, Mimi. Everything okay with Maddie? Steve said you guys had a doctor's appointment for her."

There was a pause, and she heard her daughter say something to Steve about taking Madison upstairs to get changed. "Sorry, Mom. I didn't want Maddie to hear me."

"What is it?" Anxiety crept into Sheila's heart.

"We don't know anything yet, but the doctor is running some tests."

"Tests for what? What's wrong?" It wasn't like Michelle to keep things from her. It seemed like ever since John's hospitalization, her daughter tried to protect her from any additional problems.

Sheila flashed back to her husband's suicide attempt and how her kids had been such a support through the long ordeal. Was it really eight years ago?

She glanced over at John snoozing in his recliner chair. God had gotten them through a pretty scary time. Were they about to enter another one with their granddaughter, Madison?

143

Michelle's voice interrupted her thoughts. She was saying something about bruising.

"Kids get bruises all the time, honey. You used to have a dozen bruises at any given time when you were her age — from tumbles off the bike to dodge ball at school. I even remember asking the pediatrician about it. He said it's normal."

"Maddie's bruises aren't normal, Mom. And she gets them in places kids don't normally get bruises."

Sheila could hear the concern in her voice. "What are the tests they're running?"

"They did a blood panel, and on Monday they're doing a bone marrow biopsy."

Sheila's heart stopped. It sounded serious. Really serious.

"Mom? Are you there?"

Sheila swallowed back her fears. "How are you doing with all this, sweetheart?" She tried to picture how Michelle would handle it if Madison were diagnosed with a serious or even life-threatening disease. Hadn't they been through enough with all the infertility issues? Was it possible they might lose their precious, long-awaited daughter?

"I'm doing the best I can not to let Maddie see my concerns, but it's really hard, Mom." There was a pause and then, "When the doctor said they were going to test her for leukemia, I almost fell apart. It seems unreal. She's always been so healthy." Michelle's voice trembled slightly, and Sheila could tell she was fighting to maintain her composure.

"Why didn't you call me?"

"There's no need for you to worry, Mom. We really don't know anything yet."

"But I could come up there. Help out, maybe," Sheila offered.

"We're fine for now. Thanks for offering, though. I'd love to see you, but with school and everything, it's a pretty crazy time right now. Plus, I know how hard it is for you to leave Dad."

"Well, you let me know if you need me, honey. Your dad is doing great. And I'm sure Tim would come stay with him if you needed me up there."

"What's new with Tim these days?"

Sheila smiled. "You know your brother. Always has some new adventure going on. He's learning how to make surfboards now. He's got some notion of starting his own company."

"Good for him. I'm glad he's starting to think about the future and not just the next wave."

There was a short pause in the conversation, then Michelle added, "I've got to get going, Mom. Time to fix dinner."

"Okay. Promise me you'll call if you need me, and let me know what the doctor finds out."

"I will. Promise."

As Sheila rested the receiver back in its cradle, the magnitude of her little granddaughter's medical possibilities engulfed her. Reaching for the phone again, she dialed her parents' number, needing to hear her father's voice. His steadfast faith had a way of calming her fears.

As she waited for an answer, she thought, I should have asked Michelle about Thanksgiving. It would be good for all of us to be together again.

CHAPTER SIXTEEN

Steve couldn't sleep. He wandered down the hall and peeked into Madison's room, the nightlight casting a warm glow on his sleeping daughter's face. He leaned against the doorframe and gazed at her, watching her small form nestled under the fluffy pink comforter.

She looked so peaceful.

Heaviness pressed on his shoulders as he quietly entered the room. Easing himself down onto his knees beside her bed, he gently brushed some stray curls from her face. She stirred slightly but did not awaken.

Sitting back onto his heels, Steve replayed the appointment with the doctor. Maddie seemed so healthy – a happy little girl with some bruises. How could it be possible that they were about to test her for leukemia?

He felt a sudden urge to take her in his arms and whisk her away. Somewhere where needles and biopsies and doctors would not be a part of her future. Where he could be her knight in shining armor and protect her from the dragons of life.

Though she was only five years old, he couldn't remember life without her. How could he fathom the possibility that they might lose her?

He thought back to how badly Michelle had wanted a baby and how he'd almost let her down because of his infertility and his resistance to the procedures the doctor had recommended.

But medical science had opened the door for conception, and a DNA test had confirmed his paternity. Madison was their miracle child. Probably the only child they'd ever have.

Her smile, her bright curiosity, and her contagious laugh – they were the greatest gifts God could have given them. Was He going to take them all away now? Was this the end of their happy ever after?

Please, Lord. Please don't take our precious little girl. Steve's face contorted with pain at the very thought. *Take me, God. She has her whole life left.*

It seemed like he sat there for hours, pleading with God, as he laid out his case in his best possible form. This meant so much more than the issues he pled in court on a weekly basis. This time he couldn't afford to lose, no matter what.

Eventually the numbness in his feet and legs caused him to wrestle to his feet. As he turned to walk out of the room, he saw Michelle standing in the doorway watching him. She held out her arms, and he moved into them. Their tears mingled as they held each other.

"Hi, Dad. It's Sheila."

Phil could tell something wasn't right. Sheila never was one for hiding her feelings. "What's wrong, honey?"

"It's Michelle. Well, actually Madison. There's something going on with her, and the doctors are running tests. They said it might be leukemia."

"Oh, Sheila. I'm so sorry to hear that. How's Michelle handling it?" Phil wrapped one arm around his wife, Joan, who'd come to stand next to him.

"She's worried. What mother wouldn't be? But she's trying to maintain a hopeful outlook."

Phil nodded, taking a deep breath. "And you? You sound very upset."

"I feel like I need to be there – to help out and give Michelle moral support."

"But?"

"But she says I should stay here with John until they know more."

"If you need us to come and be with John, we will. We'd be happy to help," Phil offered, giving Joan a squeeze.

"I just don't know how Michelle will handle this if it turns out to be cancer, Dad. You know how her world revolves around that little girl." Her voice was trembling.

"What exactly did the doctors say?" he asked.

"I don't know all the details, but Maddie's been getting some unusual bruises, and they ran a blood test. Now they are scheduled for a bone marrow biopsy on Monday."

"Okay. We will put Madison on the prayer chain up here, and we'll be ready at a moment's notice if you need us to come down." He gave Joan another squeeze as she searched his face for information.

"Thanks, Dad," Sheila replied.

"I know it's hard at times like this, honey, but try to trust God with the outcome. He won't allow anything into Madison or Michelle's life without a plan to ultimately bring blessings. I honestly believe that."

"I know you do, Dad. Thanks."

Joan nudged Phil and gestured toward the phone. "Your mom wants to talk to you. Keep us posted on whatever you hear, and be sure to tell Michelle that we're praying and will help in anyway we can."

"Okay. Thanks." Sheila's voice sounded a little calmer.

Handing the phone to his wife, Phil began praying that God's peace would rest on his daughter, granddaughter, and great granddaughter through whatever ordeal lay ahead. As a pastor, he'd counseled many parents through difficult times and mountains of concern, but now his heart ached for his own family, and he found himself pleading with God in ways only a father and grandfather could.

Monday morning finally arrived, and Michelle and Steve forced themselves to remain upbeat as they got Madison ready for the drive to the hospital.

"Don't forget Teddy," Michelle said, gesturing to the threadbare stuffed animal resting on Maddie's pillow.

Madison scooped him up and nestled him into her neck, as they started downstairs.

"When do we get to go out for ice cream?" the little girl asked.

"After you take your little nap at the hospital," Steve replied.

"And I get to pick any kind I want, right?"

"That's right, princess. Any kind you want," he promised.

"I don't like going to hospitals, Daddy. They smell funny."

"I know, Maddie. But you won't be there very long. And you will be asleep most of the time."

"But Teddy gets to stay with me," she added for reassurance.

"Yes. Teddy will be with you while you take your nap."

"But the doctor will give me a shot first." Her face wore a worried expression.

149

Michelle sighed as she glanced at Steve.

Steve knelt down beside their daughter. "Yes, honey. You will have to get an IV. It's like a shot, but it only hurts for a second. Just a little pinch."

"Like the blood test?"

"Like the blood test." He gave her his most reassuring smile. "Mommy and I will be with you when you get the IV. You can hold my hand."

"And Teddy will be there, too."

"Yep."

Madison looked her teddy bear in the eyes. "We have to be brave, Teddy. Don't be scared." She hugged him tight, and Steve could see her eyes beginning to fill.

"Let's get going, pumpkin, so we can get finished at the hospital and get your ice cream."

Maddie nodded her head as she rubbed her eyes with the back of her hand.

When they walked into the hospital lobby, a receptionist in bright, teddy bear print scrubs greeted them. "Look, Daddy! She has teddies all over her shirt."

"She sure does," he observed.

A nurse soon appeared and escorted them to the room where the IV would be started. Madison cried briefly but stopped when Steve suggested she might be scaring Teddy.

Soon it was time to begin the procedure, and Madison's gurney was rolled out of the room, Teddy in her tight grip.

Michelle took one look at Steve, and they both began to tear up. "Why is this happening?" she asked.

"I don't know, babe." Pulling her close, he stroked her hair and back.

With arms around each other, they walked out to the sitting area to wait.

"I heard something on the radio this week that made me think about Madison," Steve said.

She turned toward him. "Really? What?"

"It was a Bible study from Genesis about Abraham."

"Why did it remind you of Maddie?"

"For a couple of reasons. First, because the pastor talked about how Abraham had to wait a long time to have his son, Isaac."

Michelle nodded, remembering their journey with infertility that had made her wonder if they'd ever have a child.

"He also talked about how God commanded Abraham to sacrifice Isaac."

"What? Are you telling me you think God is going to take Madison from us?" Michelle couldn't believe her husband was saying this.

"Wait. Let me explain," Steve said. "It was really a test of Abraham's faith and trust in God. Abraham took Isaac and placed him on the altar, ready to obey God. He knew that Isaac was a child of promise and that God was even able to raise him from the dead if need be in order to fulfill that promise."

"Go on."

"What I'm saying, Michelle, is that maybe God wants us to put Madison on the altar – to say we trust Him with whatever is going to happen here. That we believe He loves her as much or more than we do, and that He will get us all through this just like He did with Abraham and Isaac, when He supplied a substitute sacrifice at the last minute."

Michelle just stared at him for a few moments. "How do we do that, Steve? I mean, how do we put her on the altar?"

"I guess we just pray and tell God that we are trusting Him to do the right thing and that we will still love and obey Him even if this doesn't turn out the way we hope."

"Can you honestly do that?" she asked.

"I don't think we have a choice."

She paused and then asked the question she feared most. "Do you think God is going to take her?"

"I really don't know, Michelle. But I don't think we should focus on that right now. I talked to Ben about this for a while the other night. He was saying that when you don't know what is going to happen, and you're plagued by a thousand questions, the best thing to do is to focus on what you *do* know."

"Like what?"

"Like how faithful God has been to us. Everything we know about Him from scriptures and from what we have seen in our own lives."

Michelle thought about it and replied, "I *want* to trust God, Steve, but I'm so scared."

"That's okay, honey. I'm scared, too. I think God understands that. But I also think He wants us to trust Him."

She looked him in the eye, as if searching for that trust.

"I mean, look at all God's done for us over the past few years. Think about your dad and the miracles in his life." He reached out and touched her. "And just the fact that we *have* Maddie for our daughter is a miracle itself."

"Yeah, you're right."

"And what about your teaching job at a time when it's almost impossible to get one? Or the great friends Ben and Kelly have become, and how much we love our church? There are lots of ways God has met our needs and blessed us."

She sighed deeply and nodded. "I know."

He leaned over and kissed the top of her head, then took her hand in his and began to pray. Pouring out his heart to God, he shared the fears and hopes they were wrestling with, and then finally placed their daughter squarely in God's hands. "May *your* perfect will be done in her life, Lord," he prayed, as Michelle clung to his hand and tried to hold back her tears.

By the time Dr. Morris came out to tell them the biopsy was finished, they were both spent. But there was also a new peace in their hearts that somehow God would get them through whatever might lay ahead.

CHAPTER SEVENTEEN

Michelle got to school early the next morning to read through any information left from the substitute teacher and to organize her plans for the day. Glancing at her planner, she noticed that she'd scheduled another supervised visit at the park for Amber and her brother that very afternoon.

How did I forget about this?

Kelly was keeping Madison at home with her for the day while she rested from her procedure. Michelle had hoped to pick up Maddie right after school and have a quiet afternoon watching a Disney movie before having pizza delivered for dinner. But she hated to cancel on Amber.

Besides, Madison loved going to the park. Even though she was a bit sore from her biopsy, Michelle knew she'd probably want to go.

Right before the bell rang to signal the passing period to the first class of the day, Amber shuffled in, not looking very well. "Are we still going to the park today?" she asked.

"I don't know," Michelle began. "Are you feeling okay? We can postpone if you'd like."

Amber headed to her desk at the back of the room. "No. I want to see Jack. I'll be fine. I just have a headache."

"Okay, then, we'll go," Michelle promised.

Other students began streaming into the room, and she walked to the podium, ready to begin her day. As she called the class to order, a few students expressed their relief that she was back. "That sub was crazy," one of them piped up.

"Yeah. She didn't know what she was talking about," another offered.

Michelle made a mental note to talk to Cassie and get some recommendations of better subs she could request for the future. She might need someone fairly frequently if Madison's biopsy came back positive. *Oh, Lord. Please don't let it be so.*

It was apparent she'd need to go over the lesson from the day before instead of moving forward with her original plans. *Now I'll be a day behind on the material for the next benchmark assessment,* she groaned inwardly. The pressure to excel in the standardized tests continued to hover over her like a gray cloud. *Guess we'll have to skip the guest speaker I was hoping to have from the local theater group.*

It was such a shame that many of the enrichment activities that brought her subject to life and piqued the interest of her students had to be shelved to focus on the nuts and bolts they needed to know for their annual tests.

Am I really making a difference here, God? she wondered.

Then her eye caught Amber watching her every move, and she knew she was there for a purpose — something that God had planned and that had more far reaching impact than grammar and literature.

The day flew by, and Michelle was able to catch most of the kids up to speed on what the substitute should have taught the day before. Hopefully the results of their homework would indicate that any confusion they had while she was gone had been replaced by a clear understanding of the lesson.

As she packed up her bag that afternoon and got ready to leave, Amber showed up. "Ready?" Michelle asked.

"Yeah."

"Okay, we've got to pick up Madison at the sitter."

"She didn't go to school today?" Amber asked.

"No. She had a medical procedure yesterday, and she's a little sore, so I let her take the day off." Michelle hoped that explanation would suffice, not wanting to discuss Madison's tests with her student.

"Oh," was all Amber said in reply.

The hour and a half at the park went well, although Jack's arrival was delayed by an emergency the social worker had to address before picking him up. Amber stayed close to Michelle and Madison while she waited for her brother, and Maddie clearly enjoyed the extra attention.

Amber's really good with kids, Michelle observed silently.

The teen seemed to sense just how much Madison could handle in her somewhat fragile condition, and she kept her laughing and playing without overdoing it as Michelle watched them with gratitude. She was exhausted from the emotional ordeal of the day before and from the sleepless nights leading up to Maddie's biopsy.

Now if she could just hold it together until they got the results.

When Jack arrived, Michelle expected Amber to take off for the other part of the park as she'd done the last time they were there together. Instead, she asked Jack if it was okay if they played with Madison, too. He seemed fine with the idea, so the three of them swung on the swings and climbed on the jungle gym.

Soon Michelle could tell that Madison was having a hard time keeping up. She suggested that Maddie come join her on the bench for a few minutes, and she willingly complied.

That gave Amber and Jack some time to talk. Before long the social worker appeared to pick them up, thanking Michelle for taking the time to help bring the two together for another visit.

As they left, Amber looked back.

"Bye bye, Amber!" Maddie called out.

Amber smiled and waved back, then turned and walked away, giving her brother a playful shove as they neared the car.

"Why does Amber look so sad sometimes, Mommy?" Madison asked.

Michelle hugged her close. "I think she misses her mom, honey."

"Oh." Maddie's face dropped. "I wish you could be her mom and take care of her like you take care of me," she replied.

"That's sweet, Maddie. I'm glad you care so much about Amber. She needs friends."

"I like her. She doesn't treat me like a baby," Madison replied.

Michelle ruffled her daughter's hair. "And who is treating you like a baby these days?"

Maddie looked up at her and grinned. "Daddy!"

"You might as well get used to that, sweetheart. You're always going to be Daddy's little girl." Michelle's heart swelled with emotion. *Please, God. Let it be so.*

Amber's mother was sitting in a chair by the window. Adam had driven Amber to the halfway house, hoping that after Amber talked to her mom she'd see that having an abortion was the only answer.

Amber cleared her throat. "Mom?"

Stacy turned toward her. "Amber? I didn't know you were coming. Is the social worker with you?"

"No. I came alone," she admitted

Stacy frowned. "How did you get here? You didn't hitchhike did you?"

Amber shook her head. "Adam brought me."

Her mom looked confused. "Who's Adam?"

"My boyfriend. You remember. I told you about him." Amber waited for recognition but none came. "It's not important. I just wanted to talk to you."

Stacy nodded. "Okay. What do you want to talk about?"

Her mom's expression looked distant and confused. Must be the meds. Amber took a deep breath and tried to figure out how to begin.

"I've got a little problem, Mom."

Her mom's brow furrowed as if Amber spoke in a foreign language that she could not understand.

"Mom?" Amber prompted.

Stacy searched her face. "What dear? What is it?"

"I need your help."

"Help? What kind of help?" Her mom looked scared.

Amber tried to choke the words out. "Mom, I'm… I'm…"

"What? You're what?"

An attendant entered the room. "Sorry to interrupt, but it's time for Stacy's group therapy session."

"Oh. Right." Stacy said, standing up. She turned to Amber. "I'm sorry, honey. Guess I have to go. Call me later."

"Yeah. Later." Amber turned away, tears threatening to expose her vulnerability. She walked out of the room without looking back.

"So how did it go?" Adam asked hopefully.

"Just peachy," she replied, sarcasm dripping from her tongue as her tears slipped out of the corners of her eyes.

Adam didn't say another word. He started the car, and they drove back in silence.

When they pulled up in front of Amber's foster home, she opened the car door and was about to slide out when he stopped her. "Wait a minute."

"What?" Amber tried to keep her voice steady.

"Obviously your mom isn't going to be able to help you. You need to make a decision pretty soon. Isn't that what the lady at the clinic said?"

"I know what she said, Adam. Quit bugging me." Amber pushed away from him and got out of the car.

"Call me when you get your head straight," Adam replied.

"Right." She slammed the door and went inside.

"Amber? Is that you?" Cecilia called from the kitchen.

Great.

"You're late. Your social worker called and said something about you visiting your mom." Cecilia wiped her hands on a dishtowel and threw it over her shoulder. "What's going on?"

"I just wanted to talk to her. Is that a crime?"

Cecilia paused and looked her in the eye. "Of course not. But you need to let me know what you're doing when you don't come home after school."

"Sorry." Amber knew her voice didn't sound sorry at all, but she was sick of the third degree every time she went anywhere.

159

"Call Ms. Blackwell. She wants to talk to you," Cecilia added.

"Fine." She tromped up the stairs to her room and shut the door. Grabbing some sweat pants from the dresser, she peeled off her jeans, which were getting tighter by the day now. After changing, she plopped down on the bed and rummaged through her backpack to retrieve her cell phone.

Punching in the social worker's number, she laid her head on the pillow and closed her eyes.

"Bonnie Blackwell," the familiar voice answered.

"It's Amber."

"Amber – I'm glad you called. Hold on a second."

Amber could hear muffled voices in the background, and then Ms. Blackwell was back on the line.

"They called me from your mom's rehab today," she began.

Amber didn't reply.

"What's up? I thought we agreed that I'd coordinate those visits," Bonnie said.

"Sorry. I just needed to talk to her," she replied, hoping her voice didn't give away the gravity of her issue.

"That's fine, honey. But it's my job to help you arrange that." Bonnie paused and then added, "You know your mom's not well, and her schedule is pretty controlled over there."

"Yeah. Like I said, sorry," Amber replied, pacing the floor nervously.

Silence filled the phone line.

"What are you doing right now?" Bonnie asked.

Sinking down onto the bed, she said, "Nothing. Why?"

"How about if I come over there and take you for a bite to eat?" Bonnie's voice sounded calm and kinder than Amber remembered. But she wasn't sure where this was leading.

"Why?" she asked.

"So we can talk. Maybe I can help with whatever you were going to talk to your mom about."

Amber's heart began to pound. Should she confide in her social worker? Would Bonnie try to force her to have an abortion just like Adam was doing?

Bonnie's voice cut through her thoughts. "Amber? Are you there?"

She stood and started pacing again. "Yeah."

"What do you say? Want to go for burgers somewhere?" Bonnie sounded like she really cared.

Amber gazed out the window for a moment then replied, "Uh…sure. Yeah."

"Great. I'll call Cecilia and tell her I'm coming to pick you up."

A few minutes later, Amber heard the house phone ringing. She walked over to the full-length mirror. *I'm starting to look fat,* she thought as she examined herself from the front and side. She pulled open the closet and grabbed a bulky pullover to hide her expanding waistline.

It wasn't very long before she heard Cecilia calling her name.

"Coming!" she replied, quickly running a brush through her hair and bounding down the stairs.

Bonnie was waiting in the front room. Tessie and Todd were fighting over a toy in the corner, and Cecilia was pulling them apart.

"Need a hand?" Bonnie asked.

"No, I've got it," Cecilia replied as she grabbed the toy in question. "You two go and wash up for dinner." Tessie scowled at Todd and marched out of the room with him closely following in her tracks.

Turning back to Amber and Bonnie, the weary foster mom said, "You two have a nice time."

"Thanks. We will." Bonnie looked at Amber and tipped her head toward the door. "Ready?"

"Yep." Amber slung her purse over her shoulder and followed Bonnie out the front door.

The car ride was awkward as Bonnie tried to make small talk, and Amber worried about what she would say to explain her predicament.

"How's school?"

"Fine."

"Are you enjoying the park days with your teacher and Jack?"

Amber nodded.

"Mrs. Baron is quite a lady to offer to do that for you guys."

"Yeah. She's cool," Amber replied, picturing the scene at the park and how cute her teacher's little girl was. Her heart yearned for the love she saw between that mother and daughter. What would her teacher think if she knew Amber was pregnant?

"You seem lost in thought," Bonnie observed.

Amber just looked away and gazed out the window.

Once they were seated at the restaurant and had ordered their meal, Bonnie reached across the table and touched her hand. "Tell me what's going on," she asked in a soft voice.

Suddenly, Amber began to cry. Her cheeks flushed in embarrassment, and she tried to brush the tears away, but they kept coming.

"It's okay, Amber. Take your time." Bonnie pulled some tissue out of her purse and handed it to her.

As Amber pressed the tissue to her eyes, the waitress appeared with their food.

"Could you please pack that up to go?" Bonnie asked.

The waitress nodded. "No problem. Be right back."

Bonnie paid for the meal. "Let's go somewhere quiet," she said, picking up the bag of food.

Amber just nodded, sniffling into the tissue.

Ten minutes later they were sitting on the park bench. Bonnie pulled out a burger for each of them and handed one to Amber. There was a pause, and Amber noticed Bonnie bowing her head as if in prayer. When she looked up, she said, "I want to help you, Amber. Please tell me what's going on."

The words came tumbling out faster than Amber could control. She poured out the entire story of her relationship with Adam, the unexpected pregnancy, and the pressure she was under to abort the baby.

Bonnie set her burger down and pulled Amber into her arms, holding tightly as she sobbed. "That's right. Get it all out," the social worker said.

Amber imagined the arms that held her were her mother's arms. And she thought about the little baby growing inside her. She wanted to be there for her baby in ways her mother couldn't be there for her.

After she'd regained her composure, she pulled back and looked into Bonnie's eyes. "So now you know what a mess my life is," she said with a nervous laugh.

Bonnie smiled a sad smile. "You've known about this for a while, haven't you?" she said.

"Yeah."

"What do you want to do?"

Amber was caught off guard. She'd expected to be told what to do. Instead, Bonnie was offering her the opportunity to choose. "I don't know. I feel all mixed up," she replied. "I was hoping Adam would understand, and maybe we could get married or something."

"But that's not an option," Bonnie replied, finishing her thought.

Amber nodded. "All he can say is 'get the abortion and it will all be over' but..."

"...you're not sure that's what you want."

"Yeah." Amber gazed out over the park and pictured Maddie laughing as she pushed her on the swing. "I really care about this baby. It's not the baby's fault my life is a mess."

"I'd like to help you sort this out. You have choices, and you're entitled to know all of them."

"Okay. I'd like that," Amber replied. "I tried to get Adam to take me to this place called Living Water. The lady was really nice on the phone. They have information on lots of choices, at least that's what she said. But Adam said no, that I was crazy not to just go get the abortion."

"I'm sure he's really scared, Amber. This is a grown up situation, and he's probably feeling like he's just a kid himself."

Amber nodded.

"First order of business is to get you to a doctor," Bonnie said next. "You need to have an exam and learn how to take care of yourself right now, too. I know a good OB GYN. I'll see if I can get you an appointment with her this week."

"Okay. Thanks." Relief dispelled the heavy weight on Amber's heart. Maybe there was hope.

"After we get that taken care of, we can begin to go over all your options. You don't have to do anything you don't want to do, Amber. Maybe you should take a little break in your relationship with Adam right now until you figure this out," she suggested.

"Yeah. He told me to call him when I did."

"Okay, so that's decided." Bonnie reached over and squeezed her hand. "Feel better?"

"Yeah." Amber smiled. "Thanks."

"Let's eat," Bonnie suggested, as she retrieved her wrapped burger from the bench.

Amber slept better that night than she had in weeks. She remembered how Bonnie had bowed her head before eating, and she said a little prayer of thanks to a God somewhere far, far away.

CHAPTER EIGHTEEN

Michelle awoke in a sweat. Images from her dream shot through her mind.

Madison in a hospital bed surrounded by IVs and machines. Nurses with grim expressions and no words of encouragement or comfort. Soft moans coming from their daughter's soul. And Michelle could do nothing.

A sickening feeling clutched her gut. What would happen to their precious daughter? Pulling her knees up to her chest and hugging the comforter, Michelle began to weep, crying out silently to God. Her own moans mingled with her prayers, and soon Steve was awake, pushing himself up on his elbow and reaching out to her.

"Honey, what is it?"

Michelle turned to him, tears streaming down her face, "I had a dream about Maddie." Her chest heaved as she willed herself to stop crying. "We can't lose her, Steve. We just can't."

"Oh, babe…" Steve sat up and pulled her into his arms. As he held her and stroked her hair, the dam broke, and her tears became a flood of fear.

They sat together praying, crying, and rocking in each other's arms for quite some time. Finally the storm passed just as daybreak peeked in through their window.

Michelle glanced at the clock. She yearned to sink back under the covers and sleep, but she knew 180 eighth graders awaited her at Magnolia, and it was time to start another day.

"I'll make the coffee," Steve offered, heading out the bedroom door in his boxer shorts.

She washed her face with cold water and stared into her red-rimmed eyes. A fear she hadn't seen since her father's suicide attempt stared back at her. She averted her eyes and quickly dressed for the day. Somehow she had to wipe this expression from her face before Madison awoke.

Steve returned a moment later with a steaming cup of coffee. She forced a smile and thanked him.

Come away, Michelle.

She sensed the Lord tugging on her heart. As Steve started his shower, she glanced at her devotional book and Bible in the basket by the rocking chair in the corner. The clock on the nightstand urged her to move on with her day, but the weariness in her bones knew better.

Sipping her coffee, she flipped open the devotional. She hadn't read it in over a week now. Seemed almost impossible to fit in a quiet time with God during her busy mornings getting ready for school.

Rather than turning to the page for that date, she read the message where she'd left her marker.

Do not worry about tomorrow. Today has enough trouble of its own. Matthew 6:34

Soaking in the words of that verse, she read on.

How often we are enticed by worry and fear to peek behind the veil and see the future. In the process of seeking hope, we are engulfed in anxiety. For it is not our place to know what tomorrow holds.

Corrie Ten Boom, a woman well acquainted with hardship and sorrow as she struggled to survive in a Nazi concentration camp, would often recall the words of her father as she sought to make it through another day.

"Corrie?" he would say, "When we are going on a journey, when do I give you the ticket for the train? Is it when we get to the station?"

"No, Papa. You give it to me when the conductor comes."

"That's right. And so it is with God. He gives us the strength we need to meet each day's challenges at the moment we need it. He doesn't give us the strength for tomorrow today."

Like the manna in the wilderness, God's grace is sufficient for today. He promises to walk with us through this day and to be there when we need Him tomorrow. If your heart is heavy, if fear and anxiety are your companions this morning, ask yourself if you are trying to borrow trouble from tomorrow. Rather than focusing on the unknown that awaits you, focus on what you do know.

God is for you. He is more than able to accomplish what concerns you. And just as He led the Israelites through the wilderness for forty years and helped Corrie survive a brutal season in her life, so He will meet you at every turn in the road and provide what you need at the moment you need it.

A short prayer followed at the bottom of the page, and Michelle read it slowly, making it her own.

Thank you, God, for your promise to strengthen me for the day ahead. Help me to keep my eyes on you and not the circumstances that threaten my tomorrows.

Peace. God's mantle of peace rested on her heart as Michelle closed her eyes and whispered her own prayer of thanksgiving. Although she'd missed her meetings with God for a handful of mornings, He'd brought her to this message when she needed it most. Like the ticket for the train, she had what she needed to face another day.

Lunch break had just begun. Michelle retrieved her sandwich from the mini refrigerator she kept in her room. Seemed like there was rarely time to eat in the lounge with all the papers she had to grade and the lessons she had to plan.

"Mrs. Baron?" a voice from the door caught her attention.

"Amber! Come on in." Michelle gestured toward her desk.

"Can we talk?" the girl asked.

Michelle sat down, placing her lunch off to the side of her desk. "Sure. What's up?" She pulled a chair up next to hers and offered it to Amber, who sat down nervously.

"I went to see my mom," Amber offered.

"Really? How's she doing?"

"The same."

Michelle could see the disappointment and frustration that ate at her student. "I'm sorry, Amber."

"Yeah. I wanted to tell her something."

"Maybe I can help. What's on your mind?" Michelle asked, giving Amber her full attention.

Squirming slightly, Amber looked up at the ceiling. "I'm pregnant," she blurted out.

Michelle was stunned. An eighth grader pregnant? Maybe she was being naïve, but she thought this was something that happened in the high schools, not the middle schools. "Are you sure?" she asked, trying to sound calm.

Amber nodded. She stared at her hands in her lap and then started crying.

Michelle moved closer and took Amber's hands in her own. Taking a deep breath, she asked, "How can I help you?"

Amber shook her head and pulled a hand free to wipe her tears with the back of it.

"Here," Michelle offered her a tissue.

Blowing her nose and mopping her eyes, Amber tried to compose herself.

"Have you told anyone else?" Michelle asked.

Amber looked away. "Yeah. My boyfriend and the social worker."

"What did they say?"

Looking back into her eyes, Amber replied, "Adam says I should have an abortion."

Michelle tried not to flinch. "And the social worker?"

"She said I have choices, and she'll help me figure it out." Amber reached for another tissue, tossing the first in the trashcan at their feet.

Michelle nodded. "That sounds good. Did she say anything about school?"

She shook her head. "No. Do you think they'll make me leave Magnolia?"

"I really don't know, Amber. I've never had a student who was pregnant before." She put her hand on Amber's shoulder. "Do you want me to talk to the counselor? We could go together if you'd like."

"Let me see what Ms. Blackwell says first. I guess the school doesn't have to know if I decide to have an abortion." She started crying again.

Michelle sighed and handed her another tissue. "You've got a lot to think about for someone your age. Maybe the counselor could help."

"Maybe. Just don't say anything yet, okay?" Amber asked, blowing her nose and wiping her eyes.

Michelle wracked her brain trying to remember the rules about mandatory reporting the principal had given her. Was she legally required to report this disclosure? She'd have to check with Cassie. "How old is Adam, Amber?"

Amber studied the floor. "He's seventeen."

"Do his parents know about this?" she asked.

"His mom's dead. No way he'd tell his dad. He just wants it to go away – to pretend it never happened."

Amber stood and tugged on her tight jeans then sat down again on the edge of the chair.

"And you?" Michelle asked.

Amber made eye contact with her again. "I feel bad for the baby."

Michelle nodded.

Amber picked up the picture of Madison and looked at Michelle's daughter. "I wish I could be a good mom like you are for Maddie. She's really lucky to have you."

"We're lucky to have each other," Michelle added, taking the picture as Amber handed it back to her.

"If they kick me out of school, will we still be able to have our park days?" she asked.

"I'll do everything in my power to keep that up," Michelle offered.

"But you don't know if the school will let you?"

"I just have to talk to a few people, especially the social worker, but also the principal," she explained.

Amber nodded.

"But I promise I'll try. And I'll do whatever I can to help you keep up your studies."

"Thanks, Mrs. B," Amber said, standing again. "Guess I'd better go."

Michelle joined her on her feet and gave her a hug. "I'm glad you told me, Amber. Please let me know whatever I can do to help."

"Okay. Thanks." Amber picked up her backpack and walked out the door.

Michelle sank into her chair and buried her face in her hands. As she prayed for wisdom for her troubled student, the passing bell rang.

Standing up, she grabbed her untouched lunch and headed to the back of the room to return it to the fridge. Maybe she'd get a chance to grab a bite or two between classes later in the afternoon.

Pulling a post-it note from her desktop, she scribbled a quick reminder to talk to Cassie about the mandatory reporting issue. One more thing to address in an already busy day.

CHAPTER NINETEEN

Michelle opened the door to Cassie's room and peered inside. Her friend and mentor was leaning over a file drawer in the front corner of the room.

"Cassie?"

"Michelle! Hi, come on in." Shoving the file drawer closed with her hip, Cassie turned and walked toward her. "You look tired. Everything okay?"

"Actually, no. Do you have a minute to talk?"

"Sure. Want some coffee? I've got a little left in the pot." Cassie walked to the back counter and reached for the carafe. Turning to Michelle, she held out an empty cup in a question.

"I'd love some. Thanks." Michelle sunk into one of the student seats in the front row facing Cassie's desk.

As her friend handed her the cup, she asked, "School issue or personal?"

"Both."

Cassie nodded. "Do tell."

"I had a horrible nightmare about Maddie having leukemia. And I've got a pregnant student," Michelle blurted.

"Whoa. Rewind that. Tell me about Madison, first. What did the blood test say?" Cassie leaned forward, hugging her coffee mug in her hands.

"It was inconclusive, so we had to do a bone marrow biopsy. We had that done on Monday."

"That's why you were out."

"Yeah."

"How'd she do with it?"

"Okay. She's such a little trouper."

"So how long do you have to wait for the results?"

"A week to ten days."

"That's a long time for you to have to wait," she replied. Then she added, "I'm sorry to hear about your dream. I can't imagine how you're able to concentrate on teaching right now. And what's this about your student being pregnant?"

"She asked me not to tell anyone, but I'm not sure if this is a mandatory reporting thing or not."

"Is the father an adult?" Cassie asked.

"No. Her boyfriend is from the high school. He's seventeen."

"A little old for an eighth grader," she observed.

"Yeah."

"This isn't Amber Gamble, is it?"

Michelle hesitated. "I'm not sure if I should answer that."

"Got it. You didn't tell me," Cassie smiled knowingly. "So what's she going to do?"

"She doesn't know. The boyfriend wants her to have an abortion, but she's not sure she wants to do that." Michelle shuddered involuntarily.

Cassie paused then asked, "Does anyone else know?"

"Her social worker."

Cassie looked relieved. "Okay. That's good. So that covers any mandatory reporting thing if she really does know. You might want to confirm that. You already have a contact there, right? Because of your park days, I mean."

"Yeah. She's a great lady. I really like her."

"Well, that's where I'd start if I were you. Call her and just make sure she really knows about all this. Then you can offer any assistance you'd like, but don't overburden yourself right now, Michelle. You've got a lot on your plate with Madison, not to mention your first year of full time teaching."

Michelle nodded. "So what would happen to her if she decides to go through with the pregnancy? Will she have to leave Magnolia?"

"I think our district leaves that up to the principal and the school counselor to decide. Do you think she'd want to stay here? Seems like she'd be setting herself up for a lot of fall out socially speaking."

"I got the feeling she'd want to stay. Her life's in such upheaval right now with an absentee mother and being separated from her brother. Magnolia seems to be the one place that's consistent."

"She must feel safe with you to confide in you like this," Cassie observed.

"Yeah. I feel like we've come a long way since September," Michelle agreed.

"I'd like to help her if I can. Especially if she decides to have the baby. I was thinking maybe I could offer to tutor her after school if she can't attend classes here."

"That's really sweet of you. But, like I said, don't overextend yourself." She walked around to the front of the desk. "Promise me you'll let me know as soon as you hear anything about Maddie's biopsy. And don't hesitate to call me if you need any help getting a sub or coming up with a lesson."

"I promise," Michelle replied, rising to her feet. "Thanks, Cassie. I'm really glad I have you right down the hall."

Cassie smiled and gave her a hug. "Me, too."

When Michelle got to Kelly's house to pick up Madison, the little girl was having so much fun baking cupcakes that she hated to drag her away.

"Look, Mommy! I made a happy face!" she exclaimed gleefully, showing off her candy artwork.

"I see," Michelle replied with a smile.

"She's welcome to stay here for dinner, if you'd like," Kelly offered. "It would give you and Steve a little time to yourselves."

Michelle looked at her daughter with mixed emotions. As they awaited the results of the bone marrow biopsy, each day with Maddie evoked heightened appreciation for the gift she was in their lives. On the other hand, Michelle was happy to see her enjoying a carefree time with her friends, not knowing what hardships might be looming around the corner.

"Can I, Mommy? Please?" Madison begged, licking some frosting off her fingers.

Michelle nodded. "Okay, sweetheart."

"Yay!" came the chorus from all the kids.

"Thanks, Kelly. Looks like you'll have a busy evening."

"What's one more when we're having fun?" she replied. "I'll have Ben run her home around eight, okay?"

"Are you sure? We can pick her up," Michelle offered.

"I'm sure. You two have been at work all day. Take a break and enjoy your dinner together."

"Okay. I owe you one," Michelle replied.

They hugged each other, and she headed home.

"Steve? Is that you?"

"Hi babe," he said as he walked into the kitchen. Placing his briefcase on the floor, he put his hands on her shoulders and kissed her lightly. "Where's Maddie?"

"She stayed at Ben and Kelly's for dinner."

"Oh. I thought we weren't doing that on school nights."

"They were finishing making cupcakes, and she was having so much fun – I didn't have the heart to drag her away from it. Ben's bringing her home around eight."

Steve nodded and picked up the mail on the counter. Thumbing through it, he asked, "How was school today?"

"You would not believe what Amber told me," she replied.

He looked up from the mail. "Try me."

"Steve, she's pregnant."

He set the mail down and looked directly at her. "What? How old is she, twelve?" his voice was incredulous.

"No, she's fourteen."

He shook his head. "Still, it's hard to fathom a fourteen-year-old in middle school getting pregnant."

Michelle nodded as she sunk down into a chair. "Yeah. I was pretty stunned myself."

Steve joined her at the table. "Do you know the boy?" he asked.

"No. He's in high school."

"Figures. From what you've told me about Amber, she's a sitting target for this."

She nodded. "I was just starting to make headway with her. She's really good with Madison, too. I hate to see her in this predicament."

"Do you think her mom knows?"

"She tried to tell her, but her mom's really going through her own problems right now," Michelle replied. "She did tell her social worker, though."

"That's good. What's she going to do? I suppose the boyfriend's disappeared."

"He wants her to get an abortion."

"Of course." He shook his head in dismay.

"But she's not ready to decide yet. She's hoping I can help her with the school part of all this, especially if she decides to have the baby."

"What does that mean for you?" Steve seemed concerned. "We've got Maddie to think about, too, especially now."

"I know. It's basically a matter of finding out the school policy. I'll talk to the principal tomorrow. Cassie thinks he'll leave it up to Amber to decide whether she wants to stay in her classes on campus or do a home school program."

"What do you think she should do?" he asked as he leaned against the counter and studied her response.

"I don't know. I hate to see her have an abortion. We know firsthand how many people are eager to adopt babies. But staying in class…that will be rough. I'm thinking of offering to tutor her outside of school if she chooses the home school route."

"Don't make any promises until we find out about Madison."

"Of course," she replied, nodding in agreement. Just the mention of Madison drew them into each other's arms. "This waiting is killing me."

"I know. Me, too," he agreed, holding her close.

Later that evening, after Madison was home and settled in bed, Michelle sat in her rocker and began praying. She pled with God on behalf of her daughter, for her health and for a chance to grow up. Then she turned her prayers to Amber, asking God to give her wisdom beyond her years.

Over a week had passed since the biopsy, and Michelle could not sleep the night before the appointment for Madison's bone marrow test results. Several times, she crept out of their room and peeked in on their sleeping daughter. Would their lives change radically in the morning?

Although Maddie looked so peaceful as she slept, Michelle's heart was deeply troubled. Thanksgiving was around the corner. How she hoped and prayed they would be thanking God for the test results they were about to receive.

Finally around five, she fell into a restless sleep, only to be awakened an hour and a half later by the buzzing of the alarm clock. She could feel her hands shaking as she applied her make up.

"Are you okay, babe?" Steve asked, hugging her from behind.

"I guess. I'll just be glad when today's over," she replied with a sigh.

"Me, too. Want me to wake Maddie up?"

"Yeah. That would be great. I'll be ready in a few minutes."

Steve left the room, and Michelle stared at herself in the mirror. "Get a grip," she said softly. The last thing she wanted was for Madison to see her nervous or upset.

I am with you. I will never leave you nor forsake you.

Michelle paused and let the words find a home in her heart. Then taking a deep breath, she ran the brush quickly through her hair and headed downstairs.

As they sat around the kitchen table for breakfast, Michelle noticed that Madison was playing with her cereal rather than eating it. "Are you okay, sweetheart?" she asked.

"Do I have to go to sleep at the doctor's office again today?"

"No, Maddie. The doctor's not going to do any tests on you today," Steve replied. "We're just going to talk to him."

"No shots?" her voice asked with a quiver.

"No shots," Michelle promised, taking her daughter's hand in hers. "Shall we pray?"

Madison nodded, extending her other hand to Steve, and the three of them bowed their heads and thanked God for the meal and another day together as a family.

While they sat in the waiting room of Dr. Morris' office, Michelle tried to keep herself and Madison distracted with a stack of books they'd brought along. Meanwhile, Steve was busy on his iPad working on a closing argument for a case he'd be presenting in court the following week.

Finally it was their turn. As they walked through the reception door into the hallway of examining rooms and offices, Michelle and Steve both took Maddie's hand in theirs as if to guard her on both flanks.

They glanced at each other and exchanged reassuring smiles, but Michelle could tell that Steve was equally apprehensive. They'd spent almost two weeks sharing a rollercoaster of emotions, and now the ride was about to end.

The little girl who walked between them was a culmination of their love for each other and a difficult journey of overcoming the infertility issues that had threatened to leave them childless. Would they still be holding her hands a year from now? Would they even have a daughter by then?

The nurse led them to a paneled office at the end of the hall. An impressive mahogany desk dominated the room with shelves of medical books backing it.

"Dr. Morris will be with you in a moment. Just make yourselves comfortable." She gestured to three chairs that faced the desk. "Would you like a coloring book?" she asked Madison.

Madison looked up at Michelle then shook her head.

"Okay. I'll let the doctor know you are waiting."

Several minutes passed as they sat together. Michelle had just begun to read one of the books to Madison when the door opened, and in walked the doctor, glancing up from the open file in his hands to greet them warmly.

Steve rose to his feet and shook the doctor's hand, and Michelle, who was now holding Madison on her lap, extended her own hand as well.

Seating himself behind the desk, Dr. Morris spread open their file for one last perusal, then laced his hands together and sat upright smiling. "Well, we have good news and maybe not so good news."

Michelle hugged Maddie as she sat forward in her seat. Steve reached over and took her hand in his.

"The good news is the bone marrow came back normal. No sign of leukemia."

Michelle felt her body start to shake with relief as her eyes filled with tears. Steve squeezed her hand and shot a smile her way. The worst fear was behind them.

"You mentioned some not so good news," Steve said.

The doctor glanced down at the file again and then back up at them. "There's still a concern about the bruising and bleeding Madison's been experiencing. Her blood work indicates she likely has a condition called Von Willebrand's disease."

As the doctor continued his explanation, words like antigen, ristocetin cofactor activity, and platelet functions were all Greek to Michelle. "Can this condition be treated?" she asked, eager for concrete information she could understand.

"Yes, most definitely. Von Willebrand disease is a lifelong condition. There are no cures, but it is not terminal. There are varying degrees of the disease. Some people need ongoing treatment with medications and infusions, others may only need special treatment before undergoing surgery, dental extractions, or in the aftermath of a trauma such as a car accident."

He paused and then continued. "And as Madison reaches adolescence, she may need to take prophylactic contraceptives to control heavy bleeding during her menstrual period."

"What do we do right now?" Steve asked, voicing the same question Michelle was thinking.

"Right now, I'd like to test the two of you for hereditary factors. I'll also give you a prescription for a nasal spray you can try with Madison. If it helps to prevent the bruising, I'd recommend continuing with it indefinitely. You should see her gums improving as well."

Michelle and Steve nodded.

"If she continues to have nosebleeds that are difficult to stop, we may need to adjust the dosage or try other options. But for now, this is the least invasive method of treating her condition.

"If she responds well, we're on the road to alleviating her symptoms, and I can just monitor her twice a year. I'd like to see her again in three weeks. By then I'll have the results of your blood work as well, and we can get a pretty good idea of how your daughter is doing with the medication."

The doctor reached for a pad on the corner of the desk and began writing. First he handed them each a lab order for their own blood work, then he gave Michelle a nasal spray prescription for Madison.

"She'll use this every day for the next three weeks. If you have any questions or concerns before then, please call. I'll also want to know if she experiences any of those bad nosebleeds again."

"Okay. Thanks," she replied. Then turning Madison, she helped her scoot down off her lap. As the doctor stood, she and Steve joined him on his feet, again shaking hands and thanking him for the information.

"We'll see you in three weeks, then," Dr. Morris said as he reached down and patted Madison gently on the head. "Bring Teddy next time," he added with a smile.

Madison leaned against Michelle. "Okay," she said with a grin.

On the way home, they stopped by the lab for Michelle and Steve to have their blood work done, then dropped off Madison's prescription at the drug store. "Want to get an ice cream?" Steve asked their daughter.

"Really, Daddy? Before lunch?"

"Yep. My treat," he replied, catching Michelle's glance and sharing their relief over the diagnosis.

"Yippy!!!" Maddie squealed, jumping up and down.

An overwhelming feeling of joy surged through Michelle. Before all of this, any type of disease or condition in Madison would have rattled her. Now, the replacement of leukemia with this treatable, albeit lifelong condition was like a gift from above.

"Off to the Igloo!" Steve announced as they piled into the car.

CHAPTER TWENTY

During her conference period the next day, Michelle made a call to Amber's social worker.

"Bonnie Blackwell," came the now familiar voice.

"It's Michelle Baron," Michelle said.

"Michelle, how can I help you?" the social worker asked.

"I'm calling about Amber."

"Is she having problems in class again?"

"No," Michelle replied, trying to figure out how to broach the subject of Amber's pregnancy.

"That's good. I know she really appreciates the time you're giving her and Jack for their meetings at the park," Bonnie said.

"I'm happy to do it," she replied.

"So what can I do for you today?"

Michelle began twisting a strand of hair at the nape of her neck. "Amber came to me and confided something, and I want to make sure she was telling the truth when she told me you knew."

"About?"

"About her condition." Michelle replied, hoping Bonnie would understand what she meant.

"I see." There was a pause on the line, and then Bonnie continued. "Tell me what she told you. I'm pretty sure I know."

"She said that she's pregnant," Michelle had trouble even saying the words.

"And what did you say?"

"I tried not to show her how stunned I was. This is the first student I've known of to get pregnant in middle school, so I was pretty shocked." Michelle waited a second and then added, "I told her I'd help however I could."

"Have you discussed this with your principal yet?"

"No. I wanted to talk to you first. Amber seems like she might want to have the baby, and I wasn't sure how much you take over at this point."

Bonnie cleared her throat. "I'm glad she told you, Michelle. She's going to need all the support she can get, especially if she maintains the pregnancy. My first priority is for Amber's wellbeing. That starts with making sure she is okay physically and then helping her sort through the mental and emotional issues she will face as she makes her decision."

"She told me that you are going to go over all her options with her."

"Yes. Ultimately, it needs to be her decision."

"What can I do to help?" Michelle asked.

"Being a support to her is the most important thing. She needs adult women who will listen to her without passing judgment and who will stand with her regardless of what she decides."

"I understand."

"And if Amber does decide to have the baby, which my instincts tell me she probably will, she'll definitely need help navigating the school issues she'll face in order to continue her classes, either at Magnolia or at home."

"Right," Michelle replied. "Please let me know what I can do in that regard."

"Okay. As you know, Amber has few assets in her life. She lacks a stable family, a real home, a set of core values and principles around which she builds her framework. At this point, she's feeling very vulnerable and alone. The more support we can offer, the better the outcome is likely to be."

"I agree. I told Amber I'd find out more about her school options."

"I was actually planning on setting up a meeting with Mr. Durand to discuss those later this week. Would you like to be part of that meeting?"

"Yeah, I would," Michelle replied.

"Great. I'll let you know what we set up. In the meantime, please contact me if you see any particular red flags with Amber at school."

"Okay. Thanks."

"Thank *you* for taking such an interest in her. She is very blessed to have you for her teacher."

As Michelle hung up the phone, the word *blessed* played over in her mind. Was it possible that Amber's social worker was a Christian, too?

Michelle and Amber's social worker sat across from Daniel Durand in his office. It was the Friday before the Thanksgiving week break, and this meeting would determine Amber's options at Magnolia Middle School.

"Good afternoon, ladies. I gather this meeting is about Amber Gamble."

Bonnie sat forward in her seat. "There is a new circumstance in Amber's life. She recently confided in me and in her teacher," tipping her head toward Michelle, "that she is pregnant."

"I see," he replied, sitting back in his seat. Fixing his gaze on Bonnie, he asked, "And how can we help?"

"Amber hasn't decided her course of action yet. She'd like to know whether or not she can continue at Magnolia if she decides to go ahead with the pregnancy."

Daniel nodded thoughtfully. "Let's look over her records for this year." He sat forward and flipped open a folder on his desk. Thumbing through it, he scanned Amber's grades and teachers' comments.

"She's really improving in my class," Michelle offered. "I see more effort and less disruptive behavior."

"Hmmm…" Daniel murmured, continuing to peruse the paperwork. "Looks like she's still struggling with science. Math is passing, but barely." He paused and read a few comments. "Most of her teachers indicate they see potential, and her standardized scores show that she reads above grade level."

"I don't think she has aptitude issues," Bonnie interjected. "But with her family circumstances, she's been thrown into a situation that is particularly difficult for an adolescent. At a time when she needs stability most, she's had the rug pulled out from under her."

Michelle leaned forward. "I'd really like to help her in any way I can. I noticed her P.E. class is during my conference period. Maybe I could tutor her and help her with her homework during that time."

Daniel nodded. "We could issue her a waiver for P.E. But are you sure you want to give up that planning time? This is your first full time year, after all."

"I'd like to give it a try."

"What's being done to cover her medical bases?" he asked, looking to Bonnie.

"I'm taking her for a physical in a couple of weeks. She'll have full prenatal coverage from the state if she needs it."

"I'd like Amber to talk to the school counselor before we make any decisions about her continuing at Magnolia. Karen's great with the kids, and I think she'll be an important asset to Amber, no matter what decision she makes."

Bonnie and Michelle agreed.

"Okay. Let's start there, and we'll meet again with Karen after she's talked to Amber." Daniel pushed his chair back and stood to his feet, extending his hand to Bonnie, who grasped it in a firm shake.

"Thanks so much for meeting with us," she said.

"My pleasure. I only wish it were under better circumstances," he replied. Turning his attention to Michelle, he added, "Thanks for reaching out to Amber, Michelle. You are really making a difference here."

She nodded, her heart soaring with the affirmation.

Thank you, God, she prayed silently as they turned and left the office.

Rushing to pick up Madison, she was eager to go home and pack for their trip to Seal Beach. It would be great to see her family again for the Thanksgiving break.

She'd had quite a first quarter at school and was looking forward to a relaxing holiday catching up with her parents, brother, and grandparents. She glanced at her daughter and smiled as she thought of how much fun it would be to watch Madison interact with all of them, too.

CHAPTER TWENTY-ONE

Thanksgiving break was a wonderful and relaxing time for Michelle, Steve, and Madison. Michelle's mother pampered them with delicious home-cooked meals morning, noon, and night. Uncle Tim romped with Maddie and took her to the surf shop, returning home with a little girl's hang ten t-shirt decked with hibiscus flowers.

Michelle watched Madison cuddle on her grandfather's lap and savored the joy in John's eyes as he held her close. Great grandparents Phil and Joan also clearly delighted in their precious little girl, with Grandpa Phil playing hide and seek in the back yard, and Joan helping Maddie create handprint turkeys for table decorations.

Michelle's lifelong friend Kristin and her husband were in town visiting Kristin's parents, so Michelle and Maddie joined her for a walk on the pier and a little treat at Ruby's Diner. Madison spotted the bronze seal statue and wanted her picture taken with it, bringing back a flood of childhood memories for both Michelle and Kristin.

"Remember when we used to hang out here?" Kristin asked with a wistful smile.

Michelle nodded. "Seems like only yesterday." She looked down at her daughter and smiled as she reflected on how Madison would also have memories of Seal

Beach, even though it would be about visits to her grandparents rather than as her childhood home.

Above all else, Michelle's favorite time of the weekend was the beginning of Thanksgiving dinner as everyone in the family held hands around the table while Grandpa Phil asked a blessing upon the food and their lives.

Seeing her father's hand firmly grasping Sheila's on one side and Joan's on the other triggered a heart-swell of gratitude for God's grace and mercy. Memories of her father's struggle to survive after his suicide attempt were starting to fade as memories of his newfound faith took their place.

Thank you, Lord, for all you have done for our family, she prayed silently, squeezing Steve and Madison's hands as they all said their amens.

The next few weeks passed quickly as Michelle tried to keep her students focused on *A Christmas Carol.* It was clear they were ready for their two-week vacation, but this unit was a department requirement and included an essay.

By having them take turns reading parts in the script form of the story, she was able to keep them interested and engaged. A follow-up viewing of the movie version solidified the characters and plot in their minds and helped her walk them through their essay responses.

A week before break, Bonnie Blackwell called and left a message on Michelle's cell phone. Amber's OB appointment would be the following day.

Dr. Miller rolled her stool back from the examining table. "You can sit up now," she said to Amber.

Bonnie moved forward from her place in the corner of the room and stood next to Amber, who had requested her presence during the exam.

"You are fourteen weeks pregnant," the doctor began. "Everything looks good to me. The nurse found a strong heartbeat, and you seem like a healthy young lady." Looking over her paperwork, she asked, "No drinking or drugs?"

Amber hesitated.

"It's important that you tell me the truth, Amber. We're not just talking about you now. There's another life under consideration."

Bonnie put her hand on Amber's shoulder in a show of support.

"Just a little weed," she confessed under her breath.

Dr. Miller waited for her to lookup. "How much is a little?"

"Like maybe once or twice a week," she admitted.

"You need to stop that completely while you decide what you want to do."

Amber nodded.

"How about cigarettes?" the doctor asked next.

"No," she replied, and then added, "I've smoked a couple of times, but not since I found out I was pregnant."

"Okay. That's good." She looked Amber in the eye before continuing. "You've got an important decision to make here, young lady. If you want to terminate this pregnancy, the sooner you do that, the better."

Amber nodded. "That's what they said at the clinic."

After a short pause, the doctor continued. "If you decide to maintain the pregnancy, we'll need to set you up with a series of follow-up appointments."

"Would it be possible for me to have an ultrasound to see the baby?" Amber asked.

The doctor looked at Bonnie with a questioning expression, and she nodded an affirmative response.

"Okay. We can actually do one here in the office. Let me get the nurse." She got up from her stool and walked out the door, Amber's file in her hand.

Several minutes later, a light tap on the door revealed a young, African-American nurse pushing a cart toward the examining table. She smiled warmly at Amber and adjusted the end of the table to provide a footrest.

"Just lay back and relax," she instructed. "I'm going to put some gel on your abdomen, and then we'll get a look at your baby."

The gel felt warm on Amber's skin. "I expected that to be cold," she said with a smile.

"Oh, we've got a warmer for the gel now. No more shock factor," the nurse added, returning Amber's smile. She placed the ultrasound wand firmly on Amber's abdomen and began moving it in slow circles.

Soon a whooshing sound emanated from the machine. "There's the heartbeat," she said.

Amber listened carefully, studying the monitor's image.

"Here's the head," the nurse explained. "And the little rear end." She continued to move the wand. "Do you see the arms and legs?"

Amber nodded, her heart beating loudly in her ears.

It really is a baby, she thought, as she gazed in awe at the picture on the screen. She could even see its tiny heart beating.

"Looks like it might be a boy," the nurse added. "It's still pretty early to tell for sure, but sometimes we get a good angle, even as early as this."

Immediately Amber thought of her brother Jack. She could remember him as a baby, and she tried to imagine what it would be like to have her own baby boy.

Would he look like Adam? Or maybe like her or Jack? She was mesmerized by the images on the screen and was sad when the nurse lifted the wand, announcing they were finished.

"Everything looks good," she told Amber as she wiped the gel from her abdomen with a towel. "You can get dressed. They'll book your next appointment at the check out desk." She rolled the machine out the door, calling over her shoulder, "See you next time."

"I'll meet you out front," Bonnie told her.

Amber appreciated the brief time alone to savor the images of her baby as she dressed. There was no way she could have an abortion now.

Not after seeing him.

Amber sat at the far side of the front seat of Adam's car. "You don't have to be a stranger," he said, patting the spot next to him.

The December air was cold, and his invitation was tempting. "I think I'd rather sit here," she replied.

Adam started up the car. "Whatever."

They rode in silence for the few miles to the beach, and then Adam turned off the motor. "I can't stay long," he said. "My dad's all over me about my grades and homework."

Amber looked at him and cleared her throat. "I just wanted to tell you that I decided what I'm going to do."

"Oh yeah? Okay. So what did you decide?"

"I decided I'm going to have the baby."

Adam was silent for a long time. Finally he asked, "You really can't let go of this, can you?"

"I saw him, Adam. I saw his heart beating, and his arms and legs, and everything. He's a real baby, not a bunch of tissue like they said at the clinic. The nurse said she thinks it's a boy."

"Great. Well you do whatever you want," he added.

"I want to be with you and be a family...to be a mom to him," she stammered.

"That's not going to happen. I already told you I'm not dropping out of school to raise some kid." He looked her in the eye. "I mean it, Amber. You're on your own if you do this. That kid will end up with a messed up life just like yours."

"Thanks," she replied sarcastically.

"Hey, you made up your own mind, remember. I told you what I thought you should do."

"Yeah. You made that pretty clear."

"So, if you're not going to listen to me, and your determined to ruin your life, then I think maybe we should take a break."

"What do you mean?"

"I mean, I'm not going to hang around and be your boyfriend, and pretend everything's fine, when it's not." He paused and studied her face for a moment. "If you think you're going to change my mind about being a dad to this kid, you're crazy."

"Great. Thanks for the kick in the gut."

"Whatever." Adam reached for the keys and started the motor. "I'd better get home before my dad has a stroke."

Amber just looked at him through her tears and shook her head.

Jerk. I don't need him anyway.

She turned away and stared out the window as the car pulled away from the curb.

As soon as she got back to her foster home, she went upstairs and collapsed on her bed, crying for what seemed like hours. Thankfully Cecilia had taken the kids to dinner at some fast food joint, so no one interrupted her meltdown.

When she finally pulled herself together, she picked up her phone to call Bonnie. Hopefully this conversation would go better than her little talk with Adam.

As Michelle stopped to pick up the paperwork in her mailbox early that morning, she noticed she'd missed a call from Bonnie Blackwell. *Maybe I can reach her before class starts,* she thought as she hurried directly to her room.

"Bonnie? It's Michelle Baron. Sorry to call so early," she began.

"No problem. I'm about to leave for the office."

"What's up?"

"Amber's made her decision, and I'd like to come by and talk to you later today," Bonnie said.

"Okay... I could meet with you during my lunch break or after school."

"Let's meet for lunch. I'll come by at noon."

"Great. See you then," Michelle replied.

The first few classes were hectic. The kids always seemed so much rowdier after they'd had a sub, and with Christmas break looming large, Michelle was constantly trying to reel them in.

When at last the morning was over, Michelle hurried to scoot her last straggling students out the door before Bonnie arrived. Grabbing a quick bite of her sandwich, she heard the door open and Bonnie's friendly, "Hello!"

"Come on in. I'm eager to hear about Amber," Michelle said, shoving her sandwich back into the brown bag.

"Don't let me stop you from eating. We can talk while you have your lunch," Bonnie encouraged her.

Michelle waved off her suggestion. "It's okay. I can eat during my conference period."

They sat together at a table on the side of the classroom. "So what's the verdict?" Michelle asked.

"She's decided to have the baby."

Michelle nodded, trying not to look too relieved. "Okay, so how can I help?"

"She's going to need a lot of understanding and patience," Bonnie began. "Your friendship will mean the world to her right now. Any time you can give her will be a great gift."

"I'd like to keep doing our park days," Michelle began. "Maybe we could set up one or two during the Christmas break."

"Good. I know she treasures those, as does her brother."

"And I was thinking about something else, too," Michelle added tentatively.

"What's that?"

"I thought I'd offer to take her to church with us." Michelle watched Bonnie's face for her reaction. It was hard to read.

"Have you discussed that with Amber?"

"No. I wanted to mention it to you, first."

"I have no objection to you doing that, Michelle. But you are crossing a line here that might be problematic in a couple of ways."

Michelle leaned forward. "Go on."

"First, there's the church-state issue since you are her teacher and this is a public school. I'd recommend you discuss this with your administrator to find out how your idea would go over with the district."

Michelle nodded. "Okay."

"And then there's the new territory of embracing Amber into your family life. I know you've done that to some degree with the park situation. But this would be on a non-school day and would include your husband in the event as well.

"Are you sure you want to mix that part of your life with your outreach to Amber? She may become more dependent on you than you realize."

"Yeah. I see what you're saying. It just seems like something that could really help her – you know, give her a support system that she doesn't have right now." Michelle paused, grasping for the right words. "The youth group and pastor at our church are really great. I know she'd feel welcomed, in spite of her condition."

Bonnie smiled. "Talk it over with your husband and with the principal, and let me know what they say. If you still want to go forward with the idea, I'll speak with Amber and her mother about it. It's definitely not something we can do behind her mother's back. She'll need to be informed and give consent."

"Does she know about the pregnancy?" Michelle asked, recalling her conversation with Amber about her failed attempt to tell her.

"No. Amber and I will be going to see her later this week. I've had the rehab center clear her counseling appointments for an afternoon, speaking of which, you and I need to meet again with Mr. Durand and the counselor and set something up for Amber."

They discussed possible times they were both free, and then Michelle picked up the school phone and dialed the office. By the time they'd set up an appointment with the principal and another with the counselor for Amber, the bell rang, and lunch break was over.

"I'll be eager to hear how things go with Amber's mother tomorrow," Michelle said as Bonnie walked to the door.

"I'm sure Amber will be happy to talk to you about it. Thanks again for all you are doing for her," Bonnie added warmly as she waved and left the room.

After Steve tucked Madison into bed for the night, he went back downstairs to work on some legal briefs. Before he could get settled with his paperwork, Michelle walked into the room and sat down beside him.

"Can we talk?" she asked.

"Sure. What's up?" *Hope this doesn't take too long. I've got to finish this work before morning.*

"I'm wondering how you would feel about me inviting Amber to go to church with us?"

"Didn't we talk about this once before?" he asked, trying to be patient.

"Yes, but I really think she needs as much support as she can get right now." Michelle put her hand on his knee. "She's decided to have the baby. I just feel like the church could be a good support system for her. She's going to have a rough road ahead, and I'm really proud of her decision. It would have been much easier to have an abortion."

Steve nodded in agreement, praying for wisdom about Michelle's request. "Are you sure you're not crossing a legal line here as her teacher?" he asked.

"I talked to the social worker, and she said to discuss it with the principal, and she'd talk to Amber's mom. But there's no point in doing that if you aren't on board for this." She looked at him with those big hazel eyes that always melted his heart.

"Okay. I guess we could give it a try. But only if the principal and her mom give you the thumbs up. You don't want to take a chance with your job."

His wife threw her arms around his neck and kissed his cheek. "Thanks, honey!"

"Okay. Anything else? I've got to finish going over these briefs and make a few corrections before tomorrow."

"Nope. Brief away," she said, patting his knee again as she rose and walked out of the room.

He shook his head with a smile and reached for the file in front of him.

Michelle caught up with Cassie as they both hurried to class the next morning. "Hi, friend," she said. "Hey, I need to talk to you about something. Do you have a minute before class?"

"Sure. Come on in." Cassie unlocked her door and swung it open, propping it with her foot as she gestured Michelle inside. Letting the door fall closed afterward, she dropped a pile of papers on her desk and turned back to face her. "So what's up?"

"I told you about Amber being pregnant."

Cassie nodded.

"Well, she's decided to have the baby, and I'd really like to help her in whatever ways I can. Steve and I have agreed to invite her to church with us. Her social worker says it's okay if Daniel clears it on this end, and Amber's mom says it's okay on the other. Bonnie's going to talk to Amber's mom, but I thought I'd talk to you before I ask Daniel."

"Like I said last time we talked, I think it's great that you want to help her, Michelle. Just be careful with the overlap between your life as a teacher and your family time." She paused, as if waiting for that part of her response to sink in.

Then she continued. "I honestly think Daniel will be supportive of the idea. He's always open to additional support systems for the kids, especially the needy ones like Amber."

"That's what I wanted to hear. I wasn't sure how he'd respond, and I'm still a first year pro-bee."

"He'll be straight with you. If there are legal issues, he'll let you know. But don't worry about the probationary status thing. If anything, he'll respect you all the more for taking such a personal interest in Amber."

"Thanks, Cass. That helps." Michelle gave a mock salute and added, "Off to the trenches."

She could hear Cassie chuckle as she walked out the door.

CHAPTER TWENTY-TWO

Michelle's meeting with Daniel Durand went well. He was receptive to her offer to invite Amber to church cautioning only to keep it separate from school.

Any invitation extended or follow-up discussions and arrangements would need to be made on her own time, not during the course of the school day. In addition, the first time Amber expressed a negative on the subject, Michelle would need to drop the whole matter.

He explained about the importance of asset building in the lives of troubled students and went on to give Michelle a list of suggestions along that line provided by the district. Activities listed included organized sports, scouts, clubs, and church youth groups.

Michelle's heart sang as she left his office, certain that God was going to be able to provide Amber with a wonderful support system through their young church. I hope Amber's mom will be okay with this, she thought as she hurried back to her classroom.

That night she called Bonnie and gave her the go-ahead to talk to Amber's mom. "Be sure she knows that she's welcome to join us, too," Michelle offered, noticing Steve's raised eyebrows in the background.

"Are you sure you want to do all this?" he asked after she hung up the phone.

"Positive," she replied. "This could be a whole new start for both of them, Steve."

"I guess."

"You don't sound very convinced."

"I just don't want you getting your hopes up, honey. Amber and her mom have lots of baggage. And there's more on the way," he added, clearly referring to the baby.

"All the more reason the church could be just what they need," she countered.

"Hey, you don't have to convince *me*, honey. Just don't be too disappointed if they don't jump into this full force. Sometimes God's timing isn't our timing."

"I know," she replied, wishing he were more enthusiastic but understanding his practical perspective. It wasn't that long ago that she and Steve lived a life independent of God and faith. She knew it sometimes took a life-shattering event to show someone his or her need for Him. For now, she'd just pray that Amber's mom gave the thumbs up for at least Amber to attend church.

Her prayers were more than answered when Bonnie called two days later to tell her that Stacy Gamble had not only approved Amber's attendance, but had tentatively agreed to accompany them as well. She explained that she'd told Stacy about Amber's pregnancy and her decision to go ahead with having the baby.

Amber's mother had been overwhelmed. The idea of a teacher reaching out to them and offering to take them to church was like a life raft in a sudden storm.

"Can I talk to you after school today?" Michelle asked softly as she leaned over Amber's desk.

"Sure," Amber replied in an equally hushed tone. "Am I in trouble?"

"No, nothing like that." Michelle continued on her patrol of the classroom, observing her students at work on the assignment for the day.

After the final bell had rung to dismiss school for the day, Michelle began to feel a knot of nerves forming in her stomach.

What's the matter with me? I can't believe I'm so nervous about this.

"Here I am," Amber said, as she walked into the room.

"Great," Michelle replied, retrieving her water bottle from her desk and swallowing some of the cool liquid to clear her throat. "Have a seat."

Amber sat down and plunked her backpack on the floor.

"I talked to Bonnie Blackwell the other day. She told me about your decision about the baby."

Amber looked at her, watching for her response.

"I'm really proud of you, Amber. This isn't going to be the easy way."

Amber seemed relieved to hear her verdict. "I know. I just couldn't do it – I mean the abortion. Not after I saw the baby in the ultrasound."

Michelle nodded. "I remember that moment with Madison – how she looked so perfect even in her tiny form."

"Yeah. They told me at the clinic that it wasn't even a baby yet."

"Well, that's how they make it easier for women to decide to terminate their unplanned pregnancies, Amber. But I'm glad you got to see for yourself."

"Me, too."

"So, what's your boyfriend – Adam, right? – What does he say about your decision?"

"He thinks I'm crazy. He basically broke up with me." She paused then added, "Jerk."

"Guess it's a lot easier for him to walk away from this," Michelle observed.

"Yeah. No sweat for him. He'll just find another girlfriend and go on with his life." Amber took a deep breath and then exhaled loudly. "Whatever. He acted like he cared about me until all this came up. What a loser I am to fall for that crap."

"He's a kid. He'll grow up someday. I'm not excusing his behavior here, but it doesn't surprise me either," Michelle explained. "Don't be too hard on yourself about that relationship. I'm sure at the start, you both cared about each other. But this is a big deal, even for adults, and you're making some tough decisions for a fourteen-year-old to have to make."

Amber nodded. "Thanks for understanding."

"You got it," Michelle replied, with what she hoped would come across as a warm, non-judgmental smile.

"Was that all you wanted to talk to me about?" Amber asked. "My foster mom is getting pretty freaked out these days if I don't punch in right after school."

"Well, there's actually one other thing. But before that, would you like to call home?"

"Sure." Amber flipped out her cell phone and dialed. After a pause, she said, "It's me. I'm still at school. My English teacher wanted to talk to me."

There was another pause, then, "No. I'm not in trouble. Here, talk to her yourself." Amber handed the phone to Michelle.

"This is Mrs. Baron," she said.

"Is Amber in some kind of trouble again?" Cecilia asked.

"No. I just wanted to talk to her for a few minutes. It won't take long."

205

"Okay. No problem. And hey, thanks for taking her to the park to meet up with her brother. I know that means a lot to Amber."

"My pleasure," she replied, handing the phone back to Amber, who said goodbye and flipped it shut, then asked, "So what else did you want to talk to me about?"

"Well, I know you're going to need a lot of support over the coming months, and my husband and I were wondering if you and your mom might like to come to church with us some Sunday. We go to a pretty small church with some great young people, and I think they could be good friends to you."

"Really? Even though I'm pregnant?"

"Yeah. Even though you're pregnant." Michelle smiled.

"Isn't that against your religion? I mean getting pregnant when you're not married?"

Michelle paused before answering, praying for the right words."That's a tough question, Amber. First, I guess you'd say our church isn't really about religion."

"What do you mean? Isn't that what a church is? Where people talk about religion?"

"The people in our church aren't about religion or judging other people, Amber. They're about trying to love people the way God loves us. They're about helping people get to know God for themselves."

Amber's eyes were big, and Michelle could see that she was soaking in every word. "Wow. I've never heard of a church like that."

"So, do you think you'd like to come with us sometime?"

"Yeah, I guess. But wouldn't you get in trouble if you took me? I mean isn't there some law about separation of church and state or something?"

"Actually, that's why I had to wait 'til after school to talk to you. But I checked with Mr. Durand, and he said it was okay as long as your mom agreed."

"So you have to ask her first?" Amber looked skeptical about the response that might come from her mom.

"Bonnie already talked to her, and she said yes. In fact, she said she'd like to come, too."

"No way," Amber said incredulously.

"Way," Michelle countered with a smile. "I'm serious. Ask Ms. Blackwell yourself."

"Uh, okay, so when would we go with you?"

"To church?"

"Yeah."

"How about during Christmas break? Ms. Blackwell says that your mom can get a ride from the rehab center, and we'll pick you up if your foster mom can't bring you and drop you off."

"Okay. I'll ask Cecilia and tell you tomorrow." Amber seemed to be getting really excited about the idea. She picked up her backpack and before she left, she added, "Thanks, Mrs. Baron. Thanks a lot!"

Michelle gave her a quick hug, backpack and all. "You're welcome, Amber. I'm praying for you, and for that little baby."

Amber nodded, tears welling up in her eyes. Then she turned and walked out of the room.

CHAPTER TWENTY-THREE

The holiday break finally arrived. It was the Sunday before Christmas, and Michelle was on edge as she hurried her daughter. "Just pick out something," she said, holding out a couple of outfits for Madison's approval.

"I don't want those," her daughter pronounced. "I want my new jeans."

"They're dirty. You've worn them the past two days." Michelle placed the outfits on the bed and turned back to Madison. "You've got five minutes to be dressed." She turned and walked out of the room, almost colliding with Steve in the hallway.

"Easy there," he said. "What's the problem with Maddie?"

"She won't get ready for church, and I'm tired of arguing with her," Michelle replied.

"Mommy won't let me wear my new jeans," Madison whined from the bedroom. Michelle's parents had sent their gifts up early, and they'd allowed Madison to choose one to open before Christmas. She'd been glued to her new, glittery jeans ever since.

Steve looked at Michelle and raised his eyebrows in a silent question.

"I've already gone over this with her," Michelle said. "Those jeans are dirty. I practically had to peal her out of them last night."

Steve sighed and walked into Madison's bedroom. "I'll take it from here," he said over his shoulder.

"Thanks," Michelle replied curtly. Then she hurried downstairs to get their breakfast.

Fifteen minutes later, the waffles were on the table, and Madison and Steve appeared. "Smells great!" Steve offered.

Madison gave Michelle a stoic expression and took her seat.

Really? Michelle thought. *Purple leggings and a red and green tee shirt?* She was about to say something when Steve caught her eye. Shaking his head, he warned her not to make it an issue. At least Maddie had relented on the jeans.

Michelle retrieved the butter and syrup from the counter and sat with her family. After a brief prayer of thanksgiving, she quickly downed her waffle, keeping one eye on the clock. "Hurry up, honey," she urged Madison, but the little girl slowly swirled her waffle on her fork.

"Madison," Steve spoke sternly. "Listen to your mother. We've got to hurry, or we'll be late for church."

"Fine," the little girl replied sourly. "I'm not hungry anyway." She pushed away from the table.

Michelle looked at Steve, who shrugged his shoulders. "Okay, then. Let's clear our plates and brush our teeth," he directed to Madison, who sullenly complied.

By the time they got to church, Michelle was exasperated. "Not the best mood for welcoming Amber today," she muttered under her breath.

"What?" Steve asked.

"Nothing." She peeked in the mirror on the visor and touched up her lipstick. Plastering a smile on her face, she turned to Madison in the back seat. "Here we go."

Madison pointed out the window and said, "Mommy, I think I see Amber."

Michelle followed her gaze and spotted her student standing alone by the walkway. She wondered how long the girl had been waiting. "That's her. Let's go," she said.

Madison jumped out of the car and ran toward the lonely figure. "Amber! Amber!" she called.

Michelle could see the relief wash over Amber's face as she spotted them coming.

"Hi Maddie! You look cute!" Amber said, as the little girl threw her arms around her waist.

Madison turned and smiled smugly at her mom. "Hold my hand and I'll show you where we go," she said to Amber as she released her grip.

Smiling, Amber replied, "Okay. You show me."

Steve took Michelle's hand, and they followed the girls to the auditorium that served as a sanctuary for the little church each Sunday.

"Have you seen your mom?" Michelle asked, glancing around at the people who were seated in their folding chairs.

"Nope. Probably won't come," Amber replied.

"Time to go to your Sunday school class, Maddie," Steve said, holding out his hand to her.

"Can't I stay with you in the big church today?" Madison begged. "I promise I'll be good. Please."

Michelle could see Steve's resolve softening. "What do you think?" he asked her.

"I guess just this one time," Michelle replied, seeing the first genuine smile directed at her from Madison that morning.

"Thank you, thank you!" Maddie exclaimed. "I want to sit by Amber!"

Amber looked pleased, but didn't say a word.

"Okay, pumpkin, but if you start talking or goofing off, I'll take you to your class," Steve warned.

Shortly after they took their seats, the worship team began playing an upbeat song of praise. They all rose to their feet, and Michelle noticed Madison taking Amber's hand in hers as she sang loudly. Although the words were displayed on a screen next to the band, Amber seemed shy about singing. She watched Madison and smiled, but did not join in.

Soon it was time for Ben to deliver his message for the morning. Directing them to the second chapter of the gospel of Luke, he spoke of Jesus' mother, Mary, and the dilemma she faced. He explained the Jewish culture of the day and how many in her village had probably shunned her.

Amber was engrossed in the message. Michelle saw her place her hand on her abdomen a couple of times, and she knew Amber was probably thinking of her own baby and the ways her peers at school would respond when her pregnancy became obvious to them.

Madison behaved fairly well, seeming to follow Amber's lead by carefully focusing on what her friends' father was saying. Once or twice, she tugged on Amber's sleeve and whispered something to her, but Steve's stern eye quickly put a stop to it.

After the service, Michelle asked, "So what did you think?"

"I really liked it," Amber replied. "Too bad my mom didn't show up. No surprise there."

Michelle didn't know what to say. She'd also hoped Stacy would come, but from all she'd heard so far, it didn't seem like Amber's mother was very good with following through on things, especially when it came to her kids.

"I'm sorry, too," she said. "Maybe next time."

"Yeah," Amber replied, but she didn't sound hopeful.

"Can Amber come over?" Madison asked.

Steve shot a concerned look at Michelle. Amber must have noticed it because she replied, "I have to go home, Maddie. I've got homework to do."

"Oh." Madison looked deflated.

"Maybe we could get a quick bite to eat together before we take Amber home," Michelle suggested. The idea seemed to go over well with everyone, and they headed to a local eatery for lunch.

When they dropped Amber off in front of her foster home an hour later, Michelle could see that some of her shell had fallen away. She looked a little happier, a little more at peace than Michelle had seen her at school.

Between their park days and now church, she knew God was giving her an opportunity to make a difference in Amber's life.

It seemed only a few days had passed since their last trip to California for Thanksgiving. Now they were traveling again. Although the plan had been for Michelle's family to come to Sandy Cove to celebrate Christmas, the tail end of a bout with bronchitis left her father too depleted to make the trip.

There was no way Michelle was willing to forego this special holiday with Maddie's grandparents and great-grandparents. So Steve booked their flights, and they headed south for a weeklong stay that would take them from Christmas to New Year's.

While they gathered for meals and gift exchanges, Michelle savored the time with these people she loved so very much. Noticing a definite slowing in her grandfather's movements, she couldn't help but wonder how many more Christmases they'd have with this precious, godly man.

Thank you, Lord, for his love, compassion, and spiritual leadership in our family, she prayed silently, tears pooling as her heart swelled with emotion.

Madison was walking on air throughout their stay. The princess to all, she especially loved the playfulness of Uncle Tim, who taught her to 'surf' on a sofa cushion on the living room floor and promised to one day get her a real board of her own.

Michelle noticed how well her father had overcome so many hurdles in his long road to recovery. She winced inwardly as she recalled the moment she'd first heard of his attempt to take his own life. Had it really been eight years since then? In some ways it seemed like yesterday. In other ways, it felt like a lifetime ago.

Now she saw a man who had found a solid foundation compared to his once sifting sand. No longer did he rely on self-sufficiency and pride to navigate life, but had turned to the God of her grandfather, who'd become Michelle's foundation as well.

Watching him interact with Madison, she hoped he would become for their daughter what her grandfather was for her – a role model of deep, abiding faith throughout life's varied circumstances and challenges.

By the time they got settled back into their home in Sandy Cove, school was about to resume.

CHAPTER TWENTY-FOUR

Amber was walking to class the first morning back from break, when she overheard some of her friends talking.

"Did you hear about Amber?" one asked.

"Yeah. She got knocked up by Adam."

"What a skank."

"Yeah. Hoe. You should see what Adam posted on Facebook." They shook their heads and laughed.

"Really?"

"He's finished with her. That's for sure."

"Adam's really hot," one of them gushed. "Guess he's fair game now," she added happily.

Amber felt her face flush bright red.

"Oh, hi Amber!" one of them called out to her.

The others tried to suppress their smiles.

"Saw you with Mrs. B at the park last week," another said. "Are you competing with Katy for teacher's pet?"

"Right," Amber replied sarcastically. She hurried past them to her locker.

Amber avoided eye contact with Michelle as she walked into the classroom, and Michelle noticed her scooting her desk away from the group of girls she'd hung out with earlier in the year.

Throughout the class period, Amber seemed to avoid all glances Michelle sent her way. As Michelle made her usual rounds up and down the aisles during work time, she paused at Amber's desk momentarily and whispered, "Everything okay?"

Amber just shrugged.

She noticed two of the other girls passing a note across the aisle. "I'll take that," she said, reaching for the paper. The girl reluctantly handed it over and then buried her face in her work.

"I think Adam's going to ask me out now that he's dumped Amber. Can't wait to go to their secret spot on the beach. But no way I'll be as stupid as her. What a loser! LOL."

Michelle flinched. No wonder Amber was so quiet and withdrawn.

When the bell rang, Amber disappeared before Michelle could try to flag her down. Knowing Amber had her appointment with the school counselor that afternoon, she hoped Karen would be able to help Amber deal with the snide remarks of her so-called friends.

Near the end of the day, the school phone in Michelle's room rang. "Michelle Baron, room 107," she said as she answered.

"Hi Michelle, it's Karen Stafford in counseling."

Michelle pressed the phone to her ear and glared at a couple of noisy kids, lifting one finger to her lips in a quiet sign. "Hi Karen. What's up?"

"Amber Gamble didn't show up for our appointment today. Was she in class this morning?"

"Yeah, she was."

"She must have left school after your class. Her other teachers have her absent. Any idea where she might have gone?"

Turning away from the class and speaking in low tones, Michelle said, "No. She did seem upset, though."

"About what?"

"I think some of the girls are giving her a hard time."

"Yeah. That's not surprising."

"I intercepted a note between two of them," Michelle added.

"I'll come down and pick it up, if you still have it."

"Yeah. It's right here on my desk."

A few minutes later, Karen peeked in the door. The class was busy working on an assignment, and Michelle was able to slip out into the hallway to talk to her for a minute. "Here's the note," she said, handing it to the counselor.

Karen glanced over it and shook her head. "Friends, right?"

Michelle nodded. "Yeah, supposedly."

"Okay. I'll keep this and pull in the girls to talk to them. Would you jot down their names on the back?"

"Sure." Michelle flipped the paper over and wrote the students' names.

"The meeting I was supposed to have with Amber today is really important. Daniel won't let her stay at Magnolia unless she's willing to work with me," Karen said.

"I know. I'll see if I can talk to her about it. Maybe I'll call her foster mom and see if Amber went home."

"Okay. Let me know when she wants to meet. I'm pretty free most afternoons this week."

Michelle nodded. "Will do. Thanks, Karen."

As she walked back into the room, she found several students chatting and a couple out of their seats. "Back to work, gang," she said sternly.

After the last student had left for the day, Michelle picked up the phone and dialed Amber's foster home.

"Hello?" Cecilia's voice answered.

"Hello. This is Michelle Baron from Magnolia Middle School. Is Amber home?"

"No. I was just heading out the door to pick her up."

"So you haven't seen her all day?"

"No. Why? Wasn't she in class?" Cecilia sounded weary and concerned.

"She was in my first period class, but didn't show for the rest of the day. Any idea where she would be?"

"Hmmm… the beach maybe? I know she goes there sometimes with Adam, but he hasn't been around lately." She paused as if thinking of other possibilities. "She did go see her mother one day not too long ago, so I guess it's possible she might be there, too. Should I come down to the school?"

"Let me call her social worker and get back to you," Michelle replied.

After Michelle talked to Bonnie and explained the incident that morning, they decided it would be a good idea for Bonnie to call Amber's mom.

That attempt led nowhere.

"I've got to go pick up my daughter," Michelle said. "Please let me know when you find her."

"I will, Michelle. She probably just went down to the beach to think. That girl's got a lot to process right now." Then Bonnie added, "How did it go at church yesterday?"

"Great. She seemed to really like it. Her mom didn't show, though."

"Figures," Bonnie replied. "I'll call you when I know more."

"Okay, thanks. I'll be praying," Michelle added before hanging up.

It was nine o'clock that night when Michelle finally received a call from Bonnie Blackwell. "I'm sorry to disturb you so late, but I told you I'd call," she began.

"Did you find her?" Michelle asked hopefully.

"No. No one's been able to track her down," Bonnie replied. "I've tried her mom, the beach, and just driving around town, but she's nowhere. You haven't heard anything at all?"

"Nothing. I can't imagine where she could have gone. Were you able to check with her boyfriend, Adam?"

"He hasn't heard from her and didn't seem too eager to help with a search."

"What a prince," Michelle said under her breath.

"What?"

"Nothing." Michelle glanced at Steve who was watching her from the other side of the room. "Can you hold on a sec?" she asked.

"Sure."

Michelle turned to Steve. "No one can find Amber. She's still missing."

Steve stood from his seat. "Want me to drive around and see if I can spot her?"

"Steve's offering to drive around and look if that would help," Michelle told Bonnie.

"I don't think that's necessary. The police have been notified. Since she's a minor, they'll have all the squad cars keeping an eye out. Let's give her a little more time. Hopefully she'll show up pretty soon."

"Okay. Let me know if there's anything I can do," Michelle replied.

"Will do," Bonnie promised.

Amber crouched in the shadows under the overpass. Her phone had been ringing for hours. Some of the calls were from her foster mother and some from the social worker. None from Adam, of course. And none from her supposed friends.

I am such a loser. They're right. I'm just a skank, and now I'm having a baby. There's no way I can be a good mom to him. What am I thinking? And all that church stuff. Sure, it sounds good. But all those people are better than me. They don't make the kind of stupid mistakes I've made. It's too late for me.

As cars whizzed by, she sunk deeper and deeper into her self-condemnation. But whenever she thought about the alternative – the option of having an abortion – she just felt worse.

What was she going to do? And who could she really count on? Her mom? No way. Her foster mom? She had her hands full with the two brats. Her friends? What friends? And Adam – well he was clearly not going to help her.

Mrs. Baron was really nice. But she had a family of her own that she needed to take care of. Plus she was busy teaching. Sure she'd help when she could, but other than her social worker, Amber really didn't have anyone.

As she pulled herself into the shadows and hugged her sweatshirt tightly to her chilled body, she felt a strange sensation. It was almost like a butterfly was fluttering around in her lower abdomen. Instinctively, she knew it was her baby.

He was moving!

She placed her hand over the area but couldn't feel anything. A moment later the flutter repeated itself. Amber's eyes filled with tears. *What am I going to do? How am I going to take care of a baby?*

Her heart broke as she pictured the innocent little boy who was growing in her womb.

You deserve a better mom than me. She began to cry as she again hugged her arms to her chest and started rocking back and forth.

Suddenly, she heard the sound of crunching footsteps coming down the slope from the bridge.

"Who's there?" a man's voice demanded.

CHAPTER TWENTY-FIVE

Amber pushed herself to her feet, heart pounding.

"I said, who's there?" He slurred his words slightly, and Amber could see that he was staggering toward her, a brown paper bag clutched in one hand with the neck of a bottle protruding from the top.

She started to run past him, but he grabbed her arm and pulled her close, his breath reeking with the pungent smell of alcohol mixed with decaying teeth. "What's ya doing in my pad, sweetie?" he asked, leering at her through bloodshot eyes.

"Let me go!" Amber struggled to free her arm, but his fingers dug in deeper.

"What's the hurry?" he asked with a grin. "I haven't seen anything as purty as you for quite some time. Especially here by my bed." He laughed as he drew her closer and attempted to kiss her lips.

Amber pushed hard with her free arm and knocked the bottle from his hand. Swearing, he released his grip on her momentarily then lunged at her as she began to run away. Tackling her to the ground, he rolled her over and began pressing his body down on her, nuzzling his scruffy beard into her neck. "You smell good," he moaned. "We're gonna have a real good time tonight!"

Amber screamed as loudly as she could, fighting with all her strength to push him off. As he began clawing at her clothes, she heard another voice call out from the distance. "Get away from her!" A beam of light flashed down on them as a police officer rushed down the hill from above.

The man scrambled to his feet and took off without looking back. Amber pushed up to a sitting position, hands shaking as she brushed herself off.

"Are you okay?" the officer asked.

She nodded, turning her head to the side so he wouldn't see her tears and shame. What kind of loser was she to be putting herself and her baby in danger like this?

"Here, let me help you up," he offered, holding out a hand to her.

She grasped his hand and stood. Her clothes were covered in dirt and one leg of her jeans had a wet spot of alcohol from the spilled bottle next to her.

"What were you doing down here after dark?" he asked her.

"I just needed some time to think," she stammered, feeling stupid.

His next question surprised her. "Your name Amber?"

"Yeah. Why?"

"We've been looking for you for a couple of hours now. There's a missing person on you."

"Oh. Yeah, that's me. Missing a brain…" she muttered.

"Huh?"

"Nothing."

"You sure you're okay? He didn't do anything to you, did he? I've seen that guy around here. Sleeps under this bridge most nights. If you'd like to press charges, we can bring him in."

Amber shook her head. "It's okay."

"Let's get you home, then." He gestured toward the hill leading up to the bridge. "My squad car's up there." He leaned into the radio clipped to his shoulder and spoke to the dispatcher. "I've got the 10-57. She's okay. We're coming to the station."

"10-4," came the reply. "I'll notify the subject's guardian."

Amber followed the officer up the hill and climbed into the backseat of the squad car. The steel grill separating her from him added to her sense of shame.

Maybe Adam's right. I'm not ready to be a mom.

Then she flashed back to the ultrasound image of her baby, and she began to cry.

"Hey, are you sure you're okay?" the officer asked, studying at her in the rearview mirror.

She sniffled and nodded, turning her head to stare out the window so he wouldn't see the tears streaming down her face.

"There's a great social worker at the station, who can talk to you if you'd like," he offered.

"Already have one," she replied.

Apparently he got the message that she didn't want to talk, and they drove the rest of the way to the station in silence, other than the occasional radio calls that peppered the air.

When they arrived, he opened her car door and again offered his hand to her. She pushed herself out of the car without taking it, and shuffled into the station behind him. When they got to the front desk, Bonnie Blackwell was waiting. She took one look at Amber and drew her into an embrace. Immediately Amber felt her shell crack, and she was suddenly a little girl, desperately needing a mom herself.

They stood for several minutes, Amber crying and Bonnie soothing her with a calm voice and gentle strokes as she held her close. Finally, the storm passed, and Amber shuddered once or twice then turned to thank the officer. But he was already gone.

"Ready to go home?" Bonnie asked. "We can talk about all this later. Right now, I think you need a shower and a warm bed."

Amber nodded. "Yeah. Thanks."

They walked arm-in-arm out to Bonnie's car, Amber leaning on her for support as her legs threatened to buckle beneath her.

"We found your daughter," Bonnie spoke into the phone.

"Thank God," Stacy replied. "Is she okay?"

Bonnie hesitated for a moment. "We need to talk, Stacy."

"What? What is it? Did something happen to Amber?" Stacy sounded panicky.

"Amber's okay for now. But she needs you. She needs you to be home. To be a mom again."

Stacy was silent on the other end.

"I know it's hard. You've been through a lot. I understand. But Amber's got some big issues facing her, and she needs her mom back. I'm helping her as much as I can, and her foster mom is hanging in there with her, but she needs you."

"I'm not ready yet," Stacy replied defensively. "Whenever I get alone, I lose it. All I can think of is running away. I'm just not cut out to be a mom. Especially by myself."

"It's never easy to be a single mom. I get that. But you need to try, Stacy. For Amber's sake. Jack's, too."

"I should have never had kids," she said in response. "I don't know how to do this."

Bonnie took a deep breath, mentally counting to five. "I'll help you, Stacy. We'll work on it together. But I need you to want this. It's really up to you. Your counselors are waiting to see signs that you are ready to tackle parenting again. The kids won't just be dropped in your lap. I promise I'll be available to help."

"If I just had a man. Someone who could be a father to them. That's what I need."

"No. You need to believe in yourself. You need to determine in your heart and mind that you are going to do this for them," Bonnie urged. "I'd like to meet with you and your psychiatrist and see if we can work out a plan for you to go home."

Silence.

"Okay?" Bonnie asked.

A pause and then Stacy replied, "Okay."

After hanging up the phone, Bonnie closed her eyes and rubbed the back of her neck. What a day. Tomorrow she'd meet with Amber and then call Stacy's psychiatrist.

She was just about to get into bed, when she remembered she'd promised to let Michelle know when they found Amber. Retrieving her cell phone from the end table, she flipped it open and sent a quick text.

Police found Amber. She's okay. Will be talking to her more tomorrow. Hope I didn't wake you.

A moment later the reply appeared on the screen. *Thanks! So glad she's okay.*

Bonnie sat across from Stacy Gamble. She reached out and touched her knee. "I'm on your side, Stacy. We both want what's best for the kids, right?"

Stacy nodded, her brow furrowed.

"It's time to move on. You need to put the past behind you and start the journey of life again without your husband. He's not coming back, and the kids need you. Especially now. Amber needs to know you'll be there for her throughout this pregnancy, and afterward."

Stacy looked up. "Do you think she wants to keep the baby?" she asked.

"She doesn't know what she wants yet. Her only decision is that she's not having an abortion." Bonnie's cell phone rang, and she pulled it out of her purse to see the caller ID, then silenced the ring.

"Here's the way I see it, Stacy. I think Amber is craving a family and the kind of love that never gives up. She may try to find that with this baby if she feels she's lost it with you."

"But she's too young to be a mom," Stacy argued.

"Yes. She is. And that's why she needs you. She's going to need all the adults in her life to rally around her and support her now – to help her make wise decisions about the future for herself and for the baby."

"Do you think she'll put it up for adoption?"

"I don't know. We'll broach that subject later. But first, I want to try to get her home with you and Jack, to remind her that she has a family who loves her."

"Okay. I'll try," Stacy replied, but she shook her head skeptically. "I've never been very strong."

"Like I said, I'll help you. Promise." Bonnie picked up her purse from the floor. "I'll be there for your appointment this afternoon. Then we'll begin planning your release and return home."

As she walked out the door, she glanced back to see Stacy gazing out the window, deep in thought. *Please help her be strong for Amber,* she prayed silently.

Bonnie picked up Amber after school let out. They drove to the beach and settled on a bench overlooking the crashing waves. Clouds were moving onshore, and Bonnie knew it would likely be raining soon.

"So tell me what happened yesterday?" she asked.

"Some stupid girls were dissing me in the hallway. One of them sounded like she's planning to pick up on Adam. They all knew," she added, placing her hands protectively on her swollen abdomen.

Bonnie sighed. "I'm sorry, Amber."

"They were supposed to be my friends…"

"Yeah. That happens. Girls this age are kind of fickle like that."

Amber rolled her eyes. "Whatever."

"So you took off?" Bonnie asked.

Amber nodded. "I needed to think." She paused then shuddered. "What a stupid loser I am. I thought I'd be safe, and no one would find me under that bridge. I was even thinking of staying there all night."

She looked Bonnie in the eye. "That man could have raped me or killed me."

"Yes. He could have. But he didn't. Someone was watching out for you."

"The cop?"

Bonnie smiled. "I was thinking of someone else."

Amber stared at her intently. "God?"

"Maybe. What do you think?"

"Yeah. I guess," Amber conceded.

"Mrs. Baron told me that you really liked her church. Tell me about it."

Amber smiled slightly. "It was cool. They had guys playing the guitar for the songs, and the pastor guy was easy to understand and kinda funny." She paused, and then added, "It's different than how I pictured church."

Bonnie nodded. "Sounds like a friendly place."

"Yeah. Everyone was nice." Then Amber's expression changed. "But they all seemed like good people, you know? I doubt if they'd like me if they knew I was pregnant."

"Mrs. B knows, and she still likes you," Bonnie offered.

"Yeah. She's cool." Amber nodded in agreement. Gazing out over the ocean, she added, "Looks like it's going to start raining."

"Yep." Bonnie patted her knee. "Wanna go get a hot chocolate?"

Amber smiled. "Sure."

They walked back to the car as the heavy drops started dotting the sand. "Hop in," Bonnie said, clicking the remote unlock button.

Soon they were at the local coffee shop, Amber warming her hands on a mug of hot chocolate while Bonnie sipped her cappuccino. "I have some news for you," she said.

"What?"

"Your mom is going home. You and Jack will be moving back in a week or so after she gets settled."

Amber leaned forward. "Really?"

"Yeah."

"Is she okay now?" Amber seemed concerned.

Bonnie looked at her and a wave of compassion swelled her heart. Here was a teenage, pregnant girl who'd just lost her boyfriend and whose friends had abandoned her, and she was worried about her mom's state of mind. Stacy had better pull herself together. This backwards relationship wasn't going to serve either of them well.

"Your mom's going to be fine, Amber. She knows you and Jack need her. She's ready to put the past behind her and start being a parent again," Bonnie said, hoping she was right.

"Okay. That's good news," Amber admitted. "Jack will be really happy."

"How about you?"

"Me, too, I guess. But I don't know how long I'll be living with them. Depends on what happens with the baby. I might have to figure out a way to get my own place.'

"Amber, you are only fourteen."

"I'll be fifteen right after he's born," she interjected.

"Okay, fifteen. That's still too young to be on your own."

Amber shrugged and looked away.

"I promised your mother I'll be there to help all of you get through this."

Amber nodded but didn't make eye contact.

"Are you going to church with the Barons again on Sunday?" Bonnie asked, hoping a change of subject might help them reconnect.

"Maybe. If she wants me to."

Bonnie smiled and patted her hand. "I'm sure she'd like that. She was really worried about you last night."

"She was?" Amber seemed surprised.

"Yeah. She made me promise to call when we found you."

"She's cool," Amber replied, her countenance softening again.

"Yeah, she is," Bonnie agreed. "Well, I'd better take you home. I've got a meeting with your mom and her psychiatrist in an hour."

They walked out the door, bracing against the rain with Bonnie holding out an umbrella for them both, and Amber pulling her sweatshirt hood over her head.

CHAPTER TWENTY-SIX

The meeting with Stacy's psychiatrist went well. The doctor agreed with Bonnie that it was time for Stacy to step back into life and resume her role as a mother.

In spite of Stacy's hesitation, she pressed, "You'll never know if you don't try, Stacy. The last thing we want is for you to get so comfortable here that it becomes your new normal."

To reassure her of their support, a schedule of visits from Bonnie and follow up appointments with the doctor were established.

"As you achieve success in this, your confidence will build," the psychiatrist promised. "Just keep taking your medication, and we will walk you through the weeks ahead."

She nodded and smiled slightly. The only indication of her anxiety was the unconscious nail biting that persisted throughout their meeting. At one point, she mentioned the idea of beginning to date, but both the psychiatrist and Bonnie urged her to focus on her kids.

"One step at a time," Bonnie encouraged, hoping she would be able to handle the new challenges of parenting a pregnant teen.

As she accompanied Stacy back to her room, Bonnie offered to help with the actual move back home. Stacy readily accepted the offer, and they set up the details. If all went well, by the following week both kids would be back home living with their mom.

Then they could figure out how to best help Amber.

Stacy stood looking around the family room of their house. So many memories whispered to her from every angle. Memories of rocking babies, of snuggling with the kids and her husband on the couch, of homework on the coffee table, and a cat who had scratched the fabric to frays on the easy chair.

A photograph of the family poised on the end table pierced her heart. The four of them had been happy, hadn't they? What had she missed? What caused the break in their marriage, and why did she leave this picture as a reminder of days that could never be recaptured?

She sank in a heap of floor.

How am I going to make it without him?

Exhaustion. Tears. Medication. Those were her new and constant companions.

Then the sound of a car pulling into the driveway caused her heart to race.

"Get up. They're here," she said aloud to herself. Standing, she smoothed her hair nervously as she braced for the responsibilities ahead.

"Hello?" Bonnie's voice called from the open door.

"In here," she replied, walking toward the hall to the door.

They met in the entry — Amber and Jack eyeing her, with suitcases clutched in their hands.

"How are you today?" Bonnie asked with a smile.

"Fine," Stacy lied, every ounce of her wishing for an escape. She glanced down at Amber's swollen abdomen and cringed inwardly.

"Go on in, kids. You can put your stuff in your rooms," Bonnie said.

Amber and Jack brushed past her and down the hallway, splitting at the first set of open doors.

"How are you really?" Bonnie asked again.

Stacy's hand shook as she brushed a stray hair from her face. "I'm trying, but it's hard." She turned and started walking back into the family room with Bonnie on her tail. "Have a seat," she offered.

As they sat facing each other, Stacy glanced once again at the family photo.

"There will be more good times," Bonnie said.

"Yeah. I guess." She sighed wistfully then looked back at the social worker. "When will you be back?"

"I'll stop by mid week and see how you're doing."

Stacy nodded. Three or four days on her own with the kids. She'd manage somehow. Besides, they'd be at school most of the day.

"You can call me anytime," Bonnie broke through her thoughts to remind her.

Jack walked into the room, carrying a basketball. "When's dinner?" he asked.

Dinner. She hadn't gotten that far yet. It'd been a while since she'd had to cook for her family.

I think there's a box of mac and cheese in the cupboard...

"Pretty soon," she replied.

"Okay. I'm going out back to shoot some hoops." He paused and glanced over at Bonnie. "See ya."

"See ya," she replied with a wink.

Stacy could feel Bonnie's eyes examining her. She moved her nail bitten hands underneath her to hide the evidence of the jagged cuticles and stubby chewed off nails.

"Are you okay for dinner tonight?" Bonnie asked.

"I think I can feed my own kids," she replied defensively, immediately regretting her tone of voice. "I mean, yeah. We'll be okay."

"Alright. Then I guess I'll get going." Bonnie stood and picked up her purse and keys from their resting place on the coffee table.

Stacy also arose to her feet, feeling a bit lightheaded. A flush of anxiety threatened to overtake her, and she heard in her mind the voice of the therapist.

Take three deep breaths. It'll help you get your bearings.

She breathed in slowly, trying not to reveal her state of near alarm.

Thankfully, Bonnie didn't seem to notice. But she did reach into her bag and pull out a business card, handing it to her. "Anytime. I mean it. Cell phone number is at the bottom."

Stacy took the card from her. "Thanks, Bonnie."

Amber was sitting on her bed, back propped against the headboard, when her mom walked into the room. She pulled an ear bud from her iPod out of her ear, letting the music still fill her from the other side.

"Is mac and cheese okay for dinner?"

"Sure. Whatever," she replied. "You're the mom. You decide."

Her mother looked suddenly very vulnerable and fragile. "I just thought you might have certain things you like and don't like, now that you're... you know..."

"Pregnant?" Amber replied. "You can say the word, Mom. It's not like I've got some plague or something."

"I know. I guess I'm still having a little trouble getting used to the idea."

"Join the crowd," Amber replied, and then wished she hadn't. Why was it so easy to be mad at her mother? It was her dad who messed up. "Hey. I didn't mean it that way."

Her mom nodded, took a deep breath, and walked out of the room. Several minutes later, Jack came in, looking upset.

"What did you say to Mom?" he demanded. "She's in the kitchen crying."

Oh great. Now she'd done it.

"Why do you have to be so mean to her?" he asked.

"I don't know. She just gets to me." Amber stood up, setting the iPod on the dresser. She could feel Jack staring at her. "What?"

"You're getting really fat, Amber," he said as he checked out her stomach.

"Don't be such a jerk, Jack."

"Well you are. Just look in the mirror." He gestured toward the reflection from the closet door.

"I know what I look like. I don't need you to tell me."

"Whatever. If I were you, I'd go on a diet," he suggested. "And you might want to apologize to Mom."

"Thanks for the advice, pal. Now get lost." She reached for the door handle, eager to close it behind him.

After he left, Amber slumped down on the edge of the bed. She'd wanted to come home for a long time. Now that she was here, it didn't seem like home anymore.

She'd already made her mom cry, and now her brother had seen her without her sweatshirt on to hide her swelling abdomen. How was she going to tell him about the baby?

Someone, please help me. Who could she count on now? Her mom was still a wreak. Her dad was off with his new girlfriend. And her brother couldn't stand the sight of her.

And then, without warning, a response from an unknown source. *I will help you, Amber. I will be with you. I will never leave you.*

Was she losing her mind? Or was there someone who really could help her?

Stacy watched her kids eat their mac and cheese as she tried to convince her stomach to comply. A feeling of rolling nausea kept her from taking another bite.

Everyone was silent, and she suspected there was something wrong between Amber and Jack. But she didn't know how to fix it or what to say to break the tension that hung in the air.

Jack glanced over at Amber, who was scarfing down her second helping. She looked up at him, her eyes daggers. "What?"

"Nothing," he replied, looking back down at his own food.

Stacy needed some fresh air. She pushed away from the table. "I'll be out on the back porch."

Then she left the kitchen without looking back.

Michelle noticed Amber hanging back as the other students exited the classroom. "How are things?" she asked as she collected stacks of papers from the front of each row.

Amber looked troubled. "Not so good. Can we talk at lunch?"

"Sure. I'll be here."

"Thanks," Amber replied, slinging her backpack over her shoulder and pushing the door open. "See ya."

After she was gone, Michelle shook her head. She thought things would be better for her student now that she was home with her mom and brother. But Amber looked more unhappy and anxious every day.

When lunchtime rolled around, Michelle hurried the last few students out of the room and left a note for Amber on the door.

RUNNING TO THE OFFICE FOR A MINUTE. BE RIGHT BACK.

When she returned, Amber was leaning against the wall beside the door. "Come on in," Michelle said, unlocking the room.

Amber complied and took a seat in the front row.

"So what's up?" Michelle asked, pulling her lunch out.

"Besides my mother being a wreck and my brother thinking I'm fat?" she asked as she rolled her eyes.

"Not going so well at home, huh?"

"You could say that."

"Have you talked to your social worker about it?" she asked, offering half a sandwich to Amber, who declined the offer. "So, what about Bonnie? Did you talk to her?"

"No. She's coming by tonight to check on us." Amber pulled a granola bar out of her backpack and took a bite.

"So you haven't told Jack about your condition yet."

Amber shook her head. "How am I supposed to tell him? Just say, 'I'm pregnant, Stupid, not fat.'?"

"You could probably eliminate the 'stupid' part. But he's going to find out eventually anyway, right?"

"I guess," she admitted. "I just don't want to answer all the questions he'll have when I tell him."

"Like what?"

"Like who's the dad? Why was I so stupid? What am I going to do when the baby comes?"

Michelle nodded. "Those are tough questions."

"Yeah. And they're none of his business." Amber slouched down in her seat and finished the granola bar.

"What *are* you going to do, Amber? I mean after the baby comes. Have you thought about that?" Michelle tried to picture this girl as a mother to a newborn. *What a mess.*

Amber teared up and turned her face away.

"You don't have to answer that. I just wondered if you'd figured it out."

She shook her head.

Michelle paused, praying silently for Amber and all the difficulties she faced ahead. "Is there anything I can do to help?" she offered in a soft voice.

The dam broke, and Amber began to sob. Michelle walked over and placed a hand on her back. "It's okay, honey. Let it out." She stood there gently rubbing Amber's back as the girl's body wracked with emotion.

Finally the storm subsided. Amber blew her nose and wiped her eyes. Her voice shook as she turned back to Michelle. "What would you do?" she asked.

Michelle didn't know what to say. How could she possibly put herself in this girl's shoes and give her an answer to that question?

She took a deep breath, shot up another quick prayer for wisdom, and replied, "I honestly don't know, Amber. Being a parent is one of the best things that can happen to someone at the right time. But it's one of the hardest jobs on earth. I can't imagine doing it alone."

"And Adam's definitely not going to help me," Amber said.

"He's a kid, Amber. You both are."

"Do you think I should give the baby up for adoption?"

Michelle flashed back to her experience with little Caleb – how she and Steve had rejoiced when they heard they'd be adopting that newborn, and how devastated they'd been when the birth mother changed her mind.

"I think that's a really tough decision, Amber. It's one you need to really think about and be sure of. There are lots of couples who want to adopt babies, and there aren't many babies available." She wondered if she should tell Amber about Caleb, but something in her spirit said no.

"I wish my dad would come home," Amber said. "Then maybe he and Mom could help me raise my baby."

Michelle nodded. "That would sure help."

"Do you think I'd ever get to see him again if I gave him up?" Amber asked.

"Probably not. But you'd have to ask the adoption agency about that. Maybe your social worker could give you more information." As she was speaking, the bell rang.

"Yeah." Amber paused then added, "Thanks for everything." She stood up. "Guess I'd better go."

"Amber came and talked to me at lunch today," Michelle said to Steve that night as they sat around the dinner table. "She asked me if I thought she should consider adoption."

"What's adoption, Mommy?" Madison asked, her mouth full of broccoli.

"Don't talk with your mouth full," Michelle reminded her.

"Adoption is when a mommy and daddy get a special gift from God," Steve told their daughter.

Madison swallowed her food. "What kind of gift?"

"A baby," Michelle replied.

"Or sometimes an older child," Steve added.

"Doesn't the baby's mommy want to keep it?" Maddie asked.

"Sometimes mommies can't keep their babies, honey," she replied.

"Are you going to keep me?" Maddie asked, her brow furrowed.

"Of course we are, princess," Steve said. "You will always, always be our little girl."

"Even when I grow up big like Mommy?" she wanted to know.

Steve smiled and tweaked her nose. "Even then."

She grinned. "Can we adoption a baby so I have a brother or sister?"

"No sweetheart. We aren't adopting a baby," Michelle corrected. She momentarily thought again of little Caleb. He'd be about seven now. She prayed a silent prayer for the son they'd never know.

As if reading her mind, Steve reached over and placed his hand on hers. She looked at him and saw a glimmering of the disappointment they both had experienced those seven years ago. Then she redirected her attention to their daughter. "Finished?" she asked.

Madison nodded. "Can I go play?" she asked, pushing her chair away from the table.

"Sure. But bath time's in half an hour," Michelle replied. She watched as Madison scampered off, her braids bouncing as she left.

"How come you were so nice to me when we used to see each other at the park?" Jack demanded.

"What are you talking about?" Amber replied.

"I'm talking about how you treat me now that we're home." He paused and then added, "You're different, Amber."

"Fat and mean," she offered sarcastically.

"Yeah," he replied, turning to leave the room.

"I'm not fat, stupid. I'm pregnant." She plopped down on her bed and looked away from him.

"Funny," he replied. "You're hilarious."

"I'm not trying to be funny, Jack." Her vision blurred with tears, and she cussed softly under her breath. "It's true. I'm pregnant. I'm having a baby, little brother. What do you think of that?"

Jack stared at her, incredulous. "Does Mom know?"

"Of course she knows, moron." Amber hated talking to him like this, but the words just seemed to find their own way out of her mouth.

"You're messed up, Amber," he said.

"You think?" she replied, shaking her head.

"So what are you going to do? Have an abortion?"

"No. I'm having the baby." She studied his face for a reaction.

Jack's expression told all. "You can't have a baby. You're only fourteen."

"I know how old I am, Jack. And I *am* having a baby. It's a boy."

"How do you know?" he asked.

"They show you at the doctor's office," she replied. "It's called an ultrasound. You can see the baby in there."

Jack's eyes were like saucers. "Are you going to keep it?" he finally asked.

"Maybe. I don't know yet," she said. "But hey, think of this, little brother – you're going to be an uncle. Uncle Jack."

"Whoa…" He sat down on the edge of the bed. "I've never heard of a kid being an uncle."

"Well now you have." She picked up a throw pillow from the bed and hugged it. "Uncle Jack."

He looked at her and grinned. "Mommy!"

Amber pelted him with the pillow while he ducked for cover. As they both laughed, she felt a new sensation lifting some of the oppressive weight on her shoulders.

Hope.

Maybe she really *could* do this.

CHAPTER TWENTY-SEVEN

Amber awoke from a dream of the park. This time she was with her baby, pushing him in the infant swing as he giggled in delight. She lay still in bed, savoring the dream. It was Saturday, and she didn't have to hurry off to school.

Placing her hand over the baby's hidden dwelling, she spoke softly. "I love you, little guy." And then she felt it — a kick that startled her. "Whoa!" She sat up and called out to her mom.

"What is it?" her mother asked as she rushed into Amber's room looking panicky.

"I just felt him move," Amber replied. "He kicked really hard right here."

Stacy sat down on the bed beside her, placing her hand on Amber's abdomen. But the baby was still again.

"I was just having a really good dream about taking him to the park," Amber began. "Then I woke up and was talking to him, when all of the sudden he kicked me." She smiled excitedly.

"That's nice," her mom replied, but her face didn't match her words.

"What, Mom? What's wrong?"

"I just don't want you to get your hopes up about what it's like to have a baby, Amber. It's not all fun and games at the park."

Amber felt her mother's mood seeping into her own pores. "Yeah. Right."

Stacy stood and started to walk out of the room.

"Mom?"

"Yes?"

"Wanna go to church with me tomorrow?"

She turned and looked at Amber, but it seemed like she didn't really see her. "I don't think so, honey. I'm still pretty tired these days."

"Whatever."

A worried look clouded her mother's eyes. "I'm sorry, Amber. Maybe in a couple of weeks."

Amber looked away and nodded. "Sure."

As if to redeem herself, Stacy added, "I can give you a ride over there if you'd like."

"Okay." Amber nodded, brushing past her mother as she headed for the bathroom. "Thanks."

Ben looked out over his growing congregation. He was about to make his final point as he wrapped up his message for the morning.

"And so we see that only two of the spies had the faith required to lead the Israelites into the promised land. Only Joshua and Caleb believed that God would be faithful to protect them and provide for their every need."

He searched their faces for a moment, and found his eyes resting on Michelle's student, Amber Gamble, who was hanging on every word.

Smiling warmly, he continued, "What promised land does God have for you today? In what area of your life is He asking you to trust Him fully with the outcome, to step out in faith — trusting and believing that He will never leave you nor forsake you?"

He paused to give them a moment to consider the questions. Then he closed with a simple prayer. As the parishioners filed out of their rows, he noticed Amber's swollen middle. *Dear Lord, help her,* he prayed silently. Then he turned to greet the members of his flock.

"That was really good," Amber said to Michelle, as they walked out of the church.

"Yeah. Ben's a great Bible teacher," she replied.

Amber sighed. "I wish my mom would have stayed. She's like the ten other spies — always afraid of bad things happening."

"She's had a rough time, Amber. Hopefully things will start turning around," she offered. What else could she say? She didn't want her to know how genuinely concerned she was about the future of her family.

How did I get so deeply involved with all this, Lord? she wondered. But she knew teaching for her would always be more about the kids than the curriculum. Especially those with broken hearts and lives like Amber.

As Maddie raced up to them in the hallway, she noticed Amber's eager response. *There's really a little girl buried under her teen façade, isn't there, God? How will she manage as a mother in a few short months?*

Amber felt embarrassed and frustrated as she searched the rack of maternity clothes at the local discount store. Bonnie stayed by her side, offering suggestions. "How about these?" she asked, holding up a pair of jeans for Amber's consideration.

They looked like something her mom would wear. She shook her head and kept rifling through the rack. "Maybe we should go back into the junior department and look at the bigger sizes."

Bonnie smiled. "Okay, we can try that."

Amber tried on several pairs of jeans that were larger than her normal size, but they were too big in the rear and tight on her middle. Her eyes traveled to the surrounding racks as she eyed the styles her peers were wearing.

"You okay?" Bonnie asked.

"Yeah, I guess," she replied.

They eventually returned to the maternity section, where Amber selected the least offensive pair of jeans she could find. They purchased two pairs and left.

As they walked out to the car, Bonnie turned to her and asked, "Have you thought anymore about what you want to do once the baby is born?"

"You mean, am I going to keep him?"

"Yeah."

"I don't know. Why?"

"I thought maybe you would want to know more about adoption choices, just in case." Bonnie pointed the clicker at the car and unlocked the doors. After they climbed in, she continued, "There are county and private adoptions you could consider."

"What's the difference?" Amber asked. She was pretty sure she'd be keeping him, but just in case, it wouldn't hurt to know her options.

"County is something I can take care of for you. We'd fill out the necessary paperwork, and then after the baby is born, the county will place him with the next family on the waiting list.

"It's strictly confidential, and you would be relinquishing all rights and contact with the baby. The county screens the families, so they would be placing him somewhere safe, but you would have no knowledge of the family other than that."

Amber nodded. She didn't like the sound of it.

Bonnie pulled out of the parking lot. "With private adoption, you work with an attorney or agency. Most of the time, you have a chance to know more about the adoptive family.

"You might even get to see pictures of them and have some limited contact with them after the adoption, depending on the agreement you make through the agency or attorney."

"Oh," Amber replied. "That definitely sounds better than the county thing."

"If you want me to, I can do some research for you. Figure out a good agency or attorney we might talk to."

"I think Mrs. B's husband is an attorney. I wonder if he could talk to me," Amber said.

Bonnie looked at her and smiled. "You really like them, don't you?"

She nodded. "Yeah. They're cool."

"I don't know what type of law Mr. Baron practices, Amber, but I'll see what I can find out. If he doesn't do family law, he wouldn't be involved in adoptions. But he might know someone who is."

"Okay. Thanks," Amber replied, trying to imagine what it would be like to talk to a stranger about giving up her baby.

As scared as she was about becoming a mom, she wondered if giving him up would be just as bad as what her dad did when he left. Wouldn't it be saying to her kid that she didn't want him, didn't love him enough to keep him?

All these thoughts swam through her head as they drove to their next stop – her OB appointment for a check up.

Soon she was on the examining table again, the ultrasound wand pressed into the blob of gel on her abdomen. Almost immediately, she heard the rapid heartbeat. *Whoosh, whoosh, whoosh, whoosh.*

"Sounds good," the doctor said. She continued to study the image on the screen. "Hmmm," she murmured to herself.

"Is something wrong?" Amber asked anxiously. She didn't like the way her doctor was staring at the screen.

"It looks like you might have a little problem with the placenta," she began to explain. "I noticed it was low last time. But now it looks like it may be covering part of the cervix."

"What does that mean?" Amber tried to control herself, but she felt like she would start crying any minute. Was the baby going to die?

The doctor put the wand down and turned to face her. "It's a condition called placenta previa. It's not hurting the baby. He's fine," she said reassuringly. "But it makes your pregnancy a little riskier as it progresses."

"How?" Anxiety threatened to overtake her.

"It can endanger you and the baby during delivery. We will need to watch you carefully and schedule a C-section for the birth."

"But the baby will be okay?"

"He should be fine. But it's important that I keep a close tab on you. We'll want to monitor this with regular visits, especially as you move toward the last trimester." She took a clean towel and wiped the gel from Amber's skin. "Have you made any decisions about the baby?" she asked.

"Not yet. Why?"

"When you do, we'll need to talk about some other important considerations."

"Like what?"

"Like whether or not you want an adoptive parent or parents present when he is born, if you decide to go that route. Or decisions like breast or bottle-feeding if you decide to keep him. And we'll also want to discuss birth control for the future, regardless of which decision you make."

Amber's mind was spinning with the information she'd just heard. How did she get herself into this mess? She was supposed to be a kid being taken care of by her own parents, doing things like going to football games and school dances and figuring out what classes she was going to take in high school.

Maybe she'd better talk to someone about adoption like her social worker suggested.

Michelle was browning the meat for their spaghetti dinner when the phone rang. *Bonnie Blackwell* the caller ID revealed. She picked it up and punched the talk button. "Hi, Bonnie. What's up?" she asked as she continued to stir the meat with her free hand.

"Am I catching you at a bad time?"

"No. It's okay." She glanced out through the open door and saw Madison playing tea party with her stuffed animals. "I've got a few minutes."

"Your husband came up in a conversation with Amber today," Bonnie revealed.

"Really?" Michelle's curiosity was piqued.

"Yeah. We were talking about adoption choices, and Amber was wondering if he might know about privately arranged ones. He doesn't happen to practice family law, does he?"

"No. Sorry. He does mostly corporate stuff." Michelle paused, then added, "We do know of someone in Portland, though."

"Great. Can I get his contact information from you?"

"Actually, it's a female attorney. Hold on. I'll get her number." Michelle turned the burner off and dug into the junk drawer for her personal phone book.

Flipping to the B's she spotted Veronica Blake's number. Painful memories shot through her mind, but she silenced them quickly and gave the information to Bonnie.

"Thanks, Michelle. This is really helpful. I'll give her a call."

"Okay. You can tell her I gave you her number." Michelle took a deep breath and added, "Make sure Amber really thinks this through."

"You sound concerned," Bonnie replied.

Michelle hesitated before responding. "I just hope she's really sure before she takes this step. I've been on the other side of private adoption, and I know how much is hanging on the line for people who hope to finally have a baby of their own."

"I had no idea your daughter was adopted," Bonnie said.

"Oh. No. Not Maddie." Michelle stammered. "Steve and I almost adopted another baby before we had her."

"What happened?" Bonnie asked.

"The birth mother changed her mind after he was born." Michelle felt the old scab on her heart reopening. "We'd already told our families and decorated the nursery and everything."

She tried to keep her voice even and steady. "God had other parenting plans for us. But I know how heartbreaking it can be if a birth mother chooses you and then changes her mind."

"I'm so sorry, Michelle. I will try to help Amber understand the gravity of her decision, whichever way she goes. How would you feel about me sharing your story with her?"

"If you think it would help, go ahead. But she needs to understand that this is confidential. Not something I want her talking about with friends or other kids at school."

"Of course. I'll make sure she knows that."

After their conversation, Michelle started to put the phone book back into its drawer. She stared for a moment at the attorney's name and allowed the gamut of emotions she'd felt during that tumultuous season of her life to wash over her once again.

The struggles with infertility, the eager anticipation of little Caleb's adoption into their family, and the devastating blow when his birth mother had rescinded her decision.

"Mommy? Are you okay?" Maddie's voice invaded her memories, bringing her back to reality. "You look sad."

Michelle pulled her daughter close. "Mommy's fine, honey." She kissed the top of her head and added, "Time to wash up for supper."

CHAPTER TWENTY-EIGHT

The drive to Portland was a quiet one. Taking advantage of a release day from school for teacher planning, Bonnie was taking Amber and her mother to meet with the adoption attorney.

Amber's mom sat in front, and nervously cleared her throat periodically as if to say words that never followed. A dark sky had fulfilled its promise of rain, and the steady drone of the drops, coupled with the rhythmic swipes of the windshield wipers had a hypnotic effect on the three of them.

Amber gazed out her window, her stomach in knots. She didn't know what frightened her most – the idea of handing over her baby to a stranger, or the thought of trying to be a parent herself. The arguments bantered back and forth in her mind.

If I go through with this, it'll all be over in a few months. I can start my life over and be a kid again.

Right, Amber. Like you'll ever have that chance. Even without a baby, you'll probably end up taking care of your mother and brother. And you'll feel guilty for the rest of your life for giving away your kid.

But if I don't give him up, how will I take care of him? I haven't even gone to high school yet. I won't have a job, and even if I could find one, who would take care of him while I'm at work? My mom can barely take care of us, much less a baby.

You'll think about him all the time and never even know if he's okay. What if his adoptive parents abuse him or abandon him like your dad did? You won't be there to rescue him. He could end up in foster care, and you know what that's like.

Amber cringed. *I wish someone would just tell me what to do. How am I supposed to make this decision?*

She rested her head back and closed her eyes, allowing the warmth of the car and the sound of the rain to cause her to drift to sleep.

"Amber, wake up," her mother's voice penetrated her fog. "We're here."

She rubbed her eyes and looked out the window. They were in the parking lot of a high-rise building. The rain had eased to a slight drizzle, and Bonnie found a parking place near the entrance. "Ready?" she asked.

Stacy looked at Amber. "Ready, honey?"

"Yeah." Amber unfastened her seatbelt and pushed open the door. The three of them hustled from their spot to the covering of the walkway awning leading to the large glass door.

As they approached, the door automatically slid open, and the welcoming warmth of the foyer met them. Bonnie led them to the elevator and pressed the button for the 4th floor.

Soon the receptionist was ushering them into a large office with floor to ceiling windows overlooking the foliage that framed the complex.

She offered them coffee or water, which they declined. "Ms. Blake will be right with you," she promised as she left them sitting in chairs that faced the large desk.

A few moments later, Veronica Blake walked in and introduced herself. Bonnie took the lead in returning the introductions. "And this is Amber," she concluded.

"So I understand you are considering adoption for your baby," Ms. Blake said to Amber.

She nodded, feeling like she might lose her breakfast any moment. In addition to her churning stomach, she thought she felt the baby move.

"It's a tough decision, and one to consider thoughtfully," the attorney continued. "There are many couples who are eager to adopt. Most of them are unable to have their own children, and we connect them with babies needing a loving home."

"How do you know the people who adopt the babies are going to be good parents?" Amber asked.

"We work with social services to screen all our adoptive couples. They spend time in counseling sessions, and they undergo home visits before and after the adoption to assure that the babies are in safe homes and getting off to a good start."

She paused and seemed to be studying Amber. "What are your biggest concerns?" she asked.

"What happens if the couple gets a divorce or something? Or what if they abuse or abandon the baby? Does the birth mother know? Does she get a second chance to have the baby back?"

Ms. Blake raised her eyebrows. "You've really thought about this. I'm glad to see that.

"First, let me say that once an adoption is finalized, the baby's family becomes like any other family. Unfortunately, there are no guarantees in life. It's sad but true that some of our adoptive couples do end up getting divorced.

"And, like in the case of any divorce with kids involved, there are custody issues that need to be resolved. Usually the couples opt for some kind of shared custody, but sometimes the child ends up being raised in a single-parent home.

"I've never encountered a situation where one of the babies we placed was abused or abandoned. To be honest, those incidents are usually found among the birth mothers who opt to keep their babies. However, just like any other normal family, if abuse or abandonment are discovered, social services intervenes."

Amber sat forward. "But what about the birth mother then? Can she take the baby back?"

The attorney shook her head. "Usually the birth mother has no follow up contact or information about the baby once the adoption is finalized."

"But sometimes they do?" she asked.

"Sometimes, yes. We have arranged open adoptions where the birth mother is able to stay in limited contact with the adoptive parents. All communication goes through our office, and it usually involves exchanges of letters and pictures.

"Occasionally, adoptive parents agree to one or two follow up meetings with the birth mother at a neutral location like a park, just to reassure her that all is well with the baby's new family."

"What is your recommendation in that regard?" Bonnie asked.

"I usually recommend that the birth mother completely release the adoptive family from further communication or meetings. It seems best for all parties involved if they can move forward with starting their new lives fresh and unencumbered."

Amber slumped back in her chair and rested her hand on her swollen middle. For a moment, all was silent. Then Ms. Blake got up and walked around to the front of the desk, leaning back against it slightly.

"Amber, I know this is a really hard decision for you. One thing that most of my birth mothers find helpful is compiling scrapbooks of sorts for their babies. They include a letter, some photographs, etc. and give it to the adoptive parents to give to the child at the time they deem most suitable.

"Sometimes that is around school age, when they explain to their child that he or she is adopted. Sometimes it is when the child reaches maturity at 18 or 21 years of age.

"The point of the book is to communicate to your baby your love for him and your desire that he have the best life possible." She looked Amber in the eye. "Would that be something you might like to do?"

Amber nodded, tears starting to blur her vision.

Veronica handed her a tissue and continued, "Would it help to look at some of the applications we have in our files? We put our couples into photo albums. You can see a picture of each of them and pertinent information like careers, hobbies and interests, other children in the family – some of the benefits each couple is able to offer a child."

Amber nodded again. She rubbed the tears from her eyes. "Yeah. I'd like to look at them."

Ms. Blake walked around her desk to the bookcase behind it. She retrieved a large binder from the bottom shelf and walked back over to Amber. Pulling up a chair, she sat down beside her and placed the album in Amber's lap. Amber's mom, Stacy, scooted closer to her daughter to look at the album, too.

They paged slowly through the applications, studying the faces of the eager couples and perusing their forms. As Amber read about the potential homes for her baby, she couldn't help but contrast them with the meager potential of her own.

"This couple adopted another child from us four years ago," the attorney said, pointing to a photograph of a family of three. "They are now looking to adopt a sibling for their daughter."

Amber looked closely at the smiling faces of mother, father, and child. *This is what a family is supposed to look like,* she thought to herself. Then she tried to picture her mom, her brother, and herself with a baby in her arms.

Maybe this was for the best. But how would she pick a couple from all of these? How could she know who would be best for her baby boy?

She continued paging through the book, carefully studying the faces of the couples and glancing over their forms. Overwhelmed by the magnitude of her decision, she handed the heavy volume back to the attorney.

As she sat back in her chair, the baby growing in her womb began moving. "I need time to think," she said, directing her comment to Bonnie.

"That's fine, honey. We're just here to give you an idea of this option." Bonnie turned her attention to Veronica Blake. "Thank you for your time. We'll be in touch." She stood and shook hands with her.

Amber and her mother followed suit, and soon they were back in the car headed home. As they pulled into the driveway, Bonnie looked over her shoulder at Amber. "I've got an hour before my next appointment. Want to go to the Coffee Stop for a hot chocolate?"

Amber looked at her mother, wondering if she'd want to go along.

"Go ahead, honey. I'm going inside to lay down for a while."

"So what did you think?" Bonnie asked, as they settled into the corner booth with their hot drinks.

Amber looked off into space and shrugged. "I don't know." Then turning her focus to the social worker, she asked, "What do *you* think?"

"Really want to know?"

"Yeah."

"I think you're too young to be a mother." She reached her hand across the table and placed it over Amber's. "I've seen a few teen moms in my practice, and it's an incredibly difficult situation for everyone."

"So you think I should give him up," Amber concluded.

"I think there are many couples who could give him a good, stable home. Couples who are ready to be parents, who are financially secure and can work together to meet all of your little guy's needs."

Amber bit her lip to fight back her tears. She looked down into the cup and nodded.

"But *your* thoughts are what count here, Amber. Ultimately, this is a decision you, and you alone, will have to live with for the rest of your life and his."

The ramifications of her decision overwhelmed Amber, and she gave in to her tears. "How...how... how am I supposed to know...what's best for him?" she stammered.

Bonnie pulled a tissue out of her purse and handed it to her. "I think you just have to try to project yourself into the future a little. Try to picture yourself with a baby 24-7. That's what parenting is – a marathon that will dominate your life and options."

Amber shook her head. "I don't think I can do that."

"It's a tough challenge, even for a married couple." She paused, and Amber looked up at her. "It can be done, Amber. But your life will take a very different course. And your opportunities to get an education, to make a decent living, and to find a life partner will all be more difficult."

Amber felt her heart breaking. No matter what she chose, she knew her life would never be the same. Everything was messed up.

"So what if I decide to do the adoption?" she asked. "What would we do next?"

"Would you want to have a say in who adopts the baby?"

"Yeah. Definitely."

"Then we'd go back to Ms. Blake's office and go through her book again. I'm sure she'd let you take as much time as you want."

Amber tried to picture going through the book again. There were many couples that looked like they'd make good parents. "Okay. Then what?"

"Then after you decided which couple you'd like to have adopt him, we'd set the legal wheels in motion to get that process going."

"When would they take him?" she asked.

"Probably shortly after his birth. Many adoptive parents are present at the hospital during delivery. They spend the first few hours bonding with the baby, like a natural parent would. That's an important time when a lifelong emotional connection happens."

"So I wouldn't ever bring him home?"

"No. You'd probably see him briefly at the hospital, but that would be it."

A sense of loss mingled with unexpected relief washed over Amber. Then, as quickly as it came, the relief was replaced by fear. "What if I change my mind after I see him?" she asked, hoping Bonnie would tell her she could back out and keep the baby.

Bonnie looked at her intently. "This is a decision you shouldn't take lightly, Amber." She paused and then added, "To give you the bigger picture, I'm going to share something confidential with you. It's just between you and me."

"Okay." Amber sat forward in her seat, all ears.

"Your teacher, Ms. Baron, shared something with me that may help you with your decision."

"Ms. Baron?" Now Amber was really curious.

"Yes. You really like her, don't you?" Bonnie asked.

Amber smiled. "She's the best."

"Well, what I'm going to tell you is something she's allowing me to share with you. But it's not something you can share with anyone else. Deal?"

"Deal."

"Okay. A few years before the Baron's daughter, Madison, was born, they almost adopted a baby."

Amber was even more curious now. "Really??"

"Yeah. They were having some trouble starting a family, so they applied for private adoption through the same attorney we saw today."

"You mean, they were in a book like the one we looked at?"

"Yep."

"Whoa." Amber sat back, trying to imagine her teacher filling out one of those forms. "So what happened?" she asked.

"A young woman chose them to adopt her baby. It happened to be a boy, just like yours."

"But it didn't work out?"

"Well, they were really excited, told all their family and friends, and set up an adorable nursery to welcome him into their home." Bonnie paused, as if to let this scene soak in.

"But?"

"But the birth mother changed her mind after the baby was born." Bonnie sat back in her seat and seemed to be staring at her.

"Man. She must have been really sad." Amber imagined her teacher going into the nursery, knowing the little boy would never be coming home. Then she pictured Maddie and felt a little better. "So how did they get Madison? Is she adopted, too?"

"No. Madison is their little miracle."

"What happened with the baby boy?" Amber asked, eager to hear a happy ending.

"They'll never know." She looked Amber in the eye. "But statistically those stories don't end well. And two very loving people went through a world of heartache over that decision."

Amber nodded soberly. "Wow. Good thing they got Madison."

"Yeah. God provided. But many couples don't get those miracles, and adoption is their only path to parenthood."

"Ms. Baron is a great mom. That girl shouldn't have changed her mind," Amber said.

Bonnie reached over and took her hand again. "That's why I want you to be sure. The easiest time to do this is at birth, but if you can't be sure before then, you need to wait. The adoption can be arranged afterward."

"Okay. Thanks for telling me all this," she said. "How long do I have to decide, if I want the adoption to happen right after he's born?"

"I'd say a month before your due date."

"So I've got a few months."

"Yes." Bonnie glanced at her watch. "I've got to get going," she said.

They slid out of the booth, and Bonnie paid the girl behind the counter. Then they walked out into the drizzling gloom.

CHAPTER TWENTY-NINE

Michelle was distracted throughout the English department meeting. Although she kept trying to focus, her thoughts repeatedly drifted to Amber.

Today was the day her student was going to see the adoption attorney. The magnitude of what this fourteen-year-old girl was facing far exceeded the mundane state standards tests being discussed in their meeting.

I wonder how many stories like Amber's are untold in this school. No wonder it's hard to get kids focused on curriculum when so many of their lives are spiraling out of control.

She thought about the boy who had tried to kill himself over a humiliating bullying incident, and the girl who had been removed from her uncle's guardianship because of abuse.

In one short year, she'd seen kids come to school drunk, had money stolen from her desk, and had seen the devastating effects of peer pressure on some of her sweetest, most vulnerable students.

"So what do you think, Michelle?" another teacher asked.

She startled to attention. "About?"

"About the benchmark tests? Are you okay with dividing up the text and each of us creating quarterly tests?"

"Oh. Yeah. Sure. Just tell me which section you want me to do," she added.

After they had each received their assignment from the department chair, they broke for lunch.

"Are you okay?" Cassie asked, walking beside her as they returned to their rooms.

"Yeah. I guess. Just thinking about Amber and some of the kids."

"It's tough, isn't it?" her colleague asked. "Balancing your concern for them with the demands of teaching the curriculum."

"Yeah."

"Just remember what I told you last year. You're teaching…"

"…kids, not curriculum," Michelle interrupted.

They smiled at each other. "Wanna join me for lunch?" Cassie offered.

"I've got a ton of projects to grade," she replied, picturing the boxes of student-written and illustrated children's books that awaited her. She was eager to read through them, surprised at the receptivity and excitement the kids had shown about using their writing skills for creating pop-up books.

"Okay. Coffee mid-afternoon?" Cassie asked.

"Sounds great. I'll call you when I'm ready for a break."

They gave each other mock salutes and parted for their separate classrooms.

Amber was stretched out on her bed, listening to music and thinking about everything. She knew she couldn't give her baby the kind of life those other couples could. But she didn't know if she could hand him over to strangers.

What should I do?

The question hung in the air with no answer. Closing her eyes, she drifted off to sleep.

She dreamed she was in a hospital room holding her tiny baby boy in her arms. He was gazing up at her with eyes full of innocence and trust. She cradled him close, humming a lullaby of sorts as she drifted to sleep. Everything was peaceful. Everything was fine.

Then a nurse came in and reached out her hands for him. "It's time, Amber. Give me the baby."

Amber clung to her son. "No! Leave me alone."

"They're waiting, Amber. Give me the baby." She came closer and took him out of her grasp.

"Who are they?" Amber cried out. "Who's taking him?"

The nurse just ignored her and walked out.

"No! Stop!" Amber's voice awakened her. She sat upright on the bed.

Oh God, please help me. What should I do?

"Ms. Baron? Can I come in?" Amber stood at the door to the classroom the next morning, thirty minutes before school would start.

"Amber!" Michelle greeted her with a smile. "Sure. Come on in. I'm just finishing the last slide of my PowerPoint for today's lesson."

Amber walked over to Michelle's desk and waited while Michelle clicked the last few buttons on her keyboard to complete the presentation.

Turning to her student, she pulled a chair close and offered it to her. "How are you feeling?"

"Okay." Amber glanced around the room as if searching for words. "I went to the attorney," she began.

Michelle studied her face. "And? What did you think?"

Amber shrugged. "She's okay."

"Are you planning to go the adoption route?" Michelle chose her words carefully, avoiding the term *baby*.

Amber stood and picked up the framed picture of Madison. "Maybe." She sat back down. "I looked at the pictures of the couples in the adoption application book."

"Were there lots of couples?" Michelle asked, thinking back to the form and photo she and Steve had submitted before their miracle baby.

"Yeah."

"What did you think? Did you see any you liked?"

Amber shrugged again and gazed across the room. "They all looked pretty good."

Silence hung heavy in the air as Michelle waited for her to continue.

"Ms. Blackwell told me about you. About how you and your husband almost adopted a baby."

Michelle took a deep breath. It felt strange to be talking to a student about this, but Amber wasn't just any student. She'd become almost like family to Michelle in ways she could only begin to explain. But God had given her a tender heart toward this troubled teen.

"Yes, we did," she replied.

"And the birth mother backed out?"

"Yep." Michelle looked Amber in the eye. "It's really important that you think this through carefully, Amber."

"I know. Ms. Blackwell said the same thing." She paused and played with a strand of hair, examining the split ends and breaking a few off. "How can I be sure, though?" she asked, turning her focus back to Michelle.

"I guess you just have to try to imagine both paths. Try to picture yourself with a baby to care for day and night and to all the changes that will require in your life. Then multiply that by ten because it will be harder than you can imagine without living through it."

Amber studied her soberly.

"Then think about the option of starting your life over without the baby. Of selecting a home you think will meet his needs, and then trying to put all this behind you and move on."

She nodded. "I just can't picture handing him over." She started to tear up. "Saying goodbye…"

"Yeah. It'll be tough. There's no getting around that part," Michelle agreed.

"What if I change my mind when I see him? What if I just can't give him away?" A tear slid down Amber's cheek, and Michelle handed her a tissue.

Michelle leaned forward and put her hand on Amber's knee. "I think if you're truly convinced the adoptive couple will give him a better home and future than you can, you'll find the strength to do it."

Amber sniffled and nodded.

"Don't try to make a hurried decision if you're not sure, Amber. Maybe it would help to talk to the pastor at church."

Amber looked up at her with raised eyebrows. "Why?"

"Because he can counsel you on how to find God's peace in your decision."

She seemed to be considering this idea.

"Would you like me to set up a time for you to talk to him?"

"Could I just do it at church if I go with you this Sunday?" She seemed to be hedging for time, as if still considering whether or not she wanted to do this.

"Maybe. He usually has several people waiting to talk to him after his sermons, but we could try."

"Okay. Thanks." Amber glanced at Maddie's picture again and added, "You ended up with a really cute kid."

"We think so," Michelle replied with a smile, her own eyes also soaking in the smiling face of her daughter.

The following Sunday, Amber almost missed church because her mother wasn't feeling up to driving her there. But when Amber began threatening to hitchhike if necessary, Stacy pulled herself out of bed, threw on a sweat suit and took her.

Jack had opted to stay home and play video games, so Amber was waiting alone in the parking lot when Michelle and her family arrived.

"Amber's here!" Maddie shouted, pointing out the window toward the walkway flanking the lot.

Michelle smiled. "Yep. There she is."

"Can I come into the big church again?" her daughter asked.

"No princess," Steve jumped in. "You can talk to Amber before Sunday school. But you need to go to your class."

Maddie sighed, crossing her arms in a pout. "Okay, Daddy," she muttered under her breath.

Michelle caught Steve's eye and winked. Sometimes their daughter could be so dramatic.

Madison clicked off her seatbelt and threw open her door. "Amber!" she shouted.

Amber turned and quickly spotted them. "Hi, Maddie!" she called with a smile as she walked over to their car.

Madison immediately took her by the hand, leading her back toward the sidewalk. "Where's Jack?" she asked.

"He's not coming today. He wanted to stay home and play games."

Michelle and Steve followed the girls, also hand in hand. As Madison started heading for the sanctuary, Steve stopped them. "Remember what I said, Maddie. Sunday school for you."

"Oh, Daddy…please," she whined.

"Nope." Steve cast her a stern look.

"Better listen to your dad," Amber said.

Madison looked up at her admiringly. "Okay," she relented.

After they'd dropped her off at the K-1 classroom, they headed into the sanctuary. Ben started walking by them, glancing over as he passed, and Michelle held up a finger to get his attention. He made a comical u-turn to face them.

Michelle gestured to Amber and said, "Amber would like to talk to you after the service, if you have time."

He looked at the teen and nodded with a warm smile. "Sure. Just give me a few minutes, and we can meet in the high school room after it clears out." Heading to his seat, he threw a, *'See you then'* over his shoulder.

Amber nodded. She looked nervous.

I hope this was a good idea, Michelle thought. She took Steve's hand as they stood for the first worship song.

Amber spent close to an hour talking to Ben and his wife, Kelly, after church. Michelle and Steve had promised to wait for her and give her a ride home. Michelle and Steve watched Ben and Kelly's kids, who played with Madison in the little playground area.

After a while, all the youngsters started getting hungry, so Steve offered to go to the local drive-through burger place to pick up food.

While he was gone, Michelle sat on a bench overlooking the grass area where the kids were playing. She prayed for Ben and Kelly — for wisdom in their counsel, and for Amber — to know what to do.

Shortly after Steve returned and the three of them had begun to eat, Ben, Kelly, and Amber came out of the Sunday school building. Amber looked like she'd been crying, but she smiled when she saw Madison racing toward her. "We got you some lunch!" the little girl revealed with a grin.

"Thanks," Amber replied, pulling her into a hug. Then she turned to Kelly and Ben. "Thank you so much."

Kelly smiled and nodded. "Anytime you need to talk," she offered. Noticing the bags from the burger place, she asked her kids, "Did you guys get some lunch?"

They nodded with big grins.

"Thanks for feeding our brood," Ben said. He gently placed a hand on Amber's shoulder. "You're going to figure this out," he said. "Just remember what we talked about."

She nodded. "I will."

After Kelly and Ben gathered up the kids and left, Michelle offered Amber a burger and fries, which she readily accepted and devoured. "Guess I was hungry," she said with a smile.

"Me, too," Madison chirped, clearly enjoying her big-sister friend.

As they drove Amber home, Maddie asked, "Can we do another park day, Mommy? With Amber, I mean."

"I'd like that," Amber offered.

"Okay, then we will," Michelle promised the girls. "Maybe this week."

"Yay!" Madison cheered, and Michelle could see a smile on Amber's face as well.

CHAPTER THIRTY

It rained most of the week, but on Friday the sun peeked out, and they were able to head to the park – just the three of them.

Amber had thought about what Pastor Ben said to her on Sunday – how if she prayed about her decision, God would answer. He would show her what to do, and give her a peace in her heart about that course.

Other than her brief prayers of desperation, Amber didn't really know how to pray. Ben explained it was just like having a conversation with a good friend. All she had to do was say what she was thinking. She didn't have to say any special or fancy words. And there was no point trying to hide anything from God.

It was comforting and also a bit concerning to her that God already knew all about her. He knew about her relationship with Adam and what they had done at the beach. He knew about her mom and her loser dad. He even knew what the future held, and how things would turn out for Amber and her baby.

"So why should I pray?" she'd asked Ben. "I mean, if God already knows everything, why I should I talk to Him about it?"

"Because the most important thing to God is having a relationship with you, Amber. He wants you to know how much He loves you. And He wants to spend time with you."

"Really?" The idea floored her. How could God want to have anything to do with her after the mess she'd made of her life? But Ben was certain that He did. "I don't even know how to begin," she'd confessed.

"Begin by asking Him to be part of your life, to help you make decisions, and to show you which way to go with all the choices you have to make."

When she'd still felt confused, he had offered to pray with her for the first time. And together they'd asked God to help her. Not just with the decision about the baby, but with everything from now on. Amber felt such a special feeling afterward. It had even made her cry.

All week she'd been talking to God, asking Him to help her – to show her what to do. She was eager to tell Ms. Baron everything, but Madison pulled her off to the swing set to play.

As she pushed Maddie on the swings, she noticed her teacher watching them, smiling peacefully. A thought came to her that became a new prayer.

Thank you for Ms. Baron and her family. Thank you that they make me feel special and not like such a loser.

She was soaking in the warmth of the sun and the joy of her new friendship with God when a thought suddenly invaded her mind.

The Barons are the ones for your baby, Amber.

She stopped pushing Madison for a moment and stood there stunned. Was that God talking to her? She looked over at Michelle, and her teacher smiled and waved. Then she looked at Maddie, pumping her legs and squealing with delight as she swung higher and higher.

Images of Michelle and her husband walking hand-in-hand at church along with flashbacks of her conversation with Pastor Ben about God showing her the way to go suddenly gelled in her heart and mind.

No one could give her baby a better home than Ms. Baron and her family. He would have wonderful parents and a super big sister. She knew they'd thought of adopting before. Would they be open to the idea now?

Knowing the adoptive family would change everything. She'd be sure he was fine. There was no way she'd change her mind if they said yes. Maybe they'd even let her visit him sometimes. Of course he'd never be able to know she was his real mom. At least not until he was an adult.

But in the meantime, she would know that he was okay.

Her heart swelled with feelings she'd never experienced before — like the feelings she had when the pastor told her about God loving her and that she was special to Him. But these feelings were even more powerful, more wonderful. She suddenly *knew* this was the answer, and amazingly, she felt peace. Real peace.

Now she just had to figure out how to tell Ms. Baron what God was showing her. Please, please help her say yes, she pleaded in her heart.

As they walked to the car a while later, her teacher observed, "You seem really happy today, Amber."

"I am," she replied, grabbing Madison's hand and starting to skip, with the little girl falling into step beside her.

Amber felt a surge of energy over the next few days. She kept hoping for just the right moment to talk to Ms. Baron, and her continuous prayer was that she would say yes.

She'd stopped by the classroom before school the following day, but found it empty. Then a sub appeared, and it turned out Maddie had developed a cold that kept Amber's teacher home.

Two more days passed without her teacher being at school.

Finally, the opportunity arrived.

She was waiting at the classroom door when her teacher arrived, arms laden with paperwork and mail. "Hi, Amber. You're here early."

"Yeah. Need help with that?" Amber reached out her hands to take the papers so Michelle could unlock and open the door.

As they entered the room, she noticed how chaotic things appeared. Her teacher's desk was strewn with papers from the assignments while she'd been gone. And the desks, normally in straight rows, resembled slithering snakes. Even the floor was a mess with little papers and food wrappers littering the aisles.

"Wow," Amber said.

"Now you know why I'm always having you guys straighten up at the end of class," Ms. Baron replied.

Amber put her backpack down and offered to help. "I'll pick up the trash."

"That would be great." Michelle flipped open her laptop and started setting up for her lesson.

After she'd cleared the aisles and re-aligned the desks, Amber asked, "Anything else I can do?"

Michelle smiled at her. "Nope. That's a big help. Thanks."

She sat down in the front row and waited for her teacher to finish reorganizing her desk.

"Did you need to talk to me?" Michelle asked.

"Yeah. If you have time."

"Sure. What's up?" Michelle took a seat at her desk and directed her attention to Amber.

"I've been giving a lot of thought to the adoption idea," she began. "And I think I know what I want to do."

273

"That's great, Amber. Did talking to Ben and Kelly help?" Michelle reached for her coffee mug and took a sip.

"Yeah. They really helped me see things more clearly. Like God and everything." Amber searched her teacher's face for understanding. "They helped me understand that I can't do this without God helping me, either way."

Michelle nodded.

"So anyway, like I was saying… I've given it a lot of thought, and I think I know what God would want me to do." Amber paused. Her stomach was doing flips and her heart raced.

She took a deep breath, swallowed, and continued. "So here's the thing. I want my baby to have a good home, where I know he'll be safe. Where I can know he will be loved and taken care of the way I wish I could."

Again Michelle nodded. She seemed to be listening intently.

"Oh, God. I don't know how to say this…" Amber stammered. "But anyway, I was wondering if you and your husband would adopt him."

Michelle fell back in her chair, looking like she'd been blown by a strong wind. "Amber…" she started, "I don't know what to say."

Amber leaned forward. "Please just think about it. Don't say anything now. I know you have to talk to your husband and everything. But I hope you'll say yes." She felt the tears coming as she added, "You are the kind of mom I wish I had. If I can give that to my baby, I'll know he'll be fine."

Her teacher looked away, gazing across the empty room. Then her eyes returned to her desk and the picture of Maddie that faced her.

Amber reached for her backpack. "Like I said, you don't have to tell me anything now or even this week. Just think about it, okay?"

Michelle's gaze met hers. "You really caught me off guard. This is huge, Amber."

"Yeah. Just do whatever you think God says for you to do." Amber smiled nervously. Then she turned and walked out the door.

Knowing that she wouldn't be able to face her teacher in the classroom that day, she headed to the beach to pray, the long walk giving her stomach a chance to calm down.

Amber's words from the morning kept replaying in Michelle's head as she struggled to focus on her classes.

To add to her distraction, she was concerned about Amber's failure to show up for class. But it would be incredibly awkward to have her sitting in her desk watching Michelle teaching, when both of them knew that something critical was hanging in the air between them.

Did Ben and Kelly know about Amber's idea? Surely they would have said something to her if they did. Or would they? Michelle's head spun. *Lord, what have I gotten myself into with this student?*

When the day finally ended, Michelle hurried to leave. She needed to get home and spend some time processing Amber's request and deciding whether or not to present it to Steve.

On the way to picking up Maddie, the last words Amber had spoken that morning continued to replay in her mind.

Just do whatever you think God says for you to do.

Did Michelle dare ask God for direction on this? And what if He said yes? Could she go through another adoption process? Was she ready to begin again with another baby when she'd just started her teaching career?

And what about Amber? Would Amber expect to become like part of their family – coming around to see the baby whenever she wanted?

Michelle shook her head in disbelief and confusion.

As she stood in Ben and Kelly's kitchen waiting for Madison to collect her things, Michelle threw out a line to see if Kelly would bite. "It sounds like you and Ben really helped Amber last Sunday," she offered.

"Hope so," Kelly replied, nonchalantly. "You've really made an impact on that girl's life, Michelle."

"Maybe too much," she replied.

"What?"

"Nothing." Michelle paused, then added, "I just wonder if she's getting too attached to me... to dependent on me for the future."

"Really? Like what? How do you mean?" Kelly acted surprised, and Michelle could tell she didn't know about the adoption question.

"I don't know. It's just a question I ask myself sometimes," she answered.

Just then, Madison came back into the kitchen, her backpack in her arms. "Ready, Mommy!" she said with a grin.

"Okay, sweetie. Let's go home and fix dinner for Daddy." Michelle glanced back over at Kelly.

"Thanks, friend." She tipped her head to her happy daughter. "See you tomorrow."

"I'm glad she's feeling better," Kelly replied. Then she leaned down to Madison. "You stay well now, okay?"

"Yes, Ma'am!" Madison nodded in agreement.

"Don't worry about Amber," Kelly added to Michelle. "She'll find her way."

"Yeah. Hope so." Michelle smiled at her friend and then took Madison's hand and led her out the door.

They were both surprised to see Steve's car in the garage as they pulled in. "Daddy's home!" Madison exclaimed gleefully.

"Yeah. Looks like he is," she replied.

They found him in the kitchen, sitting at the table going through the mail. "You're home early," Michelle said.

"Yeah. I think I'm getting Maddie's cold." He turned his attention to their daughter. "How was your day, pumpkin?"

"Great! I got two happy faces on my math paper," she confided cheerfully.

"That's wonderful, honey." He looked at Michelle. "And how about you? Any happy faces today?" he asked with a wink.

She turned away and put her purse down on the counter. "Other than the mess left behind by the sub and an interesting conversation with Amber, it was the usual routine."

"What's up with Amber?" Steve asked casually, turning his focus back to the mail.

Michelle glanced over at Madison, who was listening to their conversation. "Why don't you go get changed into play clothes," she said.

"Okay." Madison picked up Max, who was rubbing against her legs, and carried him off, telling him about her day as they left.

"Honey," she began as she sat down at the table by Steve, "we've got to talk."

He looked up. "What's wrong?"

"It's Amber."

Steve shook his head. "What is it now?"

She groped for words.

Before she could begin, he added, "Honey, listen. You can't solve all that girl's problems."

"I know," she replied. "But she really hit me with a bombshell today."

Steve sat back in his chair as if settling in to listen. "Go on."

"Steve, she asked me if we would adopt her baby."

"You're kidding." He shook his head incredulously.

She looked him squarely in the eye. "No, I'm not kidding. She said that I'm the kind of mother she wishes she had, and that she wants to give that to her baby."

Steve shook his head. "There are tons of couples in the files at Veronica Blake's office. Surely she can find a couple she'll feel comfortable with," he offered.

"Apparently she's given this a lot of thought. She's convinced we are the ones."

He reached over and put his hand on hers. "What do *you* think about all this?" he asked.

"I honestly don't know. I mean I never planned on having any other kids. Especially after what happened with our first try at adoption. I'll never forget how crushed we were when Caleb's mom changed her mind."

She paused and looked away, replaying the scene in her mind. "And then all the infertility stuff with Maddie... I just thought we should be thankful that we ended up with such a wonderful little girl."

"Yeah. Me, too," he agreed.

"Here's the thing, though. The last thing she said to me has been haunting me all day. Before she left my room, she told me to 'just do whatever you think God says for you to do.' That really got to me.

"I mean, what would God say about this, Steve? Seems like He wants us to care for the fatherless, right? And isn't that what both Amber and this baby are?"

Steve took a deep breath and let it out slowly, staring at her as if searching for an answer. "I'm going to need some time with this one," he finally replied.

"Yeah. Me, too," she agreed.

Staring off into space, Steve's expression changed. Turning to Michelle he said, "Maybe it would be a good thing for Madison. Having a sibling, I mean."

She paused and then nodded.

"But still...Amber's baby... I just don't know, babe. We could really be going out on a limb here."

"Yeah. I know," she agreed.

"Let's pray about this and see how we feel in a few days."

"Good idea," Michelle replied, leaning over and kissing his cheek. "I love you, Mr. Baron."

"Likewise, 'teach,'" he said. Then he looked away, staring off into space again, as if deep in thought for several minutes before resuming his perusal of the mail.

CHAPTER THIRTY-ONE

A few nights later, Steve approached Michelle with an offer. "Want to go out to dinner, just the two of us?"

"That sounds great," she replied. It had been a long time since they'd had a date. Between school, his law practice, and their desire to spend time with their daughter, the romance of their relationship took a back burner.

The babysitter, a high school girl from the church youth group, arrived at six o'clock. "She's here!" Maddie cried out enthusiastically as she peered out the window at the approaching form.

Michelle opened the front door and welcomed the girl into their home. After giving her instructions for the evening, she grabbed her coat and umbrella, and they headed out into the cool night air.

Thankfully, the rain had subsided from earlier in the day, and the fresh smell of greenery was a pleasant fragrance surrounding them.

"Nice night," Steve observed.

Michelle reached out and took his hand. "Yeah," she agreed with a smile.

"The Cliffhanger sound good to you?"

"Perfect," she replied, already tasting the savory steak they served there.

They soon found themselves sitting at a quiet table in the corner of the large serving room. A blazing fireplace and the candlelit ambiance made it a cozy environment for the couple. They each ordered a glass of wine, a rare treat they hadn't enjoyed in longer than Michelle could remember. It was something they usually reserved for special occasions. And it seemed fitting tonight.

"It's been a long time," Michelle began, reaching across the table and placing her hand over his.

Steve took her hand and squeezed it gently. "I've missed you. Seems like we're both so busy these days."

"Yeah. I know," she replied. "Hopefully next year will be easier, now that I'm getting my curriculum organized."

"You've had a lot on your plate, that's for sure," he said. "Besides teaching, I mean."

She nodded, knowing he was referring to her investment of time and energy in a handful of needy students, Amber in particular. "I wonder if I'll ever be able to leave my job at school," she mused.

"I doubt it, Michelle. You love those kids too much."

She looked at him, trying to read the meaning behind his words. All she could see on his face was admiration. No hint of judgment. But should she be going so far beyond the call of duty? Was she robbing her family of part of her heart?

The evening proved to be relaxing for both of them. They reminisced about their first date, some amusing memories from their honeymoon, and the ways they'd changed over the years to become seekers of God's will and followers of His teachings.

As they finished their shared dessert, Steve sat back in his chair and studied her.

"What?" she asked.

"Just thinking about what Amber said about how great a mother you are," he replied. "She's right, you know. Madison is one lucky girl."

Michelle could feel herself blush. *How is it that after all these years, he can still get to me like this?*

"So have you thought about her request?" he asked, drawing her attention back to their conversation.

"Some," she answered tentatively. "How about you?"

"Yeah." He leaned forward. "I'm actually kind of coming around to the idea."

"You are?" She was amazed.

"Well, like I said before, I'm thinking it would be good for Maddie. She's missed out on the experience of having a brother or sister. And I think that might be even more important as she grows up."

"Yeah. I know what you mean. It's kind of bothered me, too. That she doesn't have any siblings, I mean. I've watched Ben and Kelly's kids play together and seen how much fun Maddie has with them."

She paused, then added, "But this baby would be quite a bit younger than her. She'd probably never really play that much with him."

"True. But she'd learn a lot about sharing the attention, being patient, and helping out. Important life skills like that."

They both sipped their coffee thoughtfully. Then Steve spoke again. "I think the one thing that really concerns me most in all of this is the fact that Amber knows us personally and lives so close to us."

"I know. That concerns me, too."

"Think I'll give Veronica Blake a call and discuss this with her. She might have some input," he said.

"Good idea. And I'll talk it over with Amber's social worker. Bonnie knows the situation really well."

Steve nodded. "Okay then. We'll just have to have another date night to discuss this further," he added with a smile. He reached for the bill, paid it, and then turned back to her. "Ready to go home, Mrs. Baron?"

"Ready," she replied.

"Veronica Blake, please," Steve said to the receptionist on the other end of the line.

"May I tell her who's calling?"

"It's Steve Baron."

"Okay, Mr. Baron. One moment, please."

After a short pause, he was greeted by, "Steve – so good to hear from you. How've you been?"

"Great. Thanks. And you?"

"All's well here," she replied. "How can I help you today?"

"I've got a personal matter that I'd like to discuss with you if you have a few minutes," he said.

"Fire away."

"Okay." Steve rubbed his forehead with his free hand. "You have a client my wife and I referred to you."

"Amber Gamble. Yes. What about her?"

"She has approached Michelle about the possibility of us adopting her baby," he began.

There was a pause at the other end. "Really?" she asked, sounding taken aback.

"Yeah."

"I see," she replied. "How do you feel about that? In light of what happened with your first adoption attempt?"

"We're both a little gun shy, I guess," he admitted. "Especially since Amber is someone we actually know –

someone who lives in our community and attends Michelle's school."

"I understand completely. So how can I help you?"

"I guess I just wanted to get your input on it. Here's the deal. We were both pretty taken aback at first.

"But as we discussed it, we thought about how it might be good for our daughter to have a sibling. And with Michelle really wanting to help Amber make a wise decision for her baby, we are actually considering saying yes.

"The main issue that's nagging at me, and at Michelle for that matter, is the proximity thing."

"Well, you know you could have some conditions written into the agreement," she suggested. "It's not unheard of to have a baby placed in a relatively nearby area from where the birth mother lives."

"Yeah. I guess the added factor here is that we know this girl. Michelle has been spending time with her outside of school, and Amber's started attending our church on Sundays."

"You know, Steve, I understand your concerns. But here's something you may not know.

"Some of my birth mothers, like the teens whose parents have basically disowned them, have actually *lived* with the adoptive parents during their pregnancies, with all their needs provided by those families."

Steve tried to imagine Amber living with them. "Wow. I didn't know that."

"Yeah. So what you are telling me is not as far out as you might think."

She paused as if to let the concept sink in. "But if you decide to go forward with it, I would definitely recommend a meeting here with you and your wife, Amber, her mother, and her social worker, in which we set up the guidelines and expectations for your relationships after the baby's birth. Whatever terms we negotiate would be part of the legal paperwork of the adoption itself."

"Okay. Yeah, I agree."

"You two give this all the time and thought you need, and then let me know if you'd like to move forward with it," she said.

"Sounds good," he replied. "Thanks, Veronica."

"Anytime."

After he hung up, Steve leaned back in his chair.

Another baby. A son.

Maybe this would be the best answer for both Amber and them.

Meanwhile, Michelle was getting her own advice.

"Be really careful, here," Bonnie said, having heard Michelle's account of Amber's request as they sat at the coffee shop talking. "Amber is a very volatile young lady right now. Her decisions are all over the map."

Michelle nodded. "I can't imagine what she must be feeling and thinking. I mean, a fourteen-year-old girl with all the hormones of pregnancy plus the issues of trying to decide what to do about the baby. It would overwhelm an adult." She paused and then added, "Poor kid."

Bonnie reached over and put her hand on her shoulder. "Michelle, you've already done so much for Amber. She sees you as her rescuer. Although I confess I didn't see this coming, it really doesn't surprise me that she approached you on this. But it's not up to you to bail her out here."

Michelle studied Bonnie's face. Was she telling her to say no?

As if reading her mind, Bonnie added, "I'm not going to tell you what to do about this. If you really want to add to your family and are open to trying adoption again, then this might, I repeat *might* work out for everyone. All I'm saying is don't feel obligated to help Amber in this major, life-altering way."

She pulled her hand from Michelle's shoulder. "I know how badly you got hurt the first time you tried to adopt a baby. As much as Amber adores you, there is no guarantee here that she wouldn't pull the same thing as the last birth mother and change her mind when she sees this baby."

She waited, as if to let that thought sink in. Then she continued, "Teens often have to go through a period of time trying to be a mother before they realize they're in over their heads. They have a misguided romantic image of how their babies will love them and be these cute little trophy bundles they can show off to their friends."

Michelle nodded. "Yeah."

"Personally, I think adoption is Amber's best option. We liked the attorney and there were many prospective adoptive couples in her book of applications. I'm sure I can help Amber select one of them, if this is not the time or circumstance for you to make such a radical change in your lives." She took a sip of her coffee and looked Michelle in the eye. "Really think about this, okay?"

"Okay," she replied. After a brief silence, Michelle added, "I think, above all else, Steve and I are concerned about Amber's proximity to us if we were to go through with it. For some reason, I'm not that worried about her changing her mind.

"It's not like last time, when we thought adoption might be our only chance to be parents. If we geared up for this, I know we'd be really sad if she changed her mind, but it wouldn't be the same as before. We have Maddie now, and with my teaching career…"

"That's another thing. Wouldn't you be taking on quite a bit trying to add a new baby into the mix with your career just getting off the ground?"

"Yes, but I know lots of teachers who have babies and go back to work."

Bonnie smiled, but her eyes spoke concern. "I'm not saying it can't be done. I'm just saying it won't be easy. Please consider everything carefully, and know that we will help Amber through all of this no matter what you decide."

"Thanks, Bonnie," Michelle replied, glancing out the window at the rain and trying to process her thoughts.

Please, God. Help me know what to do.

When Michelle got home, she went upstairs and called her lifelong friend, Kristin. They chatted for a while, catching up on each other's busy lives. Then Michelle confided in her about Amber's unusual request and all the inner wrestling she was experiencing herself.

"I'll really pray for you on this one," Kristin promised. "God will show you what to do. He has a way of making things like this clear to us, one way or another."

CHAPTER THIRTY-TWO

Michelle's Bible rested in her lap, open once again to one of her favorite verses – Jeremiah 29:11. *For I know the plans I have for you, declares the Lord. Plans to prosper you and not to harm you. Plans to give you hope and a future.*

Underlined and highlighted, the verse was flanked by dates and events carefully penned in the margins. Her father's release from the hospital, the date she'd discovered she was pregnant with Madison, and recently the first day of her school year as a new teacher.

God knew the plan for this baby. She closed her eyes and let that thought nest in her heart. A sense of deep peace flooded her spirit. A peace she'd come to realize could only come from Him.

What is my part in this plan? She asked without speaking. *What would you have me do?*

Her prayers filled the silence, and Michelle waited for an answer. Although no clear directive seemed to come, she sensed a stirring in her heart. God was going to show her what to do. It would be in His timing and His way.

As she sat reflecting on the year and how much had changed since the first day Amber entered her classroom, a myriad of emotions danced through her mind.

So much apprehension followed by frustration. Then, somehow in the midst of the antagonism and disruptions that student had brought, there began to be a new set of feelings emerging in Michelle.

Frustration was replaced by desperation to somehow make a difference. And a supernatural love began to push aside the exasperation Amber provoked. Michelle's eyes had seen beyond the rebellion to a lonely, confused kid who needed her mom. And the mother heart in Michelle rose to the occasion.

Truly it had been a work of God — one that began in the prayers of a teacher and grew into a sacred trust. Amber's heart and her special needs were given over to Michelle for this season. She wanted to be faithful to whatever God called her to do in the mind-boggling situation that faced her now.

Show me, Lord. Please show me.

The phone on the nightstand rang, startling her out of her communion. She placed the Bible on the bed and reached for the receiver.

"Hello?"

"Hi sweetheart," the familiar voice of her grandfather replied.

"Grandpa. What a great surprise!" She pushed a pillow up against the headboard and sat on the bed, stretching her legs out before her.

"How've you been?" he asked.

"Good, good. How about you? Everything okay?" she asked.

"We're fine. Your grandmother's busy in the garden, and you've been on my mind this morning," he said. "So how's the teaching coming along?"

"It's good. Really busy – a lot more work than I anticipated, but I think I'm getting the hang of it."

"Middle school. What an age," he observed.

"Yeah. Sometimes they think they're adults and other times they act like little kids," she replied.

"But you're keeping them in line?"

"Trying. There've been a few challenges," she began.

"Yeah. I remember you talking about one girl in particular," he said.

"Amber."

"That's it. How's she doing?"

Michelle hesitated. How much should she tell him? He'd always had such wise advice for her in the past. Maybe he'd have valuable insight for her now.

"Grandpa?"

"Yes, honey?"

"There's something really huge going on with Amber. I could use your advice."

"I'm all ears. What's up?"

As soon as she began to speak, Amber's story flowed from her heart in a lengthy monologue, relating the struggles and triumphs of the year, and finally the current situation with Amber's pregnancy and her request that Michelle and Steve adopt the baby.

Grandpa Phil punctuated the conversation with an occasional "um hmm" or "I see."

"...So now Steve and I are trying to decide what to do," Michelle said. "We really hadn't thought much about having another child. But as we discussed it, the idea started to sound like it might be a good one. We'd both like Maddie to have a sibling."

"But?"

"But... I'm scared, Grandpa. What if Amber changes her mind after we gear up for this? I remember how much that hurt last time. And what if she ends up wanting to be involved in this baby's life? I mean, she lives in this same community, and she'll know where he is."

"True."

"So what do you think?" She pressed the phone tightly to her ear, anxious to hear his response.

"Well, honey, your concerns are understandable. There's always a chance that Amber could change her mind or pose some problems for you later. But here's the thing, and I know you already know this – I'm just reminding you."

He took a deep breath and continued. "There are no guarantees in this life. Every person we love exposes our hearts to possible pain and difficulties. That's just a fact we can't escape. On the other hand, a life without our loved ones would be empty.

"God is not going to give you any guarantees on this matter. So if you are waiting for that before you decide, I'd say you've already made your decision."

"Yeah," Michelle replied. "You're right."

"I *will* tell you, though, that God doesn't use a spirit of fear to guide us. So, my advice is not to let fear be the rudder that steers this decision. Take some time in prayer, both you and Steve, as individuals and as a couple. Ask God to show you your place in this."

He paused, and then added, "It might not be clear right away, but He'll show you eventually. And in the meantime, your grandmother and I will also be praying."

"Thanks, Gramps. You always know what to say."

He chuckled in response. "I miss you, sweetheart."

"Miss you, too," she replied.

"When you make your decision, let us know. We're behind you a hundred percent."

"I will, Gramps. And thanks so much for calling me."

"Sure, honey. Love you."

"Love you, too." As she placed the receiver back down, her heart felt like it would burst with thankfulness for the grandfather God had given her.

That evening, Michelle and Steve discussed their conversations with the lawyer, Amber's social worker, and

Michelle's grandfather. Sitting side-by-side on the couch, they clasped each other's hands and prayed for wisdom and direction.

"Steve?" Michelle said.

"Yes?"

She leaned over and kissed him. "I love you."

He smiled and wrapped his arm around her shoulder, pulling her close. Burying his face in her hair, he whispered, "I love you, too."

Amber was waiting in the hall before school again the next morning. "Can we talk?" she asked Michelle.

Michelle braced herself for whatever would come next. "Sure. Come on in."

As she flipped on the lights and set her stuff down, she noticed Amber staring at Madison's photo. Then she turned to Michelle and asked, "Have you decided?"

"About the adoption?"

"Yeah."

"No, not yet. We're still discussing it," she replied.

"Bonnie talked to me," Amber said.

"She did?" Michelle wondered how much the social worker had said about their concerns.

"Yeah. She told me you guys are worried about me trying to butt into his life, if you adopt him."

Michelle looked at her and sighed. "Sit down, Amber."

Amber complied, leaning forward on the desk to the best of her ability with her swollen middle.

"Why don't you tell me how you envision this adoption unfolding?" Michelle said.

Amber was quiet for a few moments. Then she replied, "I know you would get to see him in the hospital. I would want to see him, too. I need to say goodbye," her voice caught.

She swallowed and cleared her throat, then continued, "I wish I could be his mom." Her teary eyes looked into Michelle's, "But I know he'd be better off with you."

Michelle could see how difficult this was for Amber, and how much thought she'd put into her decision. "What about after the hospital? How will you feel, knowing that he lives right here in Sandy Cove? Will you expect to see him, to be part of his life somehow?"

"I'll do whatever you think is best," the girl replied. Then she looked intently at Michelle again, as if weighing something in her mind. "I do have one request, though."

Here it comes.

"Okay. Tell me."

"Remember at church a few weeks ago when the pastor was talking about the spies and the promised land?"

Michelle nodded.

"So, he said there were two spies who weren't afraid – Joshua and Caleb."

Michelle smiled, happy to know that Amber was really listening in church. That in and of itself had been a giant leap for this troubled girl. "Go on," she said.

"When I heard that name, Caleb, I just really liked it. I thought to myself, 'that's what I'm going to name him'," she added.

Michelle felt her heart stop. *Caleb.* That was the name they'd planned to give the baby they'd almost adopted before Maddie had come along. She could still see the adorable nursery they'd created for him, and the large wooden letters that spelled out his name on the wall above the crib.

"Mrs. Baron? Are you okay?" Amber asked.

Michelle brought her attention back to Amber. "Yeah. I'm okay."

"So anyway, I was hoping you might consider naming him that. I mean, he'd be your kid and everything, but if you do adopt him, would you at least think about that?"

And in that moment, God spoke into Michelle's heart. *Caleb is yours. I am redeeming the years you lost.*

Michelle's eyes filled with tears. Before she could figure out how to reply to Amber, the bell rang. "We'll talk more about this later," she said, moving toward the door to prop it open. "Caleb is a great name," she added with a smile.

That night, the decision was made. They'd move forward with the adoption.

"Mommy and I want to talk to you about something, pumpkin," Steve began the next night at the dinner table.

Madison looked up from her spaghetti, a curious expression on her face.

"We were wondering how you would feel about a new baby in the family," Michelle said.

"A baby?"

"Yep, a baby boy," she replied with a smile.

"Are you going to get fat like Auntie Kelly did?" Maddie wanted to know.

Michelle and Steve looked at each other and smiled. "Mommy's not having the baby, honey," he explained. "We would be adopting him."

"Oooohhhh," Maddie replied knowingly.

"So what do you think?" Michelle asked.

The little girl gave them a serious look. "Do I have to share my room?"

Michelle smiled. "No. He'll have his own room," she replied. "We'll turn the guest room into his bedroom."

"Okay," Maddie said, seeming satisfied with her answer. "Can I hold him?"

"Sure. Whenever you want," Michelle promised.

"But not when he's crying," Madison said, shaking her head with a frown.

"Not when he's crying," Steve agreed.

Their daughter put her index finger on her chin as if she were about to make an important decision. Then she piped up, "Okay. We can adopt him."

Steve reached over and tousled the hair on her head.

"Daddy," she said with a stern voice. "You're messing up my hairdo."

CHAPTER THIRTY-THREE

"Can we talk after school?" Michelle asked in a low voice as she passed Amber's desk the next morning.

"Sure."

"Give me a few minutes after the final bell, and I'll meet you in the faculty parking lot."

Amber nodded.

Seven hours later, they were on their way to the Coffee Stop.

The short drive was filled with small talk about the day at school. Amber tried to be calm, but her stomach was in knots.

This must be about their decision about the baby.

After they'd ordered some hot drinks, Michelle led her to a cozy spot in the corner.

Facing each other across the wooden table, Amber could feel her heart pounding in her chest. She was afraid to say a word.

"So, my husband and I have spent a lot of time talking and praying about your request, Amber," her teacher began.

Please God, let her say yes.

Amber nodded. "And?"

"And we want to help you. If we can all reach an agreement about how to make this happen, we will adopt your baby."

A rush of relief flooded Amber's heart. She felt herself about to cry, but this time the tears were tears of joy. Caleb would have a good home, the kind of home she wished she could give him.

"We'll set up an appointment with the attorney," Michelle added. "Your mom and Bonnie should come with you to that meeting."

"Okay," Amber replied. "And, thanks, Mrs. B. I'm so glad you said yes." She looked away, hoping her teacher and friend would not see the tears she brushed from the corners of her eyes.

After their initial meeting with the attorney, Steve and Michelle notified family and friends about the pending addition to their family. Steve obtained all the necessary paperwork, and they went through the process they'd completed almost eight years earlier when they'd first prepared to adopt another little Caleb into their lives.

Since the baby was due during summer break, Michelle looked into the family leave options she would have for the beginning of the school year. She discovered she'd qualify for six weeks off with full pay, and the state would allow her to take up to twelve weeks with reduced pay.

A long-term substitute teacher would work with Michelle to develop lesson plans for her leave, temporarily filling her position at Magnolia Middle School.

"We really like to have the regular classroom teacher make an appearance the first day of school and on Back to School Night, if at all possible," Daniel Durand advised.

"That shouldn't be a problem," Michelle agreed.

She spent the next few weeks with final preparations for the state standards exams in the beginning of April. There was so much information to review. Would they remember all the terms and rules they'd learned at the beginning of the year?

She shook her head as she thought about how many of them had come to her without having mastered the standards from the year before, or even the year before that.

Finally, the testing week arrived. Most of the kids seemed to concentrate and do their best. But several were caught randomly filling in the answer sheet bubbles without even glancing at the questions, and several incidents involving cell phone violations resulted in two suspensions.

She felt a huge sense of relief when it was over. Easter break gave her time to develop some fun and creative projects for the final months of the year.

The kids were antsy, after testing and their weeklong spring break, but she managed to reel them in each day with some activity that either involved group work, dramatizations, games, or artistic projects.

On the night of Open House, her room was filled with these displays, as well as the rigorous essays and book reports her students had produced throughout the year.

Before she knew it, she was flipping the calendar to May. Only six weeks remaining.It had been a short year in some ways, and a very long one in others.

Amber had stopped attending regular classes as she moved into her third trimester. The comments of the other students, coupled with her own physical discomfort and fatigue, led her to the decision to finish her schoolwork at home.

Michelle stopped by Amber's house several times a week, delivering new assignments from all of her teachers and tutoring her the best she could. Amber's mom, Stacy, seemed very grateful for the assistance.

Bonnie had Amber in counseling twice a week, and it looked as if Amber had complete peace about Michelle and Steve adopting her baby boy.

"Guess what?" Stacy said one afternoon as Michelle arrived at their doorstep.

"What?"

"The kids' dad called. He wants us back."

Michelle was stunned. Stacy seemed almost matter-of-fact about the whole thing. "What do you think?" she asked, looking Stacy directly in the eyes.

"I don't know," Stacy replied. "I still love him, and the kids need a father. Especially Jack." Then, as if suddenly remembering her manners, she added, "Sorry. Come on in."

As Michelle entered, she asked, "Does Amber know about this?"

"Yes. She says I'm crazy if I take him back." Stacy admitted. "But Amber doesn't know how hard it's been for me without him."

Michelle just nodded, trying not to reveal her skepticism.

"Maybe you could talk to her," Stacy suggested.

Looking at her, Michelle could see the pleading in her eyes. "I'll try," she replied.

"Thanks. She's in her bedroom. Hopefully she's finished with the work you brought Monday."

"Okay." Michelle said, praying for wisdom as she headed for Amber's room.

She found Amber sitting on the floor, her back supported by the bed, with books and papers scattered around her. "Hey, there," Michelle said.

Amber looked up and smiled. "Hey. Come on in. Sorry about the mess." She brushed aside some of the papers, and Michelle sat down beside her on the floor.

"How's it coming?" she asked, gesturing to the paperwork.

"Okay, I guess. Here's some stuff you can take back to school with you." She gathered up several assignments and handed them over.

Michelle gave her the new paperwork, and Amber perused it. Shifting her weight and arching her back slightly, she tried to get into a more comfortable position. "Your back hurt?" Michelle asked.

"A little. I can't sit very long."

"I remember that," Michelle replied. "Would you like to go for a little walk? That used to help me."

Amber began pushing herself up. "Sure. Sounds good."

Michelle helped her to her feet.

"We're going for a walk," Amber called to her mom.

"Okay. Have fun," Stacy replied.

Once they were outside and strolling down the sidewalk, Michelle broached the subject Stacy had asked her to discuss. "So I heard your dad is coming home."

Amber rolled her eyes. "Mom's crazy."

"You don't want to give him another chance?"

"Why should we? He practically killed my mom when he left. And look what happened to me." She glanced down at her swollen abdomen.

"So you blame him for this?"

"If he would have been here and taken care of us, we never would been in those stupid foster homes. Plus he could have maybe been like a dad and kept me from sneaking out to meet Adam every night."

Michelle nodded.

"Besides," Amber added, "he doesn't want to come back here. He wants us to move where he is in Arizona. He likes it there better."

Michelle drew in a quick breath. So there was more to this tale than Stacy had let on. Her first thought was whether Amber would even be in Sandy Cove when the baby was born. "When would you go?" she asked, trying to sound routine in her question.

"Don't know. If Mom had her way, it would be yesterday."

"I see." Silence engulfed them as they continued down the street.

"Maybe I could come and live with you guys," Amber suggested. "Just until the baby's born, I mean."

Michelle didn't know what to say. She couldn't picture Steve going for that idea, and she wasn't sure she'd be comfortable with it either.

"Let's not get ahead of ourselves," she said. "Why don't you discuss your concerns with Bonnie and have her help you talk to your mom about this. Hopefully she'll be fine with waiting until after the baby comes."

Amber looked at her skeptically and shrugged. "I guess."

"Think about this, Amber. Maybe after he's born, a change will be a good thing for all of you. You could start fresh with new friends in a school where no one knew you or had any preconceived ideas about you."

Amber didn't respond, but Michelle could see she was considering the idea carefully. They walked a little farther, and then she turned to Michelle and asked if they could go back to her house. "I'm getting kind of tired."

"Sure, honey. Let's go back."

After they walked in the door, Michelle retrieved her purse and Amber's completed work and said goodbye. "See you in a couple of days," she told her student, smiling at Stacy and subtly nodding in her direction. "We'll talk later."

Stacy nodded in return.

CHAPTER THIRTY-FOUR

A shrill ringing sound awakened Michelle from her deep sleep. Sitting upright in bed, she reached for the phone before it could pierce the silence again.

"Hello?" she whispered, leaning away from her sleeping husband.

"Michelle? It's Bonnie Blackwell. Sorry for calling like this, but Amber's in the hospital. I thought you'd want to know."

Michelle swung her legs over the side of the bed and got up, walking as far from Steve as the phone cord would allow. "The hospital? Why?" she asked in hushed tones.

"She started cramping and bleeding. It's not good. They're prepping her for a C-section."

Steve turned over and asked Michelle what was going on.

"It's Amber. She's in the hospital."

He flipped on the light and joined Michelle by the bed.

"Is everything going to be okay?" she asked Bonnie.

"We don't know yet. She's bleeding pretty heavily. The doctor seems concerned. It has to do with the placenta previa they diagnosed early in her pregnancy."

"I'm coming down there," Michelle said. "I'll be there as quickly as I can." She looked at Steve, who nodded his agreement.

"Okay. We'll see you in a bit," the social worker replied.

As soon as she hung up, Michelle threw on some clothes and grabbed her water bottle from the nightstand. "I'll call you as soon as I know anything," she promised.

"Okay. Drive carefully. Those streets are slick from the rain."

Michelle nodded and kissed him on the cheek then headed for the hospital. As she drove, she thought about how scared Amber and her mother must be.

The streets were empty. Although they were wet, the rain they'd had after dinner had stopped, leaving a clear sky filled with stars. She tried to take her time as Steve had requested, but urgency pressed on her heart.

The fifteen-minute drive seemed to take an eternity, but finally she pulled into the parking lot of the ER. She remembered the hospital OB orientation before Maddie's birth, and how they had instructed the expectant parents to enter through the emergency room if they arrived after regular hospital hours.

Quickly pulling into a spot near the door, she hurried into the vacant room. She was greeted by a receptionist, who logged her in and gave her a wristband to wear. "Do you know the way to labor and delivery?"

"Yes," Michelle replied, heading for the double doors that would lead her through a maze of hallways to her destination. As she entered the waiting room, Bonnie rose to her feet and came to her.

"She's in the operating room. Stacy is with her, but she's pretty out of it. They need to get the baby out as quickly as possible and stop the hemorrhaging," she reported.

"Is there a chance the baby won't make it?" Michelle searched Bonnie's face for unspoken clues.

Bonnie took a deep breath and replied, "There's a chance neither of them will."

Michelle sunk into the nearest chair and hung her head, immediately resuming her prayers for Amber and her premature baby, who was about to make an entry into the world. Bonnie quietly sat beside her, eyes closed, seemingly lost in prayers of her own.

A few minutes later, Stacy appeared, eyes red and bleary with tears.

Bonnie walked over and wrapped her arm over Stacy's shoulder, guiding her to the seat next to Michelle.

"They…they…made me… leave," Amber's mom said between sobs. "I'm so scared for Amber. Oh dear God, what will I do if she dies?"

Michelle watched Bonnie hold Stacy tightly and murmur words of encouragement and hope. "It's okay, Stacy. We're here for you. Amber's getting the best care possible."

Stacy nodded, blowing her nose into the tissue Bonnie handed her. "She… she looks so pale."

"I know," Bonnie replied. "She's lost a lot of blood. But they're taking care of her. The doctors know what to do in cases like this. That's why they're delivering the baby early. It will be easier to stop the bleeding after he's out."

The three women huddled together under the dim lights of the waiting room, each pulling into their own thoughts and fears. It seemed they'd been that way for quite a while, when a nurse appeared at the door. "Stacy Gamble?" she said.

Stacy shot to her feet. "Is she okay?" she asked, her voice thick with concern.

"She's out of danger. We were able to stop the bleeding."

"And the baby?"

"The baby is alive. He's been moved to the NICU. You'll be able to see him in about an hour."

"Thank God," Stacy replied. "Can I see Amber now?"

"We had to put her under, so she's still asleep. But you're welcome to go sit by her bed."

Stacy looked at Bonnie and Michelle. "I've got to go to her."

"Go," they both said simultaneously.

She nodded and followed the nurse. "I'll let you know when I've seen the baby," she said.

Bonnie turned to Michelle. "Coffee?" she asked.

"That would be great," she replied.

"I saw a machine down the hall. I'll go get some for both of us."

"Okay. Thanks." Michelle dug into her purse and retrieved her cell phone. As Bonnie walked out, she punched in Steve's cell phone number.

"Hey. How's it going?" he asked.

"It was pretty scary when I got here. They didn't know if either Amber or the baby would make it. But they did a C-section, and the baby's in the NICU. Amber lost a lot of blood, but they say she's going to be okay. She's asleep right now. Stacy's with her."

"Wow. Did they say anything else about the baby?"

"Only that he's very tiny, and that Stacy can see him in about an hour."

"Do you want me to wake Maddie up and come down there?" he asked.

"No. Let her sleep. There's not much to do right now. Bonnie and I are just going to hang around here and wait. I'll call you again in a while."

"Okay, babe. Love you."

"Love you, too." She flipped the phone shut and dropped it back in her bag, just as Bonnie appeared with the steaming hot coffee.

Two hours later, Stacy reappeared at the door. She looked drained but no longer fearful. "Michelle?"

"Yes?"

"Amber's sleeping peacefully. But she did wake up for a few moments, and she told me to take you to see the baby."

Michelle's heart pounded in her chest. She was going to see little Caleb for the first time. This was so different than how she'd imagined.

In her mind, she'd pictured the three of them — Steve, Maddie and her — coming to the hospital together and spending some time with Amber before seeing Caleb and taking him home with them.

As the two women walked through the first set of doors into the NICU, a nurse showed them how to scrub their hands before entering the unit. After completing the process, they walked through the other doors.

Another nurse, who was attending to Caleb, looked up at them and smiled. "It'll just be a minute," she said. "Then you can come closer and see him."

She finished adjusting some tubing, carefully taping an IV line to his tiny arm. Then she pulled her hands out of the access ports in the side of the incubator, and gestured to them to come over.

No amount of description could have prepared Michelle for what she saw. The baby's body was half the size Maddie had been when she was born.

His skin was darker than she expected and seemed to be covered in a thin fur-like hair. Tubes and wires ran from his chest, both arms and one foot, as well as from his abdomen. What she guessed to be a respirator tube was fed into his mouth and she watched as his tiny chest lifted and fell with each breath.

Oh God, he looks so fragile.

The nurse began explaining the various machines that were monitoring Caleb's vital signs. She pointed to each wire and tube and explained its function. Michelle tried to take it all in without appearing too overwhelmed or afraid. "How long will he have to have all of these?" she asked.

"It's hard to say. The goal is to give him the kind of support he would have gotten in the womb until he can function on his own.

"There are many determining factors, such as lung development, the ability to swallow and digest, and the regulation of bodily functions and temperature that we will be monitoring. And, of course, we want to see a stable breathing pattern and heart rate as well."

"But he'll be okay, right?"

The nurse looked her in the eye. "That's the hope. But it'll be some time before he's out of the woods. Babies born this early are vulnerable to many possible complications."

Michelle nodded. Was it possible they'd lose this little one before he even had a chance to become part of their family?

But even as that thought passed through her mind, she realized he already had. Just gazing down at his tiny form and watching him take each breath with the assistance of the respirator brought a surge of love coursing through her very soul.

In an instant, he'd become her son.

CHAPTER THIRTY-FIVE

Michelle was able to see Amber the next day. As she entered the room, Stacy shifted in the chair by the window where she'd been sleeping. She looked over at Michelle and nodded, holding her finger to her mouth as a signal to be quiet. She tipped her head toward the bed on the other side of the hospital curtain.

Michelle peered around the fabric wall and saw Amber was sleeping peacefully, her long hair strewn across the pillow in clumps that clearly had not seen a brush since before Caleb's birth.

"How's she doing?" Michelle whispered.

Stacy gave her a sad smile and replied softly, "She's wiped out. But the doctor says she'll be okay." She offered Michelle her chair. "Think I'll go get some coffee."

"Okay, thanks," Michelle said, then added, "Is someone with Jack?"

"Bonnie's got him for the day. The neighbor took him last night, but she works. What about you? Don't you have school today?"

"I got a sub before I came last night. She's covering for the rest of the week. Then I'll be getting a long-term after that." Somehow she couldn't bring herself to say *when the baby comes home*, not wanting to broach the subject yet. Clearly, Amber was Stacy's primary focus, and that's how it should be.

"I'll be back in a bit," Stacy said. "Want me to bring you some coffee?"

"I'm fine. Thanks, though," she replied as she sunk down into the chair. Amber had begun to stir, and she hoped their whispers hadn't awakened her prematurely.

Once Stacy was gone, Michelle relaxed, gazing at Amber's sleeping form. She looked so childlike, so vulnerable. She flashed back to the first time she'd seen her in class. Amber had looked so hardened, like a cynical adult in a teen's body.

Now all Michelle could see was the sweet, young girl who'd been buried beneath the bitterness of her parents' split and the subsequent breakdown her mom had experienced.

Stacy was acting incredibly strong right now. Michelle whispered a prayer of thanks, knowing that Amber needed her mom now more than ever.

She paused in the midst of her prayer and thought about all the trials this young girl would face over the coming weeks and months — turning her baby over to them, all the hormone changes and physical healing that accompanied the recovery from pregnancy and a C-section birth, and the possible move away from Sandy Cove to be reunited with her father.

Stepping up her prayers, she fervently asked God to meet all of Amber's needs and to teach her how to lean on Him.

Then Michelle noticed Amber beginning to stir again. "Hey," she said softly, placing her hand on Amber's arm.

"Hey," the girl replied with a sad look.

"How are you feeling?"

Amber paused, shifted her weight slightly, and grimaced. "Not too great."

Michelle nodded. "You've been through a lot."

309

Amber sighed. "You could say that."

"Can I get you something?"

"Water would be good." She gestured to a cup and straw on the rolling table against the wall.

Michelle retrieved the cup and held it in place while she took a few sips. "It really hurts whenever I move," Amber said.

"Yeah. It'll take some time to recover from your surgery." Michelle took her hand and added, "Your mom told me the doctor said you're going to be fine."

"That's good," Amber replied, but her voice did not match her words.

Michelle reached over to brush the hair away from Amber's face. She was at a loss for words.

Amber broke the silence. "Have you seen him?"

Michelle nodded. "He's very tiny."

"They said I could see him later today," she said wistfully. "Do you think he'll know I'm his mom?"

"I think he'll know you love him," Michelle replied. "Babies can sense that kind of thing."

Amber smiled in response. "That's good."

A moment later, Amber's mom returned. Michelle backed away from her spot by the bed, and Stacy reached for her daughter's hand asking, "How are you feeling this morning, honey?"

As Amber began talking to her mother, Michelle tipped her head and waved. "I'll come back later," she promised, slipping out the door.

She heard Amber say, "Okay, see ya," in reply.

Michelle stopped at the NICU on her way out. She flashed back to the days by her father's bedside in the hospital at Bridgeport and how she and her mother had spent a little time each day gazing into the windows of the nursery.

The NICU was certainly a different kind of place. Many more nurses were constantly attending to each tiny patient. Monitors, IVs, and special lights reminded the observer of the critical care these babies required.

Now a nurse from the night before was just getting ready to leave. She spotted Michelle and gestured her into the unit, via the washing station, where Michelle meticulously scrubbed up again.

"You're still here," she said to the nurse, amazement in her voice.

The nurse smiled. "Double shift. We have a couple of little ones in here who were struggling last night. I hate to leave them until I know they're stable."

Michelle nodded. "How's he doing?" she asked, tipping her head toward Caleb's isolette.

"So far, he's doing fine. Go on over," she said. "Gloria, this is Caleb's adoptive mom," she told another nurse. "Michelle, right?"

"Yeah," Michelle replied, smiling to the other nurse. "Nice to meet you."

"Let's go have a look at your little guy," Gloria replied.

As Michelle gazed down at Caleb's tiny form, her eyes filled with tears. "You think he'll be okay?" she asked.

"He's got a journey ahead, but so far he's doing well," she said. "You know that you are welcome to come see him anytime, right?"

Michelle nodded.

"We really encourage parents to be as involved as possible. If you reach your hands in through these openings, you can touch him. Just move slowly and give gentle caresses." She inserted her own hands and showed

Michelle how to reach in and make skin-to-skin contact with little Caleb.

After Gloria withdrew her hands, Michelle took a deep breath and slowly extended her arms, reaching through the two openings until she was inches from his fragile body.

"Go ahead," the nurse nudged. "He won't break."

Michelle allowed her fingertips to touch Caleb's leg. He twitched slightly at her touch, and she began to pull back.

"He's okay. Go ahead. He might move a little like that, but just hold your hand steady."

She reached for his leg again. He moved slightly, and then was still again, except for the continuous rise and fall of his chest from the respirator. She gently caressed his leg.

It felt so soft and warm, yet almost furry, like he was covered in a soft down. She didn't remember that with Madison.

As if reading her mind, Gloria said, "He'll feel different to you than a full term baby. He's still got a covering of soft hair. It'll fall out over time."

Michelle was mesmerized. It seemed so incredible that this little boy was about to become part of their family. Someday she'd be able to tell him about this day and all he'd overcome at such a young age.

"Thank you for letting me touch him," she said.

"Just hang in there," Gloria replied. "Before you know it, we'll be able to get him off that respirator, and then you can actually hold him in your arms."

Michelle smiled. "That will be wonderful," she said.

"Coming back later today?"

"Yeah. I'd like to bring my husband and daughter. What are the rules about siblings?"

"How old is your daughter?"

"She's five."

"That's fine. We actually encourage siblings to come visit, as long as they're healthy and haven't recently been exposed to any communicable diseases like chicken pox or roseola. You'll need to bring her immunization record with you when you come."

"Okay," Michelle replied. "As soon as my husband gets off work, we'll come over."

"See you then," Gloria said with a smile.

Steve held Madison's hand as the family of three entered the NICU. She was unusually quiet and clung tightly to her connection with her dad. He glanced at Michelle, who was looking excited and nervous.

A nurse greeted them at the washing station inside the first set of doors. She supervised as the three of them carefully scrubbed their hands and lower arms, providing a stepstool for little Maddie, so she could easily reach the sink. Then they walked through the second set of doors into the actual unit.

"Hi there," Nurse Gloria said, squatting down to Maddie's level. "Did you come to meet your new brother?"

Madison nodded soberly, surveying the room and moving closer to her father.

"He's right over here," Gloria told the little girl, gesturing to Caleb's isolette. "Would you like me to take you to him?" She held out her hand to Maddie, who reluctantly let go of her dad's hand and accepted it.

Gloria looked up at Steve and Michelle and smiled. A stepstool had been placed near the isolette for Madison's visit. Gloria scooted it with her foot, and Madison climbed up.

"It looks kind of scary in there, doesn't it?" she asked the little girl.

Maddie nodded, staring at all the equipment and the tiny baby.

Gloria began pointing to various items and explained their functions in very simplified terms. Madison appeared to be listening intently, nodding after each explanation. Steve smiled to himself. She was growing up so fast. How would the addition of this new fragile life contribute to that process?

He looked over at Michelle, who was also watching Madison. Placing his hand on her shoulder, he drew her close. She flashed him a smile and then pointed to the isolette as Gloria showed Maddie how to reach inside to gently touch the baby.

Madison looked over at the two of them. Steve nodded at her. "Go ahead, pumpkin. It's okay."

After touching the baby, Maddie quickly withdrew her hand. She stared at her new brother as if watching for some kind of reaction. "Good job," Gloria said. Madison turned to them and smiled. Then she reached into the isolette and put her hand on him again.

"I think he likes me, Daddy," she remarked.

"I think so, too, honey," he replied.

"You touch him now," she ordered.

Michelle looked up at him grinning. "You heard her. Your turn now, Dad."

Steve gave a mock salute and followed her directions. As he reached the side of the isolette, he suddenly felt a wave of fear. As if tuning in to his psyche, Madison said, "It's okay, Daddy. Just put your hands in here." She pointed to the openings in the side.

He took a deep breath. "Okay, pumpkin. Whatever you say." He winked at the nurse in an attempt to hide his anxiety, but his mind was flooded with a million new concerns. The gravity of their decision to adopt was one thing, and he had come to a place of peace and confidence about that.

But this was something they could never have anticipated.

Would Caleb even survive? Would he have permanent disabilities as a result of his premature birth? The idea of a son had filled his mind with adventure. Camping, hiking, fishing, and sports – those were the things you did with a son. But would this little guy be too fragile for those types of activities?

"Come on, Daddy! What are you waiting for?" Madison chided.

Steve shook off his fears and returned to the moment. "Sorry, pumpkin. Just thinking about some things." Gloria smiled a knowing smile. She glanced at Michelle, who moved closer to the foot of the isolette.

Gloria helped Madison down, scooted the stepstool over and nudged her to climb back up. Then Steve carefully reached inside Caleb's protective world. "Hi there, little guy," he said softly, as his hand came to rest on their son.

The baby stirred slightly then stopped. Glancing up at Michelle, he noticed the tears in her eyes, and without warning, his own vision began to blur as well.

CHAPTER THIRTY-SIX

The next few weeks took on a whole new routine for the Baron family. They began preparing a nursery, and Michelle decided to delay her leave from school until Caleb was released from the hospital.

As soon as her last class was dismissed each day, she left school and picked up Madison on her way home. Steve tried to leave work by four, whenever possible. After an early dinner, they'd head straight to the hospital to spend the evening with little Caleb.

He continued to improve and was weaned off the respirator after the first few days. A tiny tube, with prongs that fit into his nostrils, continued to feed him a gentle stream of oxygen, while a machine monitored his breathing and set off an alarm whenever there was a pause in the rhythm.

Both Michelle and Steve went through a special CPR class for infants, in preparation of bringing him home. They'd have to be prepared to intervene on his behalf if the need arose.

Amber did not return to school. She gradually recovered from her C-section under her mother's watchful care. Stacy seemed like a different person, now that her husband wanted them back. He'd been out from Arizona to visit several times, and Amber and Jack were beginning to see that he really was earnest in his desire to reunite the family.

Bonnie held several family counseling sessions, in which both children were allowed to vent their anger and difficulty trusting him again. She prepped Mr. Gamble in advance, directing him not to attempt to defend or justify his choice to leave them when he did.

"They aren't ready to hear your side of this right now, and they may never be. Remember, you're dealing with kids here — kids who counted on you to be there for them. Regardless of whatever the dynamics were in your marriage, in their eyes there's no justification for abandoning them," she'd firmly asserted.

Amber's father carefully followed Bonnie's lead, accepting the verbal blows with the humility Amber and Jack both needed to see.

Although Michelle offered to continue tutoring Amber, she declined. With the exception of one request, she distanced herself from her former teacher, saying that she needed time to rest and that she'd make up her classes the following year.

"All I ask," she'd said, "is for the chance to say goodbye to Caleb before he goes home from the hospital. I want to see him one last time, without all those wires and tubes."

Michelle agreed to this request, believing it would give Amber the closure she needed – the opportunity to take a snapshot in her mind of a healthy baby, ready for his new life.

Although she was still haunted on and off by the fear that Amber would change her mind, every time those thoughts threatened her, she turned to God.

Caleb is yours, Lord. You love him more than any of us ever could. Please guard him and place him in the center of your perfect will for his life. You know what's best, God.

And then a peace would wash over her.

He's yours, Michelle. I'm giving him to you.

Finally the day arrived for Caleb's release. Stacy and Bonnie accompanied Amber to the hospital, and Steve and Michelle met them there. They'd decided not to bring Madison, choosing to spare her of the emotions they knew Amber would probably experience.

As they pulled into the parking lot, Michelle caught a glimpse of Amber, Stacy, and Bonnie nearing the hospital entrance. "Let's wait a few minutes," she said.

Steve looked at her. "Whatever you think."

"I just want to give her a little time with him before we go in. We'll have the rest of our lives with Caleb, but this might be the last time she sees him."

"Might be?" he asked.

"I know that's what we agreed to, honey, but I'm not going to close the door on the possibility that she might see him in the future. Someday, he may want to find his birth mother."

"Yeah. I guess you could be right. I just don't want to give her the impression she can drop by to visit from time to time," he said.

"That's not going to happen, Steve. They'll be moving to Arizona soon."

"You're sure about that?"

"That's what Bonnie says. And you've seen Stacy. She's a different person now."

As they walked through the hospital halls a short time later, Michelle reached for Steve's hand. He looked over and smiled a nervous smile. "Guess this is it," he said.

"Yeah," she replied, returning the grin.

Rounding the corner of the NICU, Michelle spotted Amber through the glass. She was standing with

Caleb in her arms, gazing at him intently and speaking to him.

They pushed open the first set of doors into the wash station, and Stacy and Bonnie looked up immediately. Bonnie smiled, but Stacy quickly turned to Amber, a concerned look clouding her face.

Panic momentarily gripped Michelle's heart. Had Amber changed her mind about Caleb? She tightened her hold on Steve's hand.

"It's okay, honey. Let's wash up and go on in," he said reassuringly.

She nodded, and a minute later they were in the unit.

"Amber?" Bonnie said softly.

Amber looked up, her face aglow with love, and her eyes brimming with tears. She glanced back down at Caleb, leaned over and kissed him, then walked toward Michelle and Steve.

Her voice shaking, she said to the baby, "These are your new parents, Caleb. They are going to take good care of you for me."

She looked up at Michelle, and the tears began to trail down her cheeks. Gazing down again, she whispered, "I love you." Then she extended her baby toward Michelle.

Without a word, Michelle moved forward and reached for the tiny bundle. As she cradled Caleb in her arms, her heart broke for the young girl before her.

Trying hard not to cry, she shifted Caleb into one arm and wrapped the other around Amber's shaking shoulder. She leaned over and kissed the top of her head.

They stood together, clinging to each other for several moments. Aside from the beeps of the monitors in the unit, all was silent.

Then Amber looked up at Michelle. "Take good care of him," she said, sorrow thickening her voice.

"I will," Michelle whispered.

Stacy and Bonnie moved forward and drew Amber into their arms. As she collapsed into them sobbing, they supported her weight and gently led her toward the door.

Steve came over to Michelle and stood by her side as she watched them leave. Amber did not look back.

Then the nurse brought some items over for them. "Here are a few preemie diapers and other baby products we send home with new parents. And this is the monitor you'll be using to keep an eye on Caleb's breathing patterns."

Steve took the items from her.

"You have a car seat for his ride home, right?" she asked.

"Yes," he replied. "All strapped in and ready to go."

"Good." The nurse peeked at Caleb's little face almost hidden by the tightly wrapped receiving blanket. "You be good, now," she told him.

Turning to Michelle, she said, "Call anytime. We're here 'round the clock." Then she added, "We'll miss that little guy."

"Thank you so much for everything," Michelle said.

She smiled. "Bring him by sometime. We'll send you information about our annual NICU reunion. Hope you'll join us!"

"We will," she promised. Then turning to her husband, Michelle said, "Ready?"

"Ready."

And they left for home; baby Caleb sleeping peacefully in his mother's arms.

Two weeks later, Magnolia Middle School was a
flurry of activity as the eighth graders prepared for their
graduation ceremony. Steve took the afternoon off to stay
with Caleb so Michelle could attend.

First to spot her, Katy quickly rushed to her side.
"Mrs. Baron! You came!"

Michelle smiled and gave her a hug. "I wouldn't
miss it for the world." Katy had been such a help to her
over the course of the year. How Michelle wished she'd
had more time to give this sweet, shy girl! Each student
had so many needs, but it seemed that Amber's had
dominated them all.

Soon students surrounded her, asking her
questions about the baby. She'd explained to her classes
about the adoption before taking her leave of absence,
carefully omitting the information about Amber being the
birth mother.

"Did you bring pictures of him?" one girl asked.

"I brought one," Michelle replied, pulling out a
photo of her family of four.

"Is that your husband?" another girl asked,
pointing to Steve.

She nodded with a smile.

"He's cute," the girl said. "So is the baby."

Michelle laughed. "Thanks."

Daniel Durand's voice over the school intercom
interrupted their conversation. "All eighth graders report
to your homeroom to begin lining up for graduation."

"Better go," Michelle said to all of them.

She watched the cluster of kids disperse. Only
Katy remained behind.

"Mrs. Baron?" she said.

"Yes, Katy?"

The girl looked her squarely in the eye. Something she never would have done at the beginning of the year, when her shyness was almost crippling. "Thanks."

"For what?" Michelle asked.

"For everything," she began then added, "You are the best teacher. I'm really going to miss you."

"I'll miss you, too," Michelle replied. "Maybe you can stop by Magnolia sometimes next year on your way home from high school. You'll be out a half hour before us."

"Yeah. I'll for sure come by," the girl promised. She hugged Michelle, and then took off for her homeroom.

Michelle took a seat in the section with the faculty, looking forward to sitting back and enjoying the ceremony since her substitute would be herding kids through the lines while the school counselor called out their names from the podium.

As she watched the kids parade past, she noticed how grown up they looked compared to how they'd been at the beginning of the year. Many of the boys had shot up several inches, and the girls, who wore their fancy graduation dresses, looked much more mature and lady-like.

Her thoughts wandered to Amber. Who would have thought in September that she'd miss seeing her so much at this ceremony?

All the frustration Michelle felt those first few months melted away as she'd gotten to know this hurting teen. What would become of the girl who'd given Michelle and her family a blessing they never could have imagined?

Be with her, Lord. Please help her to find a life that will be fulfilling — a life that includes the love of a good and godly man and a wonderful family of her own.

Michelle watched, as the students who had shaped her first year of teaching, officially became high schoolers. After the ceremony, she congratulated as many as she could spot in the ensuing crowd. Then she walked the hall to her classroom.

The room was vacant when she entered. Although there were some new papers on the back counter and several books scattered on desks, most things were pretty much the way she'd left them.

She walked to her desk and sat down. Gazing over the rows of seats, she reflected on her first year as a teacher. So many ups and downs flashed through her memory.

As her eyes came to rest on Amber's desk, she began lapsing into more memories. Then a knock on the door interrupted her thoughts. She looked over to see Cassie poking her head into the room.

"Hey, friend!" Michelle called out. "Come on in." She stood and went over to meet her halfway.

They hugged each other tightly. "It's so good to see you, Michelle. We've missed you around here the past couple of weeks."

"I've missed you, too," Michelle said.

"So how's the baby?" Cassie asked with a smile.

"He's wonderful. Still so tiny, but growing like a weed." Michelle gestured to a chair near her desk. "Sit down."

"I can't stay," she replied. "A bunch of us are heading over to the Coffee Stop. Want to come along?"

"I'd better get home. This is the first time I've left Caleb alone with Steve. But tell everyone hi for me."

"Okay." Cassie hugged her again. "You're coming back in September, right?"

Michelle took a deep breath. "We'll see," she replied. "It all depends on how things go this summer with Caleb."

Cassie nodded. "No problems with Amber, right?"

"None so far. They moved to Arizona last weekend. Hopefully this will work out with her parents."

"It'll be good for her to start fresh at another school in a different town."

Michelle nodded.

"Well don't be a stranger this summer. Call me, and we'll meet for lunch or something," Cassie suggested.

"Sounds good," she replied. "Enjoy your break."

After Cassie left, Michelle walked through the room, picking up the stray books and placing them in the bookcase. Then she packed away the personal items she'd left on her desk, turned off the lights, and headed for the office.

She spoke briefly with the principal, promising to let him know about September.

"We're holding your spot," he said. "If you need a little more time in the fall, you always have the option of another long-term sub."

"Okay. Thanks." She smiled and gave him a quick hug. "Thanks for being so understanding this year."

"You're a great asset to this school, Michelle. I sure hope you'll be back."

She nodded and wished him a happy summer.

Time to get home to her family. Although she loved teaching, above all else, those three people owned her heart.

Someday, I'll be back. That's for sure, she thought as she descended the front stairs and walked away from Magnolia Middle School.

NOTE FROM THE AUTHOR

Dear Readers,

Thank you for sharing Michelle's journey with me. If you have been reading this series from the start, you know that much of my life is intertwined with Michelle's. This story is no exception. Teaching was my lifelong dream, sparked in a third grade classroom where I was a student myself many years ago.

I always planned to be an elementary school teacher, but God had plans of His own. After an anxiety disorder completely robbed me of my dreams to ever stand before a classroom of students again, I fell headlong into the arms of Grace as I encountered a God I'd never known. He rebuilt my life and restored this dream that I thought I'd lost forever.

Gently leading me into a classroom of tiny preschoolers, He nurtured my confidence and moved me gradually from three-year-olds, to third graders, and finally to my ministry to middle schoolers. I spent fifteen years teaching those adolescents caught between childhood and adulthood, one day resembling my preschoolers in their silly antics, and the next inspiring my admiration with their sensitivity and insight.

I have many wonderful memories of those classrooms where hormones raged and students tried to become who they were meant to be.

But I will say, it was *never* easy.

I smile and shake my head when I overhear someone talking about the easy life of a teacher. They fantasize about a job that would give them summer vacations and a two week break at Christmas.

But they have no idea about the hardships and heartaches, the fears and frustrations, and the incredible balancing act teachers experience as they seek to meet the individual needs of so many students with so many issues, not to mention the increasing burden of a system that elevates rote test scores on standardized exams as the pinnacle of achievement.

It always made me smile when I would run into a student in a grocery store or at the mall, and they acted amazed to see that I actually lived and breathed outside of the classroom. Although good teachers carry every one of their students home with them in their hearts, people forget that they must also care for their own children and spouses and all the routine chores of life.

As many teachers know, sometimes a very special, needy student comes into a teacher's life and changes it forever. This happened to me more than once. The first year I taught junior high, I had such a student. Interestingly, he is now married to another former student of mine who started her own teaching career in that very same classroom not too long ago. I'm blessed to see those two doing so well and to have been able to maintain contact with them over the years.

Probably my most life altering teaching experience was a 7th grade boy who graced my room with his presence two years in a row about ten years ago.

My first impression of this young man was not good. His loud, disruptive actions made teaching that class the most difficult challenge I'd ever faced. When I first started praying for him, I confess that my prayers were *Please move him to another room, God.*

Wouldn't you know that he would end up actually needing to repeat 7th grade?

Thankfully, by the end of the first year with him, God had given me a mother's heart for this boy. I could see how vulnerable and sensitive he really was under his tough guy façade. About seven weeks into the second year of having him in my room, the administration was on the verge of expelling him, when God put it on my heart to intercede for him.

Going to the principal, I asked if there was any way I could help this troubled kid stay in school. His offer – keep him in your room all day everyday. This meant that while my other 180 kids came and went throughout the seven periods of the school day, he would remain in my room from 7:30-3:00, sitting at an isolated desk behind mine, and working on all his academic subjects while I taught my English classes. It also meant he'd have to stay with me during my prep period and lunch break.

By the end of the first week, he was calling me 'Mom.'

God used that time to stretch me as a teacher and to grow this boy in the knowledge and understanding of His unconditional love. In a public school setting, this young man's father asked me to openly share my faith with his son, in the hopes that it would help him in his struggles in life.

Lots of prayers, shared scriptures, and tears marked that year. Even to this day, eleven years later, I still pray for this young man whom God placed into my adoptive heart. Not too long ago, I received a letter from him from across the continent. In it he shared the positive impact that year had on his life as well.

And so, I have had my own Ambers and though never an actual adoption of a child, there's no denying that some of my students have been clearly placed into that position in my heart.

Each of us is called to reach out to someone, somehow. God created us for good works that He prepared for us before the beginning of time. I pray that Michelle's story has inspired you to examine your own life and ask yourself what God's purpose might be for you. There is nothing more fulfilling than finding that purpose and going forth with His guidance and blessing.

Thanks for joining me on this journey to Sandy Cove. I hope you'll continue to read the rest of the books in the series. After this letter, you'll find the beginning of book 4 ~ *Around the Bend*.

With deep appreciation and love,

Rosemary Hines

P.S. I would love to hear from you! Please feel free to email me at **Rosemary.W.Hines@gmail.com**. If you'd just like to be added to my email notification list for future releases or special offers, all you need to say in your email is "Add me!" and I'll be sure you are added to my contacts. You'll be the first to know when I'm about to run a special on one of the books or when a new book is in the works. ☺

You can also visit me on the web at **www.RosemaryHines.com** and keep up with my blogs and news on my Facebook author page: **https://www.facebook.com/RosemaryHinesAuthorPage**
And don't forget to visit my Amazon author page, where you'll find all the titles in the Sandy Cove Series:
Rosemary Hines Amazon Author

If you are new to the Sandy Cove Series and would like to travel back in time to follow Michelle's journey from the beginning of her new life in Sandy Cove, *Out of a Dream* (Sandy Cove Series Book 1)and *Through the Tears* (Sandy Cove Series Book 2) are available for immediate download on Amazon.com.

ACKNOWLEDGMENTS

Although writing is often a solitary journey, God has brought alongside many wonderful people to assist and encourage me as I have labored to complete this story. My heart swells with gratitude for each and every one of them.

Giving freely of her time and medical knowledge, I want to thank pediatrician, Dr. Nivedita More of Kidiatrics Medical Group in Rancho Santa Margarita, California. Without charge, she gave me two significant blocks of her valuable time, carefully reading through many pages of the manuscript of this book and lending accurate medical terminology and scenes to the story. Also deserving of recognition and thanks for medical consulting is Liz Drake, NICU nurse at Mission Hospital in Mission Viejo, who answered our NICU questions during one of those meetings.

Special thanks go to my editor and friend, Nancy Tumbas, who generously provides free content editorial suggestions and whose line-by-line technical editing hones and polishes the story before it ever reaches my readers' eyes. I am so blessed by her talent, skill, and attention to detail. In addition, I'm grateful for the follow-up proofing by Julie Cowell and Bonnie VanderPlate.

For their profound encouragement in this writing journey, I want to express my gratitude to Kathy Gilbert and Carol Wild, whose reviews and recommendations took my stories to over 1,000 pastors' wives at both the Calvary Chapel West Coast and East Coast Pastors' Wives Conferences in 2011 and 2012. I'd also like to thank Carol Deckard, who reviewed and recommended *Out of a Dream* at the Calvary Chapel Living Word Christmas Tea, and the Calvary Chapel Living Word Ladies Book Club who selected *Out of a Dream* and *Through the Tears* for their books of the month in January of 2012 and 2013.

On a personal note, I'd like to thank my husband, my sister, my kids and their spouses, and my many 'sisters' and 'brothers' in-the-Lord who have believed in me as a writer and encouraged me in my voyage. Special thanks go to Benjamin Hines for the cover design of *Into Magnolia*. He truly possesses a skillful eye for photographic composition and design and worked tirelessly to assist me in developing the perfect image and layout. And I also want to thank Justin Schmauser for the captivating cover photo.

Last but not least, my heartfelt gratitude goes to my readers who make this journey worthwhile, and to all the students who gave me the chance to fulfill my dream of teaching.

BOOKS BY ROSEMARY HINES

Sandy Cove Series Book 1

Out of a Dream

Sandy Cove Series Book 2

Through the Tears

Sandy Cove Series Book 3

Into Magnolia

Sandy Cove Series Book 4

Around the Bend

Sandy Cove Series Book 5

From the Heart

Sandy Cove Series Book 6

Behind Her Smile

Sandy Cove Series Book 7

Above All Else

CPSIA information can be obtained
at www.ICGtesting.com
Printed in the USA
LVHW02s1548170518
577555LV00002B/202/P

9 781542 469906